THE UNINNOCENT

THE UNINNOCENT

STORIES

BRADFORD MORROW

PEGASUS BOOKS
NEW YORK

THE UNINNOCENT

Pegasus Books LLC
80 Broad Street, 5th Floor
New York, NY 10004

Collection copyright © 2011 by Bradford Morrow

First Pegasus Books cloth edition: December 5, 2011

Interior design by Maria Fernandez

These stories first appeared, often in somewhat different form, in the following magazines and anthologies: "The Hoarder": *Murder in the Rough* and *Best American Noir Stories of the Century*. "Gardener of Heart": *Conjunctions, Paraspheres: Fabulist and New Fabulist Stories*, and *Poe's Children*. "Whom No Hate Stirs None Dances": *Bomb*. "Amazing Grace": *Conjunctions* and *Pushcart Prize XXVII*. "The Uninnocent": *The Village Voice Literary Supplement*. "Tsunami": *Black Clock*. "(Mis)laid": *Conjunctions*. "All the Things that Are Wrong with Me": *Ontario Review*. "The Enigma of Grover's Mill": *New Jersey Noir*. "Ellie's Idea": published as "Sylvia's Idea" in *Ontario Review*. "The Road to Nadĕja": *The New Gothic*. "Lush": *Ontario Review* and *The O. Henry Prize Stories, 2003*.

Library of Congress Cataloging-in-Publication Data is available.

ISBN: 978-1-60598-265-6

10 9 8 7 6 5 4 3 2 1

Printed in the United States of America
Distributed by W. W. Norton & Company

For Joyce Carol Oates
& Cara Schlesinger

CONTENTS

THE UNINNOCENT

THE HOARDER

HAVE ALWAYS BEEN a hoarder. When I was young, our family lived on the Outer Banks, where I swept up and down the shore filling my windbreaker pockets with seashells of every shape and size. Back in the privacy of my room I loved nothing better than to lay them out on my bed, arranging them by color or form—whelks and cockles here, clams and scallops there—a beautiful mosaic of dead calcium. The complete skeleton of a horseshoe crab was my finest prize, as I remember. After we moved inland from the Atlantic, my obsession didn't change but the objects of my desire did. Having no money, I was restricted to things I found, so one year developed an extensive collection of Kentucky bird nests, and during the next, an array of bright Missouri butterflies preserved in several homemade display cases. Another year, my father's itinerant work having taken us to the desert, I cultivated old pottery shards from the hot potreros. Sometimes my younger sister offered to assist with my quests, but I preferred shambling around on my own. Once in a while I did allow her to shadow me, if only because it was one more thing that annoyed our big brother, who never missed an opportunity to cut me down to size. Weird little bastard, Tom liked calling me. I didn't mind him saying so. I was a weird little bastard.

When first learning to read, I hoarded words just as I would shells, nests, butterflies. Like many an introvert, I went through a phase during which every waking hour was spent inside a library book. These I naturally collected, too, never paying my late dues, writing in a ragged notebook words that were used against Tom at opportune moments. He was seldom impressed when I told him he was a *pachyderm anus* or *festering pustule*, but that might have been because he didn't understand some of what came out of my mouth. Many times I hardly knew what I was saying. Still, the desired results were now and then achieved. When I called him some name that sounded nasty enough—*eunuch's tit*—he would run after me with fists flying and pin me down, demanding a definition, and I'd refuse. Be it black eye or bloody nose, I always came away feeling I'd gotten the upper hand.

Father wasn't a migrant laborer, as such, and all our moving had nothing to do with a field-worker following seasons or harvests. He lived by his wits, so he told us and so we kids believed. But wits or not, every year brought the ritual pulling up of stakes and clearing out. His explanations were always curt, brief like our residencies. He never failed to apologize, and I think he meant it when he told us that the next stop would be more permanent, that he was having a streak of bad luck bound to change for the better. Tom took these uprootings harder than I or my sister. He expressed his anger about being jerked around like circus animals, and complained that this was the old man's fault and we should band together in revolt. It was never clear just how we were supposed to mutiny, and of course we never did. Molly and I wondered privately, whispering together at night, if our family wouldn't be more settled had our mother still been around. But that road was a dead end even more than the one we seemed to be on already. She'd deserted our father and the rest of us and there was no bringing her back. We used to get cards at Christmas, but even that had stopped some years ago. We seldom mentioned her name now. What was the point?

Like the sun, we traveled westward across the country all the way to the coast, though more circuitously and with much dimmer prospects. I'd made a practice of discarding my latest collection whenever we left one place for another, and not merely disposing of it, but destroying the stuff. Taking a hammer to my stash of petrified wood and bleached bones plucked off the flats near Mojave, after the word came down to start packing, was my own private way of saying good-bye. Molly always cried until I gave her a keepsake, a sparrow nest or slug of quartz crystal. And my dad took me aside to ask why I was undoing all my hard work, unaware of the sharp irony of his question—who was he to talk? He told me that one day when I was grown up I'd look back and regret not treasuring these souvenirs from my youth. But he never stopped me. He couldn't in fairness do that. These were my things and just as I'd brought them together I had every right to junk them and set my sights on the new. Besides, demolishing my collections didn't mean I didn't treasure them in my own way.

We found ourselves in a small, pleasant, nondescript ocean-side town just south of the palm-lined promenades of Santa Barbara and the melodramatic Spanish villas of Montecito, where the Kennedys had spent their honeymoon a few years before. By this time I was old enough to find a job. Tom and I had both given up on school. Too many new faces, too many new curricula. Father couldn't object to his eldest son dropping out of high school, since he himself had done the same. As for me, having turned fifteen, I'd more or less educated myself anyway. It was a testament to Molly's resilient nature that she was never fazed entering all those unknown classrooms across this great land of ours. My responsibility was to make sure she got to summer school on time and pick her up at day's end, and so I did. This commitment I gladly undertook, since I always liked Molly, and she didn't get in the way of my schedule at the miniature golf course where I was newly employed.

Just as California would mark a deviation in my father's gypsy routine, it would be the great divide for me. Whether I knew it at the time is beside the point. I doubt I did. Tom noticed something different had dawned in me, a new confidence, and while he continued to taunt me, my responses became unpredictable. He might smirk, "Miniature golf . . . now there's a promising career, baby," but rather than object I would cross my arms, smile, and agree, "Just my speed, baby." When we did fight, our battles were higher pitched and more physical, and as often as not, he was the one who got the tooth knocked loose, the lip opened, the kidney punched. Molly gave up trying to be peacemaker and lived more and more in her own world. It was as if we moved into individual mental compartments, like different collectibles in separate cabinets. I couldn't even say for sure what kind of work my father did anymore, though it involved a commute over the mountains to a place called Ojai, which resulted in our seeing less of him than ever. The sun had turned him brown, so his work must have been outside. Probably a construction job—so much for his touted wits. Tom, on the other hand, remained as white as abalone, working in a convenience store. And Molly with her sweet round face covered in freckles and ringed by wildly wavy red hair, the birthright of her maternal Irish ancestry, marched forward with patience and hope that would better befit a daughter of the king of Uz than of a carpenter of Ojai—which our dear brother had by then, with all the cleverness he could muster, dubbed *Oh Low*.

The change was gradual but irrevocable, and would be difficult if not impossible to describe in abstract terms. To suggest that my compulsion to hoard shifted from objects to essences, from the external world's castoffs to the stuff of spirits, wouldn't be quite right. It might even be false, since what began to arise within me during those long slow days and evenings at work had a manifest concreteness to it. Whether my discovery of glances, fragrances, gestures, voices, the various flavors of nascent sexuality, the potential for beautiful violence that hovers behind those qualities came as the result of my new life at Bayside Park or whether it would have happened no matter where I lived and breathed at that moment, I couldn't say. I do know that Bayside—that perfect world of fantastical architecture and linked greens and strict rules—was where I came awake, felt more alive, as they say, than ever before.

The first time I laid eyes on the place was early evening. Fog, which seasonally rolled in at dusk, settling over the coastal flats and canyons until early afternoon the next day, was drifting like willowy ghosts. I wore my best flannel shirt and a pair of jeans to the interview. My head was all but bald, my old man having given me a fresh trim with his electric clippers, a memento filched from one of his many former employers. Even though it was late June and the day had been warm, I wished I'd brought a sweater since the heavy mist down by the ocean dampened me to the bone. I could hear the surf, once I crossed the empty highway, and started thinking about what questions I might be asked during my interview and what sorts of answers I'd be forced to make up to cover a complete lack of experience. There was a good chance I'd be turned down for the job. After all, I was just a kid who had done nothing with his life beyond collecting debris in forests and fields, and reading comics and worthless books. If I hadn't been so bent on getting clear of our house, pulling together money toward one day having a place of my own, unaffected by my shiftless father and moron brother, I'd have talked myself out of even trying.

As I approached the miniature golf park, I was mesmerized by a ball of brilliance, a white dome of light in the mist that reminded me of some monumental version of one of those snow-shaker toys, what on earth are they called? Those water-filled globes of glass inside which are plastic world's fairs, North Pole dioramas, Eiffel Towers that, when joggled, fall under the spell of a miraculous blizzard. What loomed inside this fluorescent bell jar was a wonderland, a fake dwarf-world populated by real people, reminiscent of snow-globe toys in other ways, too. The fantastic, impossible scenes housed in each, glass or light, were irresistible. I walked through a gate over which was a sign that read BAYSIDE—FOR ALL AGES. What lay before me, smaller than the so-called real world but larger than life, was a village of whirling windmills and miniature cathedrals with spires, of stucco gargoyles and painted grottoes. A white brick castle with turrets ascended the low sky, its paint peeling in the watery weather. Calypso's Cave, the sixth hole. A fanciful pirate ship coved by a waterfall at the seventh. And everywhere I looked, green synthetic alleys. All interconnected and, if a bit seedy, very alluring.

By lying about my age, background, and whatever else, I got the job. When asked at dinner to describe what kind of work was involved, I told my father I was the course steward. In fact, my responsibilities fell somewhere between janitor and errand boy. Absurd as it may sound, I was never happier. Vacuuming the putting lanes; scouring the acre park and adjacent beach for lost balls and abandoned golf clubs; tending the beds of bougainvillea and birds-of-paradise; spearing trash strewn on the trampled, struggling real grass that lay between the perfect alleys; skimming crud out of water traps and ornamental lagoons; retouching paint where paint needed retouching. If Bayside was a museum—and it was, to my eyes—I was its curator. The owner, a lean, sallow, stagnant man named Gallagher, seemed gratified by my attentiveness and pleased that I didn't have any friends to waste my time or his. Looking back, I realize he was quietly delighted that I hadn't the least interest in playing. What did I care about hitting a ball with a stick into a hole?

That said, I did become an aficionado, in an antiseptic sort of way. Just as I had about the classifications of seashells or the markings of dragonflies in times past, I read everything I could about the sport of miniature golf in the office bookcase, surrounded by framed photos autographed by the rich and famous who had played here long ago. The history was more interesting than I imagined. In the Depression they used sewer pipes, scavenged tires, rain gutters, whatever junk was lying around, and from all the discards built their Rinkiedinks, as the obstacle courses were called, scale model worlds in which the rules were fair and the playing field—however bunkered, curved, slanted, stepped—was truly level. Once upon a time, I told Molly, this was the classy midnight pastime of America's royalty. Hollywood moguls drank champagne between holes, putting with stars and starlets under the moon until the sun came up. One of the earliest sports played outdoors under artificial lights, miniature golf was high Americana and even now, though it had a degraded heritage, was something finer than people believed.

My favorite trap in the park was the windmill, which rose seven feet into the soggy air of the twelfth green. Its blades were powered by an old car battery that needed checking once a week, as its cable connections tended to corrode in the damp, bringing the attraction—not to mention the obstacle—to a standstill. One entered this windmill by a hidden door at the back, which wasn't observable to people playing the course, indeed was pretty invisible unless you knew it was there. Gallagher had by August learned to trust me with everything except ticket taking, which was his exclusive province when it came to Bayside, and about which I could not have cared less. So when, one evening, a couple complained to him that the windmill blades on twelve weren't working, he handed me a flashlight, some pliers, a knife, and explained what to do. The windmill was at the far end of the park and I made my way there as quickly as possible without disturbing any of the players.

Once inside, I discovered a new realm. A world within a world. Fixing the oxidized battery posts was nothing, done in a matter of minutes. But then I found myself wanting to stay. What held me was that I could see, through tiny windows in the wooden structure, people playing, unaware they were being watched. A girl with her mother and father standing behind, encouraging her, humped over the blue ball, her face contorted into a mask of concentration, putting right at me, knowing nothing of my presence. One shot and through she went, between my legs, and after her, her mom and dad. They talked among themselves, a nice, dreary, happy family, in perfect certainty their words were exchanged in private. It was something to behold.

I stuck around. Who wouldn't? Others passed through me, the ghost in the windmill, and none of them knew, not even the pair of tough bucks who played the rounds every night, betting on each hole, whose contraband beer bottles I'd collected that very morning. It became my habit, from then on, to grab time in the windmill during work to watch and listen. I found myself particularly interested in young couples, many of them not much older than I was, out on dates. Having avoided school since we came west, and being by nature an outsider, my social skills were limited. The physical urgency I felt, spying on these lovers, I sated freely behind the thin walls of my hiding place. Meanwhile, I learned how lovers speak, what kind of extravagant lies they tell each other, the promises they make, and all I could feel was gratitude that my brand of intimacy didn't involve saying anything to anybody. The things I found myself whispering in the shade of my hermitage none of them would have liked to hear, either. That much I knew for sure.

One evening, to my horror, Tom appeared in my peephole vista. What was he doing here? What gave him the right? And who was the girl standing with him, laughing at one of his maudlin jokes? He had a beer in his pocket, like the toughs. His arm was slung over the girl's shoulder, dangling like a broken pendulum, and his face was rosy for once. They laughed again and looked around and, taking advantage of being (almost) alone, kissed. At first I stood frozen in the windmill whose blades spun slowly, knowing that if Tom caught me watching, he'd beat the hell out of me and back at home deny everything. But soon I realized there was nothing to fear. This was my domain. Tom could not touch me in my hideaway world. Much the same way I used to trespass his superiority with those words lifted out of books, I offered him the longest stare I could manage. Not blinking, not wincing, I made my face into an unreadable blank. Pity he couldn't respond.

Work went well. Some days I showed up early, on others left late. Gallagher one September morning informed me that if I thought I would be earning overtime pay I was mistaken and reacted with a smiling shrug when I told him my salary was more than fair. "You're a good kid," he concluded. And so I was, in that what he asked me to do I did, prompt and efficient. Players, it turned out, were more irresponsible and given to vandalism than I'd have assumed. Since the game had so much to do with disciplined timing, thoughtful strategy, a steady hand and eye, what were these broken putters and bashed fiberglass figures about? Perhaps I'd become an idealistic company man, but the extensive property damage Gallagher suffered seemed absurd. I helped him with repairs and thought of asking why he didn't prosecute the offenders; we both knew who they were. Instead I kept my concerns to myself, sensing subconsciously that it was best, as they say, not to call the kettle black. After all, Gallagher surely noticed my long absences within the precincts of the park and by mutual silence consented to them, so long as I got the work done.

In my years of wandering far larger landscapes than Bayside, I had learned where the birds and beasts of the earth hide themselves against their enemies and how they go about imposing their will, however brief and measly it may be, on the world around them. All my nest hunts and shell meanderings had served me well, though here what I collected thus far were fantasies. I can say I almost preferred the limitations of the park. Finding fresh places to hide was my own personal handicap, as it were. And since this was one of the old courses, ostentatious in the most wonderful way—a glorious exemplar of its kind—the possibilities seemed infinite. They weren't, but I took advantage of what was feasible, and like the birds and crustaceans whose homes I used to collect, having none myself to speak of, I more or less moved into Bayside, establishing makeshift berths, stowing food and pop, wherever I secretly could. Like the hermit crab, I began to inhabit empty shells.

The girlfriend's name was Penny. Penny for my thoughts. Thin, with sand-colored hair that fell straight down her back to her waist, she had a wry, pale mouth, turned-up nose, and brown searching eyes, deep and almost tragic, which didn't seem to fit with her pastel halter and white pedal pushers. The desperate look in those eyes of hers quickly began to haunt me and, as I watched, my bewilderment over what she was doing with the likes of Tom only grew. In life many things remain ambiguous, chancy, muddled, unknowing and unknowable, but she seemed to be someone who, given the right circumstances, might come to understand me, maybe even believe in me. I developed a vague sense that there was something special between us, a kind of spiritual kinship, difficult to define. Molly was the one who told me her name. She said they had taken her on a picnic up near Isla Vista, and that Penny had taught her how to pick mussels at low tide. Very considerate of Tom, I thought, very familial.

Meantime, my brother and I had never been more estranged. Our absentee father kept a roof over our heads but was otherwise slowly falling to pieces, a prematurely withering man who spent his time after work in taverns, communing with scotch and fellow zilches. Molly had made friends with whom she walked to school these days, so I wasn't seeing much of her either. And I, always the loner, had never been more solitary. Time and patience, twin essentials to any collector, were all I needed to bring my new obsession around. So it was that I took my time getting to know Penny, watching from the hidden confines of the windmill, the little train station with its motionless locomotive, the Hall of the Mountain King with its par five, the toughest hole on the course. Having wrapped her tightly in my imaginative wings, it was hard to believe I still hadn't actually met Tom's friend.

He, who returned to Bayside again and again with some perverse notion he was irritating me, would never have guessed how much I learned about his Penny over the months. Anonymous and invisible as one of the buccaneer statuettes on the pirate ship, I stalked them whenever they came to play, moving easily from one of my sanctuaries to another, all the while keeping my boss under control, so to speak, Gallagher who had grown dependent on me by this time. She was an only daughter. Her father worked on an offshore oil rig. Chickadee was the name of her pet parrot. She loved a song by the Reflections with the lyric *Our love's gonna be written down in history, just like Romeo and Juliet.* French fries were her favorite food. All manner of data. But my knowing her came in dribs and drabs, and it began to grate on me that what I found out was strictly the result of Tom's whim to bring her to Bayside. I needed more, needed to meet her, to make my own presence known.

How this came about was not as I might have scripted it, but imperfect means sometimes satisfy rich ends. The first of December was Tom's birthday, his eighteenth. As it happened, it fell on a

Monday, the one day of the week Bayside was closed. Molly put the party together, a gesture from the heart, no doubt hoping to bring our broken, scattered, dissipating family into some semblance of a household. When she invited me, my answer was naturally no until, by chance, I heard her mention on the phone that Penny was invited. She even asked Gallagher to come. Thank God he declined. Molly and a couple of her friends baked a chocolate cake and the old man proved himself up to the role of fatherhood by giving Tom the most extravagant present any of us had ever seen. Even our birthday boy was so overwhelmed by his generosity that he gave Dad a kiss on the forehead. Molly and I glanced at one another, embarrassed. Ours was a family that didn't touch, so this was quite a historic moment. If I hadn't spent most of the evening furtively staring at Penny, I might have thrown up my piece of cake then and there.

It was a camera, a real one. Argus C3. Black box with silver trim. Film and carrying case, too. The birthday card read, *Here's looking at you, kid! With affection and best luck for the future years, Dad and your loving brother and sister.* My head spun from the hypocrisy, the blatant nonsense of this hollow sentiment, but I put on the warm, smiling face of a good brother, ignoring Tom while accepting from his girlfriend an incandescent smile of her own, complicated as always by those bittersweet eyes of hers, and said, "Let's get a picture." Tom's resentment at having to let me help him read the instructions for loading gave me more satisfaction than I could possibly express. We got it done, though, and the portrait was taken by a parent who arrived to pick up one of Molly's friends. The party was a great success, we all told Molly. That Argus was a mythical monster with a hundred eyes I kept to myself. Although the idea of stealing his camera came to me that night—Tom would never have used it anyway—I waited a week, three weeks, a full month, before removing it from his possession.

With it I began photographing Penny. At first, my portraits were confined to what I could manage from various hiding places at the park. But the artificial light wasn't strong enough to capture colors and details in her face and figure, and of course I couldn't use flashbulbs, so the only decent images I managed to get were on the rare occasions when she played during the day, often weekend afternoons, and not always with Tom. I kept every shot, no matter how poor the exposure, in a cigar box stowed inside a duffel in a corner of the windmill along with the camera. During off-hours I often took the box, under my jacket, down to some remote stretch of beach and pored over the pictures with a magnifying glass I'd acquired for the purpose. Some were real prizes, more treasured, even cherished, than anything I'd collected in the past. One image became the object of infatuation, taken at great risk from an open dormer in the castle. It must have been a warm early January day, because Penny wore a light blouse that had caught a draft of wind off the ocean, ballooning the fabric forward away from her, so that from my perch looking down I shot her naked from forehead to navel, both small, round breasts exposed to my lens. The photo was pretty abstract, shot at an odd angle, with her features foreshortened, a hodgepodge of fabric and flesh that would be hard to read, much less appreciate the way I did, unless you knew what you were looking at, whose uncovered body you were seeing laid out on that flat, shiny silver paper. Thinking back to those heady times, I realize most pornography is very conventional, easily understood by the lusting eye, and certainly more explicit. But my innocent snapshots, taken without her knowledge or consent, seem even now to be more obscene than any professional erotic material I have since encountered.

Things developed. I made the fatal step of finding out where Penny lived. Her house was only a mile, give or take, from ours. It became my habit to go to bed with an alarm clock under my pillow, put there so that only I would hear it at midnight, or one, or two in the morning, when I'd quietly get dressed and sneak out. These excursions were as haphazard as, if not more than, what I did at the park. I took the camera with me and often came home with nothing, the window to her bedroom having been dark, or worse—her lights still on, the shade drawn, and a shadow moving tantalizingly back and forth on its scrim. But there were occasional triumphs.

Milling in a hedge of jasmine one moonless night, seeing the houses along her street were all hushed and dark, I was about to give up my one-boy siege and walk back home when I heard a car come up the block. Tom's junker coasted into dim view, parking lights showing the way. The only sound was of rubber tires softly chewing pebbles in the pavement. Retreating into the jasmine, I breathed through my mouth as slowly as I could. Penny emerged from the car many long minutes later and dashed right past me—I could smell her perfume over that of the winter flowers—and let herself into the house with hardly a sound. Good old cunning Tom must have dropped his car into neutral, as it drifted down the slanted grade until, a few doors away, he started the engine and drove away.

The lateness of the hour might have given her the idea that no one would notice if she didn't close her shades. Or maybe she was tired and forgot. Or maybe she was afraid to make any unnecessary noise in the house that would wake her parents. She lit a candle, and I saw more that night than I ever had before. To say it was a revelation, a small personal apocalypse, would be to diminish what happened to me as I watched her thin limbs naked in the anemic yellow, hidden only by the long hair she brushed before climbing into bed. How much I would have given to stretch that moment out forever. Though the camera shutter resounded in the dead calm with crisp, brief explosions, I unloaded my roll. After she blew out the candle, I retreated in a panicked ecstasy, dazed as a drunk.

The film came out better than I'd hoped—the blessing that would prove a curse, as they might have written in one of those old novels I used to read. The pimply kid who handed me my finished exposures over the counter at the camera shop, and took my crumple of dollars, asked me to wait for a minute.

"How come?" I asked.

Not looking up, he said, "The manager's in the darkroom. He wanted to have a few words with whoever picked up this roll. You got a minute?"

"No problem," I smiled.

When he disappeared into the back of the shop, I slipped out as nonchalantly as possible and walked around the corner before breaking into a run, until I reached the highway and, beyond, the golf park. Gallagher mentioned that I was even earlier than usual, not looking up from his morning paper in the office. I explained I wanted to do some work on the Calypso Cave if he didn't mind. He said nothing one way or the other. Toolbox in hand, I hurried instead to the windmill, wondering what kind of imbecile Gallagher thought I was. Nothing mattered once I spread the images in a fan before me in the half-light of my refuge. Aside from having cost money to be developed, these new trophies were just as virtuous, as pure and irreproachable as any bird nest or seashell I'd ever collected—perhaps more innocent yet, I told myself, since nothing had been disturbed or in any way hurt by my recent activities. I had given the camera shop a fake name and wrong phone number. Everything was fine. To describe the photographs of Penny further would be to sully things, so I won't. She was only beautiful in her unobservance, in her not quite absolute solitude.

Spring came and with it all kinds of migratory birds. This would normally have been the season when our family meeting—which the old man called, as we might have expected, one Sunday morning—meant the usual song and dance about moving. Out of habit, if nothing else, we gathered around the kitchen table, Tom thoughtfully drumming his fingers and Molly with downcast eyes, not wanting to leave her new friends. Whatever the big guy had to say, I knew I was staying, no matter what. I was old enough to make ends meet, and meet them I would without the help of some pathetic Ojai roofer. I could live in the windmill or the castle for a while, and Gallagher would never know the difference. Eventually I'd get my own apartment. Besides, where was there left to go?

He came into the room with a grim look on his heavy brown face. "Two things," he said, sitting.

"Want some coffee, Dad?" Molly tried.

"First is that Tom is in trouble."

"What kind of trouble?" my brother asked, genuinely upset.

Our father didn't look at him when he said, "I might have thought you'd make better use of your birthday present, son."

Tom was bewildered. "I don't know what you're talking about." He looked at me and Molly for support. Neither of us had, for different reasons, anything to offer. Surely it must have occurred to my dear brother that having misplaced his fancy birthday present and kept it a secret would come back to haunt him. On a lark, I'd started using his name when I went to different stores to have the film developed. Seemed they'd caught up with their culprit.

"Much more important is the second problem."

We were hushed.

"Your mother has passed away."

No words. A deep silence. Tom stared at him. Molly began to cry. I stared at my hands folded numb in my lap and tried without success to remember what she'd looked like. I had come to think of myself as having no mother, and now I truly didn't. What difference did it make, I wanted to say, but kept quiet.

"I'm going back for a couple weeks to sort everything out, make sure she's—taken care of, best as possible."

It was left at that. No further questions, nor any answers. However, when we put him on the flight in Los Angeles, Tom having driven us down, I could tell my brother remained in the dark about that first problem broached at the family meeting. Dull as he was, he did display sufficient presence of mind not to bring it up when such weightier matters were being dealt with. The old man, waving to us as he boarded his flight, looked for all the world the broken devil he was becoming, or already had become.

Things moved relentlessly after this. Mother was put to rest and her estranged husband returned from the East annihilated, poor soul. Molly withdrew from everybody but me. Penny and my brother had broken up by the time June fog began rolling ashore in this, my year anniversary at Bayside. It fell to me, of all people, to nurture family ties, such as they were. To make, like an oriole, a work of homey art from lost ribbons, streamers, string, twigs, the jetsam of life, in which we vulnerable birds could live. I had no interest, by the way, in mourning our forsaken mother. But for a brief time, I tried to be nice to the old man and avoid Tom.

Which is not to say that my commitment to Penny changed during those transitional months. I continued to photograph her whenever I could, adept now that I had come to know her routines, day by day, week by week. Instead of hiding from her at Bayside, or downtown, or even in her neighborhood, where sometimes I happened to be walking along and accidentally, as it were, bumped into her, I stopped and talked about this or that, when she wasn't in a hurry. If she asked me about Tom, I assured her that he was doing great, and changed the subject. Did the Reflections have a new hit song? I would ask. Did she want to come down to the golf course, bring some girlfriends along, do the circuit for free? She appreciated the invitation but had lost interest in games and songs and many other things. Rather than feeling defeated I became even more devoted. My collection of photographs throughout this period of not-very-random encounters and lukewarm responses to my propositions grew by leaps and bounds. I enrolled pseudonymously in a photo club that gave me access to a darkroom where I learned without much trouble how to develop film. Hundreds of images of Penny emerged, many of them underexposed and overexposed and visually unreadable to anyone but me. But also some of them were remarkable for their poignant crudity, since by that time I'd captured her in most every possible human activity.

The inevitable happened on an otherwise dull, gray day. Late afternoon, just after sunset. The sky was like unpolished pewter and late summer fog settled along the coast. I was down near my windmill, loitering at Gallagher's not great expense, with nothing going on and nothing promising either that evening, except maybe the usual jog over to Penny's to see what there was to see, when, without warning, I was caught by the collar of my shirt and thrown to the ground. I must have blurted some kind of shout, or cry, but remember at first a deep exterior silence as I was dragged, my hands grasping at my throat, through a breach in the fence and out onto the sand. The pounding in my ears was deafening and I felt my face bloat. I tried kicking and twisting, but the hands that held me were much stronger than mine. I blacked out, then came to, soaked in salt water and sweat, and saw my brother's face close to mine spitting out words I couldn't hear through the tumultuous noise of crashing waves and throbbing blood. He slapped me. And slapped me backhanded again. Then pulled me up like a rough lover so that we faced each other eye to eye, lips to lips. I still couldn't hear him, though I knew what he was cursing about. Bastard must have been following me, spying, and uncovered my hideout and stash.

What bothered me most was that Tom, not I, was destroying my collection. He had no right, no right. None of the photographs that swept helter-skelter into the surf, as we fought on that dismal evening, were his to destroy. Much as I'd like to sketch those minutes in such a way that my seizing the golf ball from my shirt pocket, cramming it into his mouth, and clamping his jaw shut with all the strength I had were gestures meant to silence, not slay him, it would be a lie.

Lie or not, Tom went down hard, gasping for air, and I went down with him, my hands like a vise on his pop-eyed face. He grabbed at his neck now, just as I had grabbed at mine moments before, the ball lodged in the back of his throat. A wave came up over us both in a sizzling splash, knocking us shoreward before pulling us back toward the black water and heavy rollers. Everywhere around us were Penny's images, washing in and out with the tidal surges. Climbing to my feet, I watched the hungry waves carry my brother away. I looked up and down the coast and, seeing no one in the settling dark, walked in the surf a quarter mile northward, maybe farther, before crossing a grass strip that led, beneath some raddled palms, to solitary sidewalks that took me home, where I changed clothes. In no time, I was at work again, my mind a stony blank.

Whether by instinct or dumb luck, my having suppressed the urge to salvage as many photos as I could that night, and carry them away with me when I left the scene where Tom and I had quarreled, stood me in good stead. Given that I had the presence of mind to polish the Argus and hide it under Tom's bed, where it would be discovered the next day by the authorities when they rummaged through his room looking for evidence that might explain what happened, I think my abandonment of my cache of portraits was inadvertent genius.

Genius, too, if heartfelt, was my brave comforting of Molly, who cried her eyes out on hearing the disastrous news. And I stuck close to our father, who moped around the bungalow we called home, all but cataleptic, mumbling to himself about the curse that followed him wherever he went. Though they had not ruled out an accidental death—he disgorged the golf ball before drowning—our father was, I understand, their prime suspect. A walk on the beach, man to man, a parental confrontation accidentally gone too far. In fact, their instinct, backed by the circumstantial evidence of his having been troubled by his estranged wife's demise, given to drinking too much, and his recent rage toward his eldest kid over having taken weird, even porno snapshots of his girlfriend, led them in the right direction. Just not quite. Molly and I had watertight alibis, so to speak, not that we needed them. She was with several friends watching television, and Gallagher signed an affidavit that I was working with him side by side during the time of the assault. Speculating about the gap in the fence and faint, windblown track marks in the sand, he said, "Always trespassers trying to get in for free," and, not wanting to cast aspersions on the deceased, he nevertheless mentioned that he'd seen somebody sneaking in and out of that particular breach at odd hours, and that the person looked somewhat like Tom.

Our father was eventually cleared. Turned out Sad Sack was a covert Casanova with a lady friend as alibi in Ojai. This explained why our annual rousting had not taken place. He need not have been shy about it, as his children would prove to like her, Shannon is the name. Whether Gallagher'd been so used to me going through my paces—efficient, thorough, devoted—that he improved on an assumption by making it a sworn fact or whether he really thought he saw me at work that night, ubiquitous ghost that I was, or whether he was covering for me, not wanting to lose the one sucker who understood Bayside and could keep it going when he no longer cared to, I will never know. Gallagher himself would perish a year later of a heart attack in our small office, slumped in his cane chair beneath those pictures of stars who gazed down at him with ruthless benevolence.

The initial conclusions reached in Tom's murder investigation proved much the same as the inconclusive final one. They had been thorough, questioned all of Tom's friends. Certainly, Penny might have wanted him dead given how humiliated, how mortified she was by the photographs that had been recovered along the coast. Asked to look through them, she did the best she could. While she did seem to think Tom had been with her on some occasions when this or that shot was taken—they were all so awful, so invasive, so perverse—she couldn't be sure. Given that he was present in none of the exposures, that the camera used was his, and so forth, there was no reason to look elsewhere for the photographer. Penny had a motive, but also an alibi like everyone else.

None of it mattered, finally, because good came from the bad. Our family was closer than ever, and Dad seemed, after a few months of dazed mourning, to shake off his long slump. He brought his Ojai bartender girlfriend around sometimes, and Molly made dinner. Penny too was transformed by the tragedy. Before my watchful eyes she changed into an even gentler being, more withdrawn than before, yes, but composed and calm—some might say remote, but they'd be wrong, not knowing her like I did. It was as if she changed from a color photograph to black and white. I didn't mind the shift. To the contrary.

The morning she came down to Bayside to speak with me was lit by the palest pink air and the dank, hard wind of late autumn. I'd been the model of discretion in the several years that followed Tom's passing, keeping tabs on Penny out of respect, really, making sure she was doing all right in the wake of what must have been quite a shock to her. Never overstepping my bounds—at least not in such a way that she could possibly know. Meanwhile, I had matured. Molly told me I'd become a handsome dog, as she put it. Her girl-friends had crushes on me, she said. I smiled and let them play the golf course gratis, why not. Then Penny turned up, unexpected, wanting to give me something.

"For your birthday," she said, handing me a small box tied with a white ribbon. There was quite a gale blowing off the ocean that day and her hair buffeted her head. With her free hand she drew a long garland of it, fine as corn silk, away from her mouth and melancholy eyes. It was a gesture of absolute purity. Penny was a youthful twenty-one, and I an aged nineteen.

I must have looked surprised, because she said, "You look like you forgot."

She followed me into the office, where we could get out of the wind. All the smugly privileged faces in Gallagher's nostalgic gallery had long since been removed from the walls and sent off to his surviving relatives, who, not wanting much to bother with their inheritance of a slowly deteriorating putt-putt golf park, allowed me to continue in my capacity as Bayside steward and manager. Like their deceased uncle—a childless bachelor whose sole concern had been this fanciful (let me admit) dump—they thought I was far older than nineteen. The lawyer who settled his estate looked into the records, saw on my filed application that I was in my midtwenties, and further saw that Gallagher wanted me to continue there as long as it was my wish, and thus and so. A modest check went out each month to the estate, the balance going to moderate upkeep and my equally moderate salary. What did I care? My needs were few. I spent warm nights down here in my castle, or the windmill, and was always welcome at home, where the food was free. And now, as if in a dream, here was my Penny, bearing a gift.

I undid the ribbon and tore away the paper. It was a snow globe with a hula dancer whose hips gyrated in the sparkling blizzard after I gave it a good shake.

"How did you know?" I asked, smiling at her smiling face.

"You like it?"

"I love it."

"Molly told me this was your new thing."

"Kind of stupid, I guess. But they're like little worlds you can disappear into if you stare at them long enough."

"I don't think it's stupid."

"Yours goes in the place of honor," taking the gift over to my shelves, which were lined with dozens of others, where I installed the hula girl at the very heart of the collection.

Penny peered up and down the rows, her face as luminous as I've ever seen it, beaming like a child. She plucked one down and held it to the light. "Can I?" she asked. I told her sure and watched as she shook the globe and the white flakes flew round and round in the glassed-in world. She gazed at the scene within while I gazed at her. One of those moments that touch on perfection.

"Very cool," she whispered, as if in a reverie. "But isn't it a shame that it's always winter?"

"I don't really see them as snowflakes," I said.

"What then?"

Penny turned to me and must have glimpsed something different in the way I was looking at her since she glanced away and commented that no one was playing today. The wind, I told her. Sand gets in your eyes and makes the synthetic carpet too rough to play on. In fact, there wasn't much reason to keep the place open, I continued, and asked her if she'd let me drive her up to Santa Barbara for the afternoon, wander State Street together, get something to eat. I was not that astonished when she agreed. Cognizant or not, she'd been witness to the character, the nature, the spirit of my gaze, had the opportunity to reject what it meant. By accepting my invitation she was in a fell swoop accepting me.

"You can have it if you want," I offered, taking her free hand and nodding at the snow globe.

"No, it belongs with the others." She stared out the window while a fresh gale whipped up off the ocean, making the panes shiver and chatter as grains of sand swirled around us. I looked past her silhouette and remarked that the park looked like a great snow globe out there. How perverse it was of me to want to ask her, just then, if she missed Tom sometimes. Instead, I told her we ought to get going, but not before I turned her chin toward me with trembling fingers and gently kissed her.

As we drove north along the highway the sky cleared, admitting a sudden warm sun into its blue. "Aren't you going to tell me?" she asked, as if out of that blue, and for a brief, ghastly moment I thought I'd been found out and was being asked to confess. Seeing my bewilderment, Penny clarified, "What the snowflakes are, if they're not snowflakes?"

I shifted my focus from the road edged by flowering hedges and eucalyptus over to Penny, and back again, suddenly wanting to tell her everything, pour my heart out to her. I wanted to tell her how I had read somewhere that in some cultures people refuse to have their photographs taken, believing the camera steals their souls. Wanted to tell her when Tom demolished my collection of adoring images of her, not only did he seal his own fate, but engendered hers. I wished I could tell her how, struggling with him in waves speckled with swirling photographs, I was reminded of a snow globe. And I did want to answer her question, to say that the flakes seemed to me like captive souls floating around hopelessly in their little glass cages, circling some frivolous god, but I would never admit such nonsense. Instead, I told her she must have misunderstood and, glancing at her face bathed in stormy light, knew in my heart that later this afternoon, maybe during the night, I would be compelled to finish the destructive work my foolish brother had begun.

GARDENER OF HEART

I know that I have to die like everyone else, and that displeases me,
and I know every human born so far has died except for those now
living, and that distresses me and makes most distinctions . . . look
false or absurd.

—Harold Brodkey

DESPITE THE GRIEF I FELT as my train chased up the coast toward home, I had to confess that after many years of self-imposed exile it might be strangely comforting to see the old town again, walk the streets where she and I grew up. Imagining the neighborhood absent its finest flower, its single best soul, was unthinkable. Yet it seemed that my visiting our various childhood haunts and willing Julie's spirit—whatever *that* is—a prolonged residence in each of these places would be salutary for her. And cathartic for me. We had made a pact when we were young that whoever died first would try to stay alive in essence, palpably alive, in order to wait for the other. Death was somehow to be held in abeyance until both halves of our twins' soul had succumbed. Sure, we were kids back then, given to crazy fantasies. But the covenant still held, no matter how unspiritual, how skeptical I had become in the interim. Indeed, I had only the vaguest idea of what to do. Just go. Walk, look, breathe, since she could not.

For some reason, I could envision the mortuary home in radiant detail. A breathtaking late-eighteenth-century neoclassical edifice of hewn stone, two imposing stories surmounted by a slate roof and boasting a porch with fluted marble Doric columns. Huge oaks and horse chestnuts surrounded it where it perched on one of the highest hills in town, which, aside from the steeples of local Presbyterian and Catholic churches that rose to almost similar heights, dwarfed everything and everyone in their vicinity. To think that Julie and I, who grew up several doors down the block from this mysterious temple of death, used to love to climb those trees, play kickball on its velvet lawns, or hide in the carefully groomed hedges, peeping in the windows to giggle at the whimpering adults inside. What did we know. Crying was for babies and the unbrave, Julie and I agreed. We laughed ourselves sick and pissing in the greenery, and now, as I imagined, she was lying embalmed, a formal lace dress her winding-sheet, in the very wainscoted chapel whose many mourners gave us so much perverse pleasure to observe over the years of our youth.

Mother would be present at the service, and our father with his third wife, Maureen. Probably a crowd of Julie's friends would be there, few of whom, actually none of whom, I had ever met. Parents aside, I doubted I'd be recognized, so much time having passed since I bared my émigré's face in the unrocking cradle of noncivilization, as I deemed home. If only I could attend her rites invisibly, I thought, as the Acela flew by ocean-edge marshes punctuated by osprey stilt nests and anomalous junkyards where sumac grew through the windshields of gutted trucks. As Jul's only brother,

her best childhood friend, I knew what my sibling responsibilities were, even though a part of me presumed she'd find it apt—no, downright hilarious—if I chose to mourn her from our cherished outpost in shrubbery beneath the casement windows.

When I left home three decades ago, I left with collar up and feet pointed in one direction only: away. By some ineffable irony, Julie's staying made my great escape possible. Being the younger twin—she was delivered a few minutes before I breeched forth—it was as if some part of me safely stayed behind with her in Middle Falls even as a wayward spark in her soul came along with me to New York and far beyond. Julie wasn't the wandering type, though, and after college and a mandatory trip to Europe, she returned home with the idea of seeing our mom through a tough divorce (where's an easy one? I asked her) then simply stayed, as if reattaching roots severed temporarily by some careless shovel. For my part, when I left, I was gone. There were many reasons for this, an awful lot of them now irrelevant thanks to, among so much else, scathing but unscathed time.

By informal agreement my father and I rarely spoke, and my mother and I only talked on holidays or during family crises—which are essentially one and the same, by my lights—so when she called on a nondescript day that celebrated nothing, I knew, even before she gave me the news, that something was badly amiss. Her voice, raspy as a mandolin dragged across macadam, hoarse from years of passionate cigarette smoking, made her words nearly impossible to understand. If I hadn't known she wasn't a drinker, I could have sworn she was totally polluted.

Your . . . she's . . . you're, your sister's . . .

I tried to slow her down, but she was weeping hysterically. Soon enough, I who had always scoffed at weepers became one, too. As tears swamped my eyes, I stared hard out my dirty office window across the rooftops and water towers of the city. A cloud shaped like a Chagall fiddler snatched up from his task of serenading blue farm wives and purple goats, and thrust unexpectedly into the blackening sky, moved slowly over the Hudson toward Jersey. My Julie was dead, my other half. I told my mother I'd be up on the morning train and as abruptly as our conversation, call it that, began, it ended.

Middle Falls lies midway between Rehoboth and Segreganset, east of East Providence, Rhode Island. A place steeped, like they say, in history. One of the diabolical questions that perplexed me and Julie when we were kids was that if there was a *middle* falls, where were the falls on either side? We knew that Pawtucket means Great Falls and Pawtuxet means Little Falls. Yet while our narrow, timid waterfall did dribble near the main street of the village, where the stream paralleled a row of old brick-facade shops quaintly known as downtown, even in the wettest season it hardly deserved its designation as a waterfall. Nor, again, were there any neighboring falls. Be that as it may, Julie and I on many a summer afternoon took our fishing poles down there (never caught so much as a minnow), or paddleboats made with chunks of wood and rubber bands, and had a grand time of it by the cold, thin water. One of our little jokes was that Middle Falls meant if you're caught in the middle, you fall. Our nickname for the place was Muddlefuls.

Julie, much like me, was neither unusually attractive nor unattractive. We were plain, with faces one wouldn't pick out in a crowd. We each had brown hair and eyes, mine darker than hers, with fair skin. We were each slender and tall, given to gawkiness. Since her hair was sensibly short and mine a little long, I suppose that in a low-lit room it would have been possible to mistake one of us for the other. Like me, my twin sister had the thinnest legs in the world, bless her heart, with gnarly knees to boot. She hated hers—wishbones, she figured them, or scarecrow sticks—and as a result never went along with friends to sunbathe on the Vineyard or out on Nantucket. Mine were always a matter of indifference to me, and I never bothered with the seashore anyway. Two modest people with even temperaments and in good health, entering early middle age, sailing forward with steady dispositions, one a homebody, the other an inveterate expatriate, neither of us ever married. Never even came close. Some of our aversion to the holy state of matrimony undoubtedly was a function of our response to our father's philandering and the train wreck of a wife he left behind with her lookalike rug rats. At least for Julie all such concerns, from skinny legs to a broken family, had come to an end. Given the chance, how I'd have loved to take the old man aside after the funeral and let him know, just for once, how very much Jul and I always resented his failure to father us. As the train pulled into the Providence station, I found myself hoping that the embalmer had been instructed to go light on the makeup. Julie never wore lipstick or eyeliner or rouge when she was alive. What a travesty it would be for her to enter eternity painted up like some Yoruba death mask.

The autumn leaves were at peak, and those that had let go of their branches drifted like lifeless butterflies across the road in the cool-warm breeze. I made the drive from Providence—bright, rejuvenated capital of the Ocean State—to Middle Falls, and as I reached the outskirts of town I was seized by an intuition of something unexpected and yet longed for, weirdly anticipated. It was as if I were driving from the hermetic present into the wily certainty of the past. Providence, with its sparkling glass office towers and fashionable storefronts, was transfigured from the seedy backwater whose very name held it in contempt when I was a boy, while the scape around Middle Falls appeared unchanged. There were no other cars on the road so I could slow down a little, take in the rolling vistas of our childhood, Jul's and mine, and luxuriate in this New England fall day. A flock of noisy starlings cleaved the otherwise unarticulated deep blue sky. Look there, Bob Trager's pumpkin patch—Trager's, where we used to pick our own this time of year to carve into jack-o'-lanterns. Sentimental as the thought was, not to mention foolish, I wished we could walk here again just once, scouting plump ones that most looked like human heads. And, feeling a little silly in fact, I pulled over and rambled into the field among the pumpkins attached to the sallow green umbilicals of their dying stalks, and might even have bought a couple, had anybody been manning the farm stand.

I called out, *Anyone here?*

A dog or maybe a fox barked, unseen in a nearby copse of silver birches whose fluttering leaves were golden wafers, barked incessantly, madly, in response. Unnerved, I traipsed back to where the rental was parked beside the road. In a moment that felt dreamlike as déjà vu, as I stepped into the car I mistook my foot for Julie's— by that, I mean her shoe was on my foot. No question but my grief was weighing on me. On second glance the hallucination passed.

Hers was one of those deaths that leave the living in a state of questioning shock. How could this happen to someone so healthy? Yesterday she was alive, vibrant, bright. Today she's mute, still, dead. Gone in a literal heartbeat. Before my mother and I hung up, I did manage to extract from her the cause of death. Brain aneurysm. Like a blood adder born inside a rose, a fleshy pink rose, or one of those peculiar coxcomb flowers, a lethal serpent that when suddenly awakened understood that in order to live and breathe it must gnaw its way to freedom. How long this aneurysm had been lying dormant in Julie's cerebrum none of us will ever know. Her death, the doctor assured our mother, was almost instantaneous. That my sister didn't suffer a protracted demise is some consolation, though one wonders what happens in a person's mind during the irrevocable instant that constitutes the *almost* instantaneous. It's the *almost* that is appalling in its endless possibilities.

Images from days long past continued to accrue beyond the windshield, like those on some inchoate memory jug, and I knew that while they were exhilarating as an unexpected archaeological find, they were also a clear manifestation of mourning. Although I was anxious to get home—I'd be staying in my sister's room, since my bedroom had long ago been converted into a solarium in which Julie tended her heirloom orchids—I was compelled to drive even more slowly, in order to take in every detail of what I had so studiously dismissed over half my life.

A canary yellow and emerald kite in the shape of a wide-mouthed carp or Ming dragon ascended as if on cue above the turning trees, and while I couldn't see the kid at the other end of its silvery string, I easily pictured myself and Julie behind the leaves, pulling and letting out more line. After all, we had a kite that looked a lot like it, way back when. I drove across a stone bridge, a fabled one when we were young, beneath which hunchbacks and trolls loitered in the dank shadows. (Several women accused of witchcraft were hanged there centuries ago, in good old Commonwealth of Massachusetts style.) My sister and I, left so often to our own devices, and admitted addicts of anything frightening or macabre, would egg each other on to wander down here in the twilight and throw taunting stones at the shadow people who lived beneath the bridge. Once, to our surprise, we interrupted a man under the embankment who chased us—yelping, his pants caught around his ankles—halfway home under the snickering stars. Here was a telephone pole we had once tied a boy to, whom we'd caught shooting at crows, our favorite bird, behind an abandoned canning factory. I could still hear his indignant, pleading screams in the wind that whistled at the car window.

Now I saw the church spires above the sea of trees, then one by one the charming clapboard houses of our childhood, and above all that mortuary roof, gun-barrel gray against the jay-blue sky. There were the glorious smells of leaves burning; a garden of dying asters whose yellow centers were catafalques for exhausted wasps in their final throes; the blood-red cardinal acrobating about in his holly bush. Julie and I loved these things, and today felt no different than decades ago. If I didn't know better, I'd have sworn that time had somehow collapsed and, as a result, the many places my work as an archaeologist had taken me—from Zimbabwe to Bonampak, Palenque to the Dordogne—were as unreal as my campus office cluttered with a lifetime of artifacts and books, my affection for *film noir* and vintage Shiraz, and everything else I had presumed was specifically a part of my existence.

My whole adult life, in other words, was an arc of fabrication. Oddly fraudulent was how I felt, unfledged, and in the midst of this, also abruptly—how else to state it?—liberated. Liberated from precisely what, I couldn't say. But the feeling was strong. I reemerged from this small reverie to find myself staring at Julie's pale and slender hands where they lay like wax replicas on the steering wheel. The magnitude of my loss had plainly gotten the better of me. Breathe, I thought. Pull yourself together. And again the world returned to me, or I to it. I pressed forward toward the turnoff that would take me uphill, up the block where our mother awaited me.

Julie did have a boyfriend once. Peter was his name. Peter Rhodes. He was our runaround friend since forever and a day, lived across the street from our house, was all but family. Peter was more or less expected, by everyone who knew him and Julie, to become my sister's husband. Had it happened, it would have been one of those sandbox-to-cemetery relationships that are inconceivable these days. Julie and I had the curbs in on Peter Rhodes from the beginning, however, and in my heart I understood they were never meant to be. Still, we did love to work the Ouija board in the basement, by candlelight, little punks goading the universe to cough up its intimate secrets that lay just there beneath our fingertips. Not to mention overnights, when we camped out in a makeshift carnival tent of Hudson Bays and ladder-back chairs. We played hide-and-seek, freeze tag, Simon Says, all those games that children love. We learned how to ride bikes together, and together we slogged through adolescence. Peter took Julie to the prom when we graduated from Middle Falls High, and I, in my powder-blue tuxedo and dun-brown shoes, went with Priscilla Chao, a sweet, shy girl who was as happy to be asked as I was relieved that she, or anyone else, would bother to accompany me; not that I wanted to go in the first place. We four stood at the back of the gymnasium, far away from the rock band, watching classmates flailing like fools beneath oscillating lights, as our teachers stood nodding by the long sheeted tables set with punch bowls and chips and cheese wheels. In retrospect, I realize how normal—for unassimilateds—Jul and I must have seemed to anyone who bothered to watch. Throughout those years we subtly kept poor Peter at a near-far distance, especially when it came to some of our more transgressive ventures—indeed, he never knew about our passion for the mortuary home, its mourners, hearse driver, gun-for-hire pallbearers, and all the rest. Doubtless, he would have thought us not a little odd if he'd had any idea about our graveyard rambles under the full moon, headstones sparkling naughtily under their berets of fresh-fallen snow. But then no one truly knew Julie and me. A bond formed in the womb was, it seemed, as impossible for others to fathom as to break. I believe Peter married a nice woman he met during his stint as a Peace Corps volunteer in Rhodesia, having fled Middle Falls in the wake of Julie's rejection of his marriage proposal. To this day, I never wished Peter Rhodes ill. I know Julie didn't, either.

Like my sister, I went to college. A scholarship to Columbia saved me from having to lean on my father for tuition money—I'd sooner have committed myself to an assembly line in a clothes-hanger plant. After dabbling in history and the arts, I settled into the sciences and knew early on that archaeology was my calling. Just as Audubon made his sketches from *nature morte*, I believed the best portrait of a person, or civilization, was only accomplishable after the death knell tolled. Schliemann and Layard were like gods to me, just as Troy and Nineveh were secular heavens. Conze at

Samothrace; Andrae in Assyria. Grad work at Oxford was floated on more scholarships, and I'd truly discovered my métier, I felt. A first excursion to Africa, and I was all but over the moon.

As with most disciplines, archaeology is fundamentally the art of attempting to understand ourselves through understanding others. All cultures eventually connect. Language, myth, variant customs, mores, bones are like cultural continental drifts. Put them on a reverse time trajectory and they relink. They become a single supercontinent called Pangaea. My inability, my stubborn refusal to admit to having a true familial home, an ancestral hearth from which I set forth on my specialized journeying, I'd always considered a hidden asset. I had a knack for entering others' homes, that is to say ruins and burial sites, and quickly understanding, sometimes even mastering, the essential idiom of a locale and its inhabitants. Middle Falls I simply never understood. With Julie gone, if I wanted to comprehend this place of personal origin, I might be forever locked out. All the more reason to honor our covenant. Perhaps, through my twin as medium, I might come to some understanding of who I'd been and was no more.

The house was empty. I assumed our mother had gone out somewhere to finalize arrangements. The front door was unlocked, a practice Mom inaugurated after the divorce, saying there wasn't anything left to steal here (morose absurdity, poor darling, but whatever), so I let myself in. Odd, she'd obviously been baking cookies, Julie's beloved peanut butter and pecans, as the whole house was redolent with the warm scent. Maybe she planned to host a small gathering of mourners at the house after the rites. Upstairs in my old room, I saw that Julie's private garden of potted orchids and exotic herbs was as opulent as she'd described it in letters and during our monthly phone conversations (it didn't matter how distant I was, I never failed to call her). The scent, it struck me, was precisely what heaven should smell like, were there such a place. Fluid, rich, evocative, somehow soft.

I closed my eyes and breathed this sensual air, and as I did, a wave of deep tranquillity washed through me. This tranquillity even had a color, a dense matte cream, into which I rose, or sank; it was hard to tell the difference. I believed I was crying, though the cognitive disconnect, however brief, wouldn't quite allow me to know this with certainty. The episode, like some epileptic seizure of the psyche, finally passed, but not before delivering me another of the hallucinations I had been experiencing.

As I turned to leave—flee, rather—the room, I caught sight of a vertiginous Julie, alive in the mirror on the wall behind a sinuously arched blooming orchid, her dark eyes as filled with hysteria as mine must have been. Then she was gone, replaced, as before, by me—and yes, my eyes displayed a scouring dread, not without a tinge of sad disbelief.

Nothing like this had ever happened to me, and if they weren't so eminently real, I'd have insisted to myself that these *petits mals* were strictly the effects of melancholy. But something else was in play about which I had no clear insight. Some incipient voice inside me suggested that the covenant Julie and I had made as children bore more authority than she and I'd imagined possible. Placing my overnight bag on her bed, I asked myself, Could she have managed to pull it off, to linger, to keep our childhood pact?

Voices downstairs brought me to my senses. I was about to shout to my mother that I'd arrived when I realized I was hearing my father and Maureen, the last people on earth I needed to see just now. Like so many houses from the Victorian era, this one had a set of narrow back steps leading down to a pantry off the kitchen. Julie and I never tired of playing in this claustrophobic corridor, which was lit by octagonal stained-glass windows, and often used it, to our mother's exasperation, as an escape route when we happened to be hightailing it from some chore or punishment. Its usefulness in this regard was as valued now as then—having to confront my father at that moment would have qualified as both a chore and punishment—so I slipped quietly downstairs, out the pantry door into the back yard.

Some clouds intruded on the earlier pure blue above, and the temperature definitely had dropped since morning. I wished I could run back inside and grab the windbreaker I'd shoved into my bag in the city, but figured it wasn't worth the risk. Rolling down the sleeves of my shirt, I headed across the lawn (needed mowing or else I'd have walked more swiftly) and along a row of pin oaks whose leaves were ruddy red, like dyed leather. Other than the drone of distant machinery—a road crew clearing a fallen branch with a wood chipper, I guessed—the air was dead silent. Someone was burning a pile of brush nearby; a skein of transparent brownish gray floated across the middle air. Two girls, from out of nowhere, came running past me laughing wildly, paying no attention to me, nearly knocking me down in their great rush. It smelled a little like it might rain.

Once I was out of sight of the house, walking the next block over, I slackened my pace and contemplated, as best I could manage given the crosscurrents of what had been happening, what to do. Not that I needed to deliberate for long. My feet instinctively knew it was imperative to go to Middle Falls Cemetery. The graveyard was in a meadow on the far side of the town's pathetic waterfall, and getting there involved crossing down past the main street where, I expected—rightly, it turned out—no one would notice me, John Tillman, Julie Tillman's brother who defected a lifetime ago. The soda shop we'd loved to frequent was, amazingly, still there, Katzman's, one of the few Jews in this largely Christian enclave and maker of the best egg cream north of Coney Island. Ancient but still alive, there behind the counter stood, I swore, Katzman himself, who had concocted for Julie every Saturday afternoon a superb monstrosity made with pistachio ice cream, green maraschino cherries, sprinkles, whipped cream, and salted peanuts. The thought of it still makes my spine tingle, but she loved it, and good old Katzman, too. I walked on, my head crowded with memories. There was the grocery market. There was the post office. There was the combined barbershop and shoe store (its owner, Mr. Fry was his name, boasted of *head-to-toe service under one roof,* as I recollect). There was the package store whose proprietor was always lobbying, without success, for a repeal of the blue laws. And there was the florist where I'd stop on my way back to pick up a dozen calla lilies. It wasn't hard to picture my sister walking in and out of any of these places and, yes, I had to admit there was a misty comfort in village life. God knows, I'd seen trace evidence of such systemized culture clusters in my own fieldwork, and admired—from an objective distance of hundreds, or sometimes thousands, of years—the purity and practicality of intimate social configuration. In many ways it was a shame misty comfort never agreed with me, I thought, as I crossed the foot-bridge that led through another neighborhood and, finally, to the cemetery where Julie was to be buried. But one cannot change intrinsic self-truths, I didn't believe.

What did we love about this place? For one, all the carved white stones, with their cherubic faces of angels and upward-soaring doves, their *bas-relief* gargoyles, not to mention their glorious names and antique dates. The trees here were especially old and seemed to us repositories of special knowledge; the Frazer of *Golden Bough* fame knew all about this. Here was a place our minds could run as wild as the spirits of the dead. This was how we thought, two pale, skinny children with no better friends than each another. I saw, quite soon, half a hundred yards away, the pile of freshly dug dirt I'd come looking for without really knowing it. I strode between grave markers to the earthen cavity into which my Julie would be lowered to begin the longest part of any human existence: eternal repose. I peered in, curious and frankly as uninhibited as anyone who'd spent his time excavating artifacts of the long dead, and the desiccated, frozen, or bog-preserved remains of men whose hands had fashioned those very tools and trinkets. One always forgot how deep a contemporary North American grave is. My guess is that in our memories we fill them in a little, make them shallower, as if we might undo a bit the terminal ruination that is mortality. Against my archaeological instincts I kicked some soil back into the hole. Some queer corner of my soul concocted the idea that I ought to climb down into her burial pit myself and spend a few speculative moments on my back, looking upward at the now fully overcast sky, try to commune with Julie in her future resting place while there was still the chance.

I didn't. Instead, I walked back to town, forgetting, in my sudden rush to climb the hill to the mortuary and view the corpse of my dear twin, to purchase the dozen lilies I'd wanted to lay at the foot of her coffin gurney, her penultimate berth. It seemed I was moving swiftly and slowly at the same time, thoughts streaming like an ironic spring melt under a harvest moon.

She and I were in a play together in high school once. *Love's Labour's Lost.* Julie was the Princess of France, and I, who coveted the role of King Ferdinand of Navarre, wasn't much of a thespian and wound up playing Costard, the clown. I can only remember one of her lines, which went, *To the death we will not move a foot,* which I naturally misinterpreted at the time to mean that, like Julie and me, the princess had no intention of giving in to mortality. Later, I realized Shakespeare's message was quite different. All Julie's princess was trying to say was, well, *never.* As for my poor Costard, I can't remember a single word I worked so hard to memorize for the production. What made me think of this? Impossible to know, since the high school was located on the southeast edge of town and my walk from the cemetery in no way converged with it. I felt that my mind, which unlike my body wasn't used to wandering, was out of sync with itself.

Reentering the house by the pantry door, I found myself alone, the hollow ticking of the kitchen clock the only sound in the place. On the table lay a note, a memo in my mother's gracefully dated round handwriting, with the words *We've gone ahead up the hill, will meet you there, dear.* What had I been thinking? Here it was already half past four, and in my daydreamy meandering I had managed to miss the beginning of Julie's funeral. No time to change clothes. Informed by many a summer's tramping up to the mortuary grounds, my feet intimately knew the path. As I made my way, I noticed the edges of my vision were blurred, causing me to believe I'd begun to weep again, just as I had back in the city when I first learned the news of my sister's death. But when I touched my eyes to brush away the tears, I found them dry. Though this was not the first intimation that something might be wrong with me, that I somehow seemed to have lost a crucial equilibrium without which consciousness makes little or no sense, it was the first of my hallucinations I could not ignore.

I climbed the hill with a quicker step, yet it was as if I approached my destination ever more unhurriedly. What was before me oddly receded. It felt as if I were walking backward. All the while, my tearless weeping—or whatever caused my sight to smear—continued unabated, worsened actually, the neighborhood elms and oaks melting into watery pools of ocher, hazel, and every sort of red. I believe I blinked hard, several times, hoping to will away this tunneling vision. The great Victorian houses on either side of the block, dressed in their cheery gingerbread, were like shimmery globules of undifferentiated mass rising up toward the now-gray ceiling of sky overhead. By dint of sheer volition I managed to reach the top of the hill, where I left the sidewalk and made my way across the lawn toward the mortuary.

In the mideighties, I was invited to participate in a dig on the southern coast of Cyprus. The Greco-Roman port city of Kourian, which had been partially excavated in the thirties, but had since been untouched by grave robbers and classical archaeologists alike, was to be our site. Early on the morning of July 21, in 365 AD, a massive earthquake had leveled every structure in this seaside town even as it snuffed out the lives of its inhabitants in a matter of minutes. What few people might have survived the falling rubble were drowned in the monster tidal waves that followed. While we dug from room to room through the hive of attached stone houses, the discoveries made by the team were nothing shy of miraculous. The skeleton of a little girl, whom we named Camelia, was found next to the remains of a mule—her workmate, we presumed—in a stable adjacent to her bedroom. Coins littered the sandy floor, as well as glass from the jar that once held them. Here was a wrought-copper volute lamp; here were amphorae. As we unearthed the physical record of this disaster, a tender intimacy developed between the members of our team and the victims of the quake. On our final day we made a discovery that was, for me, at least, the most moving of any I'd ever witnessed. A baby cradled in its mother's arms, the woman in turn being embraced by a man who was clearly trying to shelter them both with his body. Such love and natural courage were present in these spooning bones. I could hardly wait to get Julie on a transatlantic line to tell her what we had found.

For reasons that will now never be wholly clear to me, I did decide, as I approached the mortuary with its imposing, if very fake, Doric columns, to attend my sister's funeral from the vantage of our old secret hiding place. Maybe I felt, deep down, I simply couldn't face my father. Perhaps I feared sitting next to my mother, whose tears, no doubt, would be as real as they were copious. I don't know; it hardly matters. My vision, in any case, had only further disintegrated during the moments of my memory of the dig at Cyprus, and I had to wonder if I could manage to make myself presentable in front of others inside the funeral home. Pushing aside the hawthorne leaves, my hands splaying the shrubbery just as they might if I were wading into an ocean, I peeked through the window and saw, with what sight was left to me, the mourners within. A smaller group than I might have expected, since Julie had always been the more gregarious of the two of us. It was as if I could hear her voice whispering in my ear, just then, when I remembered my sister's response to that call I made telling her about the family in Kourian.

Over the years from time to time, she'd referred to me as a gardener of stones, but that day she told me she thought I was a gardener of heart. I liked that. It was the nicest thing anyone ever said to me, before or since. As the first drops of rain began to fall, and the crumbling margins of my vision grew inward toward the center of all that I could see, I felt a strong communion with the community of the many dead, and with my sister, too. My sister, Julie, who turned from where she sat in the front row nearest the casket and gazed at her shocked and vanishing brother in the window, her brother who offered her, as best he could, a smile of farewell.

WHOM NO HATE STIRS NONE DANCES

S TILL DRESSED IN HIS SHINY BLACK SUIT and graying white shirt he wore to church and not a full minute in Mama's house, Cutts sought, found, and pulled down on the cord that hung from the trap door to the attic. His wife, Georgia, stood behind him, barefoot, having left her black pumps downstairs by the door.

"Cutts, what are you doing?" I asked. "Georgia, what on earth's he doing?"

Ignoring me, my brother climbed the ladder that dangled from a square hole in the ceiling like a tired lattice tongue. A fine, mildewed mist of dust was shaken into the warm air of the hallway with each step he took. Georgia warned him if he wasn't careful the whole thing was going to work free of its old bolts and come crashing down. "We don't need another funeral today," she added, half in joyless jest, half not in jest at all.

But whether he heard her or not, Cutts didn't say a word before disappearing into the darkness of the attic, a man obsessed.

"Well, anyway," she said, turning to me with a weary shrug, maybe a bit embarrassed that he so easily dismissed her without the slightest pretense of wedded civility.

Wanting to shift the focus away from Cutts and his rudeness, I told Georgia I had something in my eye. She took me over to the window at the end of the hall and asked me to look up. Folding her handkerchief into a pointed cone, she removed it, a little black particle of who knows what fallen from the attic.

"There you go, Jen," she said, then suggested I ought to wash my face with some nice cold water—my eyes were red from Mama's service. It was kind of her, I thought, to temporarily assume the role of big sister. After all, I was, I admit, still pretty dazed by the hard, bald, plain fact that I would no longer be my mother's caretaker. My future stretched before me like the empty plains just beyond the outskirts of town where we, now I, lived.

Meantime, there was no escaping Cutts. We heard him stomping about overhead like muffled thunder miles away in a stale afternoon, the way it plays around the perimeters of heat lightning. The thump of a chair, or maybe a lamp, its globe chipped, its wire frayed, carried from above with exaggerated weight and portent. Doing her level best to ignore him, Georgia brushed her hair in silence. When will this water ever get cold? I wondered, as my sister-in-law left the bathroom and I stared at my puffy face in the mirror.

She had been dying for years, Mama had, of a seemingly limitless variety of ailments. I nursed her through the days that led from one problem to another. During these last twelve months, however, the pain made her behave more and more peculiarly. My brother Cutts and Georgia drove out to visit her here in Lincoln in September, all the way from Maryland. But Mama couldn't recognize either one of them, and so she asked them to leave. Other than me, she never recognized anybody by then. Not the neighbors, some of whom she had known her whole life, not the kindly minister, not even Dr. Farley, whose own father had delivered her wailing into the world in the same house that stands three doors down the block. Reverend Robotham and Farley had each before witnessed this kind of gradual lapse into amnesia or whatever it was, but Cutts took it hard.

"Ephram, you get on back to your own home, or else—"

"But, Mama," I interrupted. "This isn't Ephram. It's Cutts."

"Ma, it's me, Cutts, your son?"

"Cutts?"

"There you go, that's right. Cutts. Me, your son."

"Cutts," she said again, pondering.

"Right."

"Get me some ginger ale, would you?"

And yet when Cutts returned to her bedroom with her glass of ginger ale, she let out a sharp scream. "I thought I told Ephram to get. Still here? You go on and get out of here this minute."

None of us knew any Ephram.

"She's lost her mind," Cutts whispered hoarsely in the front room. "Farley's wasting our money. How long's this been going on?"

I had never noticed how the blood vessels could stand up so tall on my brother's forehead before that moment, thick and blue as rancid meat.

That was the only time Cutts and I saw each other after he and Georgia moved east when they got married, so we'd really lost touch with one another. But I remembered that tone of his like I'd heard it every day of my life. It trembled, angry and accusing, at the edge of his teeth. Georgia understood his angular, irritable voice, too.

"Cutts," she said, quietly admonishing.

He scowled. "Old sow'll probably outlive every last one of us, and Farley? He'll retire to a big beach house in the Bahamas on any inheritance we might've hoped for."

Out in the front yard, my gnarly crabapple trees were twirling their new leaves in a coquettish display of April's promise. The spring leaves in the cherry and cottonwood trees were shimmering in the light breezes, too.

"Well, all right then," said Cutts, not noticing the dancing leaves or anything else as he backed away toward their Impala without so much as a handshake.

"Well, all right," I echoed. Maybe if he had stayed a night or two, Mama might have come around and recognized her oldest child. But he made it clear that the whole trip out had been a waste of time.

Georgia stepped forward, embraced me, a forlorn smile quivering on her lips. "Listen here, Jenny. Anything you need, just write, or call, call collect, promise? Cutts?"

But Cutts was already sitting in the car. The luggage they'd brought hadn't even been taken out of the trunk.

"Thank you, Georgia," I said.

"You take care, darling."

She turned to go.

"Oh, Georgia?"

"Yes?" turning back.

"Mama doesn't mean to be like that to Cutts. She's that way to just about everybody."

They left, not to be heard from until I wired them to say that our mother had died.

During her last month, the woman began calling out for Desmond during the night. She had never concealed her preference for Desmond over Cutts. Desmond had from the beginning been her favorite, her final born, her glory, and it was on him that she pinned a wide range of impossible hopes. Desmond would bring fortune and respect to their family, Desmond was her golden boy. The world, she felt, would be wise to spread itself willingly at his feet and provide for him a passive surface upon which he might make whatever mark he pleased, take whatever path he liked.

But for all the heroic qualities attributed him by his devoted mother, Jenny and Cutts's younger brother, Desmond, was as dim-witted as a milking stool. Be that as it may, Cutts did allow him to participate in the various escapades of the neighborhood gang, even though he was younger by several years than most of its members. Lanky, proportioned like the reflection in a funhouse mirror, Desmond stood a head taller than any of the other boys. Gamely, he trailed behind the pack, loping, slouched, knuckles swinging at his sides like a tight row of bantam eggs attached to the fronts of his fists. At his older brother's proprietary bidding, Desmond pursued whatever follies the gang did, but less for the adventure in and of itself than for Cutts's treasured attention. His wildness belied his weakness. He played a willing fool whenever called upon to do so.

If Cutts had his first taste of beer at twelve, or his first cigarette, then Desmond accordingly had his by nine. The tolls of Desmond's adolescence were an arithmetic function based on Cutts's own imperfections, needs, frenzies, to the exclusion of anything else. Desmond himself was not compulsive, but was caught as if in a vacuum that was created in the wake of his brother's will. It was always just ahead of him, drawing him on.

Cutts knew it was for his approbation that Desmond lived. He offered it only when he found it convenient or useful, when it fit into some specific scheme. If it suited Cutts, whenever any or all of the gang were in trouble, Desmond would be delivered up as the collective scapegoat. Out from under Cutts's fickle wing he would come, tacit and willing to atone for some petty theft, a water tower east of the city painted with obscenities, a smashed window, a broken arm or black eye.

In time Desmond had a worse reputation than Cutts, or any of the others. That is why when he broke the code of silence about what had happened to Jenny that one August evening, sunk now with a quarter century of other Augusts into anonymity, no one, not even his mother, believed him.

After that August, Desmond went moody, glum. He exiled himself from the gang of boys. He disappeared for days at a time. He wouldn't speak when spoken to. He died in November, just a few weeks before his eighteenth birthday. No one would ever be quite sure what had occurred. There was no looped belt nailed to a basement crossbeam, nothing as telling as that, no bridge off which he'd hurled himself into a partly frozen river. Nor were there any guns in the house. No, he simply tumbled down the stairs to the cellar floor, opened his head like an overripe melon on a flange where the railing had been detached.

Cutts found him first. Jenny had been putting out bread crumbs on the crunchy snow for late robins and meadowlarks that needed feeding for their migration south. Mr. Beechel Gray, the butcher, took the call from Cutts and passed the phone across the smooth white stone counter to Desmond's mother, who fainted on the sawdust-strewn floor when she was given the news.

•

The water, loosely cradled in my fingers, cooled my face. I soaked a hand towel under its thin, lazy stream and, hunching forward over the shallow sink while holding my hair up off my shoulder, ran the cold, wet cloth across the nape of my neck. It trickled down my back when I stood up straight. I wrung the towel, folded it, replaced it on the rack to dry. As I did, I caught myself thinking that if I ever had to go to another funeral service it might best be my own, since the three I'd attended—my father's when I was young, Desmond's in my early twenties, and now Mama's, leaving me behind in my new role of middle-aged bachelor lady—left me feeling as depleted and barren as a dead cornstalk in a winter field.

What happened next startled me out of my doldrums. I was surprised to see, reflected in the mirror, Georgia leaning, arms crossed, lightly against the jamb of the bathroom doorway. She was looking at me with an expression indescribably strange. Quizzical. Her puzzled oval face, pretty and punctuated by sharp features, whiter than the veiny marble of the sink, was set off by her black dress and dark hair. She seemed a different person than the Georgia I'd always known, little that I actually knew her.

She smiled, lips tight. "That better?"

I turned off the water and nodded at her mirrored image.

"See? I knew a little cold water would help."

She remained in the doorway as I straightened my hair, not really knowing what better to do with myself and uncomfortable given that odd look on her face.

"Didn't mean to startle you."

"Oh, not at all," I brightly lied, turning to face her with a tight-lipped smile of my own. "Just thought you'd gone downstairs is all. I guess Cutts is still up there in the attic."

"God knows what's so important he couldn't even change out of his good suit before he had to start rummaging around in all that dust and cobwebs."

What's he after? I might have begun, but Georgia made a sign for me to follow her, turned suddenly, and walked down the hallway in the opposite direction of the attic ladder, downstairs to the kitchen in the back of the house. When she turned toward me again, the color in her cheeks and neck had changed. In the haggard afternoon light, whose summer skies were gathering thunderheads in stacks of white and violet and green and gray out all the windows, her face had gone ashen.

"Can we talk for a minute?" she asked, quietly.

"Is it about the house? Because if it is, I won't know what to say, Georgia." Having literally forgotten her son's existence, Mama had willed me her house and possessions.

"No, no. Something else completely."

I stood there awkward by the stove, waiting.

"Look. I know it's a bad time, terrible time, to talk about things. But since you—we never see you, and Cutts has got to be back to work day after tomorrow, I just feel I have to talk with you now."

Georgia sat at the kitchen table on one of the hardwood chairs, and I joined her. The table was still cluttered with bottles of old medicine, handwritten schedules for pill-giving and the administration of shots, as well as a week of dishes I had not been able to bring myself to wash. My sister-in-law looked troubled. She fidgeted with a pack of cigarettes, drew one out, lighted it, and deeply inhaled, as if it were the first breath of air she had ever taken.

"About half a year ago, I don't know how to say this, about five or six months ago, I got a letter—well, not a letter exactly. It was from your mother."

"Oh?"

How Georgia thought it was possible for Mama to have mailed her a letter, I couldn't guess. Mama, invalided these past few years, and especially so during the grim final months of her life, and who only came out into the sunlight when Reverend Robotham and I carried her down into the back yard and laid her on a clean blanket next to the bed of snapdragons and black-eyed Susans she loved. I listened without questioning.

"Her name was right there on the envelope. Since she addressed it to me, not Cutts, I opened it. But, Jenny, it was the darnedest thing. What was inside wasn't a letter from your mother. It was a kind of document, like a pact, I guess you could say, and all written out longhand on this oatmeal paper?"

The word *paper* traced an upward arc, transformed itself into a question. Georgia hoped that I might by this detail—*oatmeal paper*—be prompted into recognition of something she obviously would rather not have to put into words herself.

I said, "I see."

"The handwriting was a child's."

After a long stretch of silence upstairs, Cutts continued with his noisemaking.

I asked Georgia, "Would you care for some sherry? I think I could do with a little myself." I opened the cabinet door, got out two of Mama's crystal vine-stemmed glasses and the Taylor amontillado that was her favorite, so pale, so tobacco-yellow and strong, and brought them to the table, where, after clearing a space, I set them down. I could hear Cutts banging around at the westernmost corner of the attic, then he went silent again. I knew exactly which barrel-topped trunk he was picking through now. It would take him half an hour to dissect its contents even if, as I suspected, he didn't bother to replace what he'd removed.

"It had to be years old, I knew," Georgia went on, taking a sip of the amontillado. "The way it almost came into pieces along where it was creased. Anyway, it was a pact—"

The stillness from Cutts's periphery unnerved me more than I thought it might, but I reassured myself, steeled myself, thinking, *Go on, let it happen, whatever happens, let him come down now, let him do us all the—*

"—between Cutts and your brother and—"

"Desmond?"

"Yes, and some other names, too. They'd made this treaty, I guess you could call it. It was, well—but, Jenny, I can't. What I want to ask is, is it true?"

She had put the question to the reflective, circular surface of sherry, stationary on the table before her.

I thought, *What a lovely woman. Worry can sometimes be so becoming in a person.*

That attic where everything was lost. And Father at the time downstairs, sedated. Dr. Farley had gone home, having put his syringe, his morphine, his instruments, back into that black scratched and bubbled leather bag of his. Mama and me the doctor had left to stand by the bed to prop and reprop pillows, smooth the coverlet, gaze into his eyes runny and vacant as an old horse's. Dad not knowing where he was, pushing up with his hands outstretched as if something on the ceiling threatened him, pushing and pushing it away. The deathly farrago of sounds he made so upset his poor wife, my mother, that she had to leave the room not to burst into tears in front of him. The light in the room, color of a peach. Eisenhower making a speech in his simple way on the scratchy radio. Kitchen smells, roast beef and gravy. Early evening. August. Back when.

"Desmond?" Mama hollered. "Dessie? Cutts?" Then she returned to the room, sat down on the bed, its springs complaining. "Go, would you, Jenny, and find those brothers of yours."

I ran outside into the twilight and down the street toward the places where I knew they might be hanging out. Not in the playground park. The druggist's was empty, its row of stools with mottled vinyl aligned kind of sad somehow before the long counter, Coke taps, pie racks, ketchup bottles, the stainless-steel malted cup—

Not here . . . I know where they are.

—and the movie posters I loved to stare at while I sat up to the counter drinking my cherry soda, especially the one for *Lifeboat*, Tallulah Bankhead and all those desperate men and women huddled together, waves licking the prow of their doomed boat, and as I stared into an image I myself would easily slip inside, so that it was I who held the red pony's reins in *The Red Pony*. As I ran like the wind back along the uneven concrete slabs of sidewalk, the unforgettable vision of that pony's eyes planted in my father's head by his sickness—pitiful, liquid, pleading—returned to me. Nothing in the world I could do to help him, any more than I could have saved those people in the lifeboat. But I could do what my mother asked, because I knew where Cutts, Des, and the gang were hiding.

Cutts didn't like to see him, see his father now that he was ill. He didn't like to be around anyone who was weak or sick. Besides, my dad and his oldest son never got along. Desmond would want whatever his brother wanted, no doubt, but he too ventured into the master bedroom only when Mama made him, to kiss his cancered father good night, or to say good-bye before taking the bus over to Grand Island to visit Uncle Tune.

When I got back home, I silently entered by the back porch. Mama was still in Father's room. She was reading to him aloud,

". . . shall come forth a rod out of the stem of Jesse, and
a Branch shall grow out of his roots, and the spirit . . ."

in a singsong.

Once safely past the half-shut door, up the stairs and down the hallway, I groped for the cord in the growing darkness and could already hear them stirring upstairs in the attic. It was one of their sacred places. I knew I was breaking an unspoken rule, but my mother's request and my own curiosity overrode that concern. A crack of yellow light, excited by shadows, thrown from a candle flame, flickered above me when I pulled down on the cord, releasing the ceiling ladder. The silence that accompanied this broken pattern of light seemed strange, and I had the sensation of being like Alice tipped upside down and dropped heavenward into a dreamy, maybe unfriendly, Wonderland.

I climbed the ladder, eyes fixed on each rung, where foot over foot I placed my weight. I had never been up to the attic before. Why was it they were all so quiet? I wanted to look up but was afraid I'd lose my footing. I was too terrified to scream when hands and arms came down suddenly around my body and I was lifted away free into the near-pitch air, too shocked as I gave in, my legs kicking and wheeling uselessly, these strong, strange fingers that hoisted me by my hair and my dress tight under my neck just starting to tear and my hips and arms into the horrible with hands all over my down in my—

Someone whispered, "No." Someone hit me.

Crazy old dead bitch, well it's over now. Jesus, what a pigsty. Sixty years and more with never so much as a tatty housecoat fed to the incinerator, never one single burned-out toaster tossed in the trash. Here's a milk carton filled with plaster of paris. Why? Here's a birdcage. Cockatoos, canaries, we never had any. Sight of a bird she'd be covered in hives. Allergic to everything, so was Des. What's it doing here for godsakes? And this tittied mannequin, purse-lipped, bobbed nose, always a faithful mistress to us and how we loved her, so indulgent, how many times did I? Dressed her, undressed her. Crazy kids. Good days, those, the best. Holy place this was for us, secret society, hallowed be thy shame. Wonder did dear old Ma ever wonder. Watch out, the joist. Oh, pint-size bike, tires—the rubber hard, flat. King of hearts, jack of spades, Grandma's canasta cards still there on the rim, too, clothespins over the spokes ready to go snappety-snappety-snap. Crazy. Mueller with his half arm. Rode better than any of us, feet on the butt saddle, remember? How'd he lose it? Never asked. Born that way, was it? That little nipple on the end of the stump, murder at tetherball. Menace to the prudes, freak show. Clem and Jimmy were scared of him, but a lamb he was. Wonder who, what he's sticking it into right now. Nice guy, but whacked. Might be pushing up roses, the Mule might. Skin white as a factory-fresh softball. Those red basset eyes blown straight down the pike from his mater, that sad old shrew, real guzzler. Like a barn, that one was. Me sitting on the Mule's shoulders, moonless night, peeking in at her naked as an elephant, bottle in one hand and fag in the other, sunk back in her armchair watching the black-and-white set. No husband from the word go. Poor old bastard Mueller.

There she was, always alone, always the curtains undrawn. She must've known, might have put the Mule up to it. Nuts. Here's the photo albums, won't look. Des. All of them. The old man, won't look. So sour smelling, not sweet like mothballs, but this paper, these books, the mildew. Roof must leak. Somebody's nest, tickertape, little mouse. What we need here is a piece of sharp cheddar, a trap, and ping! Who was it we made eat the mothball soaked in his own piddle? Phineas, was it? Omaha, schoolteacher now. Wouldn't his wife love to know about—

Wake up, wake up, wake *up*.

Goddamn little bitch . . . it's not as if . . . it's got to be here somewhere. It never happened, that's what happened.

"Why don't we leave him be?" Jenny advised Georgia.

They had left the kitchen, carrying their sherry glasses back through the vagaries of rooms, windows shrouded in damask and undusted lace, through the staleness of deathly still air, for the deep veranda that ran the length of the front of the house. Two phoebes shot like feathery bullets from their mud nest lodged in the rafters. The dense, earthy air had begun to move. Miles out to the horizon, a black bank gusted eastward, diligently following the columns of rain that preceded it, released from its nearest edges. They could see the storm through the vined screen at the west end of the porch, out over the plumes of big-leafed oaks and cottonwoods, as it descended toward town.

"Feel how quick this heat is breaking?"

But Georgia said nothing. She watched her sister-in-law's inscrutable face—severe, childish, intent—and marveled at how few features she shared with her brother Cutts. It seemed to Georgia as if this face were wrapped in a transparent gauze, occlusive, separated from the rest of the world, its desecrations, its filth. Jenny forbore, thought Georgia. That was the right word for it.

Rocking lightly in the porch swing, Jenny finally asked her sister-in-law, "So, you have it with you, I guess?"

"Yes."

"Go ahead and let me see it, then."

Georgia set her glass on the wicker stand. She pulled the envelope from her blouse cuff. "Here."

Jenny removed the folded piece of browned paper from the envelope, leveled her eyes at Georgia, who sat again in a chair that faced the swing. She unfolded it and read without any expression what was written.

What we done with Jenny was law, it began.

With decisive, nimble movements, she then refolded the sheet and set it beside her on the swing. "What we done with Jenny was law," she quoted, low-voiced.

Georgia could hear her own strained breathing. The answers to the questions she wanted to ask had already come through Jenny's few gestures and by the distant penciled injunction. She felt she already knew the answers, but had to pose the questions that would precede them in any case. "Jenny? What was it?"

Abruptly, disconcertingly, Jenny laughed. "It was their precinct, their holy little . . . well, wasn't it?"

"No, I mean what happened?"

And as abruptly the laughter stopped.

"My dear ridiculous Georgia, please. What do you want from me? It was a lifetime ago."

"But then what are those other names?"

"Jesus," she said, and her eyes ran the length of the rain gutter. "They all just, they all—"

Somewhere down the block two dogs began barking.

"Cutts, he?"

Jenny's lips closed into a fine, straight line.

"Desmond too?"

"No, not Desmond."

Softly the rain began to report across the roof of the veranda, and in the grass and trees surrounding the house. Jenny watched Georgia weep, drily.

Now I always liked her, always will. Way she helped me clear Mama's medicines, useless now without a patient, gather them up into a brown grocery sack, seal it with masking tape, and bury it under other garbage in the tin can out in the alley so the neighborhood children couldn't rummage it up. Way she set to washing the dishes, which I dried, both of us dressed in our mourning blacks, sleeves rolled up to the elbows. Way she had come over and held me in her arms, rocking gently, as the porch swing creaked. The way she let me take her by the hand and lead her out into the steady, light rain, around the side of the house, where the hollyhocks fell over themselves in their own abundance, into the kitchen through the back door. It was not a time to run into Cutts, was it, what with both of us in tears and him in his rage at not finding it? And the way Georgia would never ask me whether it was I who sent the letter. And also I felt assured that she would after all go back home with Cutts, because she hoped that in the passage of time I had in fact forgiven him, and how she could feel this was true because it was I who insisted I had forgiven him.

But how the matter now would never really come to rest inside her. How it would gnaw at her and in the oddest moments come up, like a nausea, outrageous, insuppressible. Cutts would never again be able to run his hands over her, push himself inside her in quite the same way as he had in times past. That was over now. And as for Georgia, I was certain she surely preferred knowing this truth about him. She will go on home to Maryland with him and they will lie down at night in their warm bed after their long journey, but it won't be Georgia asleep beside him. Not truly Georgia.

She is standing next to me before the sink. Her long, delicate hands are pushing the sponge around the stained circle of a plate, as she stares hard into the soapy water. A real sister, the one I never had.

All the while, the noise Cutts makes upstairs is growing more and more violent. His cursing filters down like a shower in a nightmare where the rain soaks its victim though it never actually gets him wet—however drenched in his own sweat he may be on awakening in his twisted bedclothes. Poor pathetic Cutts, the way he is going on up there, looking and looking. Let him break every stick of furniture, every memento, every bit of family history in that badly lit, hysterical attic.

Let him shout. Let him grind his teeth.

AMAZING GRACE

Whereas I was blind, now I see.
—John 9:25

THE MIRACLE THAT RESTORED my sight, one winter morning, was a miracle that led to many desperate others. Who could have foreseen the catastrophes that followed this moment I had dreamed of for over a decade? The only blessing that accompanied the sudden, unexpected reversal of my blindness was this: I was alone when it happened. My wife was away shopping; the two children were out. Myself, I was in my humble study, listening to an old recording of Sviatoslav Richter playing Schubert's Sonata in G Major. Thanks to Sarah, a fire crackled in the wood-burning stove, making my sanctum warm and dry—the room where I worked was an uninsulated extension added to the house in the months after my accident. A pot of nice fragrant cinnamon tea was on my desk, along with my braille Bible, some reference books also in braille, and my computer loaded with voice-synthesizing software I used to draft the many motivational speeches I gave touring the country. It has always struck me as ironic, although naturally I never mentioned it in my uplifting talks, that I made a far better living after the accident than when I was among the sighted. No one would have paid a plugged nickel to hear me speak before tragedy struck me down. Now I filled rented auditoriums and hotel convention halls, and my talks on surviving personal crises were well received wherever I went. Not that my philosophy about adversity management was more informed or refined than the next survivor's—not a vain bone in *this* body—it's just my story had all the necessary elements. The perfect life, the great disabling affliction, the season of despair, the awakening of hope, and the long road of spiritual renewal that rewards the steadfast pilgrim with a life far richer than what seemed so perfect before. Sarah, I must say, deftly supervised this unantici-pated chautauqua career of mine, from bookings to billings, and oversaw with the help of our dedicated manager every detail of our burgeoning mission. And with seldom—no, never—a complaint. She was nothing less than a stoic saint, an altruistic martyr, with just enough savvy to hold our shattered lives together, not only keeping her eye on our spiritual needs, but making sure there was always bread on the table.

One reason I have been so successful on the circuit is that I believed every word I said, or at least most every word. To the sort of individual who attends such seminars, unwavering personal conviction on the part of the speaker is nine-tenths the victory. I have often felt that if I held up an egg in the palm of my hand and proclaimed with firm faith that it was not an egg, but a flower or a shoe, say, the right audience of seekers would cry out in agree-ment, *So it is!* With conviction and what might be called a winning idiosyncrasy in the presenter—in my case, the blindness—one can bring people around to anything. That I never used my powers of persuasion to ends other than kindly inspiration, positive role modeling, carrying the simple message of hope to souls willing to listen, pleases me. The temptation to deceive was always there, somehow, but it was a human weakness never acted upon. Not that I'd have known what to deceive my acolytes about, nor that I ever made the logical next step to consider the possibility that some of them entertained deceptive thoughts regarding me. No one, I convinced myself, would want to victimize this victim. Hadn't I suffered enough? The answer was, I had not even begun my real suffering.

Not born blind, indeed I had twenty-twenty vision for thirty years. A robust, confident young man, I met my Sarah at a church bazaar—we were always active members at St. Francis Episcopal—and it was love at first sight. Her thick auburn hair drifting in gentle waves down the back of her white dress, her quick blue eyes, the exquisite mole above her lip, the warm hands that shook mine when we were introduced, her smile as sunny as dawn. How many times since my world fell into shadow have I conjured up the visual memory of that day. After a succinct courtship, we married and started a family. Rebecca was born first, and then the twins, Emma and Luke. Emma survived only a few weeks, poor little bird. My grief over the loss was so great that to this day I indulge in fantasizing about her, what her interests would have been, how her voice might have sounded. I would like to think she'd have turned out a trustworthy Milton's daughter. In my mind's eye, I always pictured her as a young Sarah, pliant as a willow and sturdy as an oak, along those lines. But we all know how ingenious imagination can be, how it sometimes finds a shining berth in the rankest mound of dung.

Time passed, our young family thrived. My job at the utilities company was going well enough; the benefits were good and hours such that I could spend quality time with my children. I worked the graveyard shift at the local power plant as a maintenance technician troubleshooting outages, servicing customer emergencies, getting people back on line when an ice storm or high wind brought down wires or blew out a transformer. In the Northeast, where we live just a mile from my own childhood home, our crew had more to do during the night than one might imagine. Always something going wrong, always some problem to remedy. I very much enjoyed the challenge, as I've told my rapt audiences, and learned a lot meeting people from all walks of life under trying circumstances. So long as I live, I will never forget the courage of the little girl—her name was Belinda, if I'm not mistaken—who, during a severe nor'easter that crippled not just Gloucester but the whole corridor from the Carolinas up to Maine, offered her mommy her teddy bear to feed to the flames in the fireplace that heated their home while our crew worked through the night to restore power. A bunch of us later pooled some cash together to buy her a new bear, bigger and fuzzier than the one she sacrificed. Duress brings out the best in us—so I often advised my Ramada listeners. In a file somewhere there is a newspaper clipping with a photograph of Belinda surrounded by her benefactors and our stuffed bear. Sarah had it up on the refrigerator for months. She thought it was a flattering shot. I must have looked pleased with myself, because in those days I was. Life was a river awash with proverbial milk and honey.

A stifling, muggy midsummer night changed all that. I wasn't even supposed to work the shift, but a massive brownout across our regional grid forced the company to call upon every available hand. My memory of that night is selective at best. I whispered good-bye to Sarah, kissed the children where they lay asleep in their bedrooms. The streets were eerily dim. Thick, steamy amber haze hung in the wilted trees. Cicadas had burrowed up from the earth to mate that year—dogday locusts, we called them—and were lustily clicking and buzzing away outside the open windows of our utility van, their boisterous droning sounding like bandsaws underwater. We were hard at work on a central routing transformer, using the headlights of the van to see, when I must have made the simplest error, crossing two clusters of wire in such a way that I sparked a high-voltage explosion. Knocked unconscious, I have no recollection of what happened in the hours that followed. My first perceptions had only to do with a searing, bludgeoning pain in my neck and around the base of my hot skull. My face was burned and my eyes felt as if they were molten.

Recuperation swallowed up days and weeks of time, all of which remains vague even now. What stands out from the miasma of my lengthy recovery was the ophthalmologist's concern that the many lesions on the corneas of both eyes were healing, as he'd expected them to, but my vision still hadn't returned. Yet one should have resulted in the other. I could make out uneasy shapes at a distance of a foot or so in front of me, but had no strong sense of day or night, of whether the lights were on or off. The doctors performed tests to determine ocular blood flow, ran an MRI against the possibility of brain damage, but found nothing that would explain the blindness. My twenty-twenty vision was now twenty-four hundred at best and when I was released from the hospital my condition was not only unimproved, but worsening. They continued to chart my progress but there wasn't much more that could be done medically.

Summer faded into fall. The once-steady stream of colleagues and friends who dropped in to visit, read me the Bible, listen to music with me dwindled. I couldn't in fairness expect otherwise. Sarah's considerate idea of building an extension onto the house, thus to spare me the trouble and danger of walking up and down stairs I couldn't see, kept me busy for a while. Not that I was able to help. But my wife and the contractor did consult with me about construction specs. Ever the clever one in our family, Sarah suggested we might save money by forgoing windows in my modest wing—they could be added later, when and if my sight returned—and used the balance of the home improvement loan to carpet the whole house. I thought it an extravagance, but she insisted it would cushion any falls I happened to take. Although my equilibrium hadn't been a problem, I commended her ingenuity.

Around Thanksgiving I lost my job. My supervisor was kind enough to give me the bad news in person. They'd held out as long as they could, he said, sitting with me in my den over some chowder Sarah served us in mugs. "Damn bad luck," he told me, his voice gooey from the thick soup if not the tacky sentiment. I nodded, trying to form an understanding smile on my lips, though I'd already begun to forget what I looked like before the accident, and had no clear concept what such a smile might look like now. Vivid silence clouded the room before I heard him shift in his seat and rise to leave. "Your workman's comp is all in order," he said, taking my free hand into his, which was clammy. I thanked him, climbing to my feet. I wanted to touch his face but hadn't the nerve to ask. As I recall, he had a dense, large nose, the by-product of a long-standing love affair with cheap scotch chased by cheaper ale. Balls and beer, the boys used to call it at work, a thousand years ago. Off the top of my head I couldn't tell you his or any of their names now.

Then came the truly dark days. Days that added up to months, a year of miserable months that vanished like voices murmuring in an empty room. Learning braille was a necessary but grim admission that my blindness was not the temporary setback my hopeful ophthalmologist had diagnosed. A second sightless Christmas came and went. Luke and Becca seemed happy with their presents, none of which I could see any more than I could their presumptive beaming faces. Sarah thanked me for the nightgown I bought her with the help of a salesperson who was kind enough to describe it to me over the telephone—rayon, beige, a few flounces edged in lace. We tried to act celebratory, to make the best of the situation, and I even indulged in a little champagne, which gave me a migraine that lasted a week. Sitting alone in my personal black hole on New

Year's Eve, I urged Sarah to go without me to a party down the street, hire a sitter, enjoy herself a little. It hardly seemed fair for her, who looked after me day and night, to stay home reading to me from Isaiah, or Job, while I followed along with my fingers. Even as I sat wallowing in my misfortune that evening, listening to Mahler and eating a bowl of popcorn my wife had placed on the side table, I guessed the busybodies were talking about none other than me and what a shame all this was for poor Sarah, who was still so young and vibrant. I drowned myself in the choral voices of the Eighth Symphony, then fell asleep in my chair. Later, Sarah woke me and led me by the arm upstairs to bed, which smelled of roses and sage. My melancholy delirium lifted for a moment, for these fragrances reminded me of the carefree, caring nights we used to enjoy, the nights of earlier intimacy that resulted in the births of our babies. Half awake, I kissed her and thanked her for all she had done to help me through this tragedy. I promised her—though she might not have heard, since I could tell by her breathing she was asleep—that I would try harder, would overcome the doldrums that had made life so tough this past year and a half. That I would do something with myself, defeat my disability in some way, learn to see anew, like blind Bartimaeus whom Jesus cured in Jericho with nothing more than a few words of encouragement.

True to my promise, the next morning I glued braille alphabet tabs to the keys of my old typewriter and sat myself down to outline everything that had conspired to bring me to my present predicament, and what I believed as I began my long journey back to life. Sarah set me up with a fresh ream of paper. The work was slow. It took a while to get a feel for producing words and phrases through the clumsy machinery of the typewriter. Not being able to review what I'd just written, I had to visualize the sentences fore and aft in my head. Initially, Sarah read me back what I'd sketched, but even she had reasonable limits as to how much time she could devote to my little project. The children weren't getting younger. She had even taken a part-time position with that contractor who built the extension, in order to supplement my benefits. He was called Jim James, a name whose triumph of redundancy might have intimated the ways matters were drifting but did not. We were grateful for the income.

At first I thought to write an article for the St. Francis newsletter about how faith in God is essential to our surviving crises, or some such, but as I got the ideas down on paper, I realized it was one cliché after another and of no use to anybody. I had to delve deeper into my reservoir of pain, so I turned some of my ideas around backward and found they came out much better. Faith alone, in other words, was not enough to carry us through. Rather, it was one oar we could use to pull our fragile ship through the turbulent waters of doubt and despair, the other oar being hope. Like that. I spent hours on end working out my thoughts, quoting passages from my King James whenever the reference seemed apropos, or sometimes, if the pretty image struck my fancy, when it wasn't.

Not only did the newsletter publish my first effort but, thanks to someone in the congregation who showed it to an editor at the local paper, reminding him who I was—the man blinded while trying to bring light to others, as he put it—I was commissioned to write a human interest article detailing the aftermath of that horrifying night. I missed the deadline and Sarah asked for an extension, which they granted. When I did turn in my manuscript I explained in an apologetic cover letter that typing on an old Royal rigged with braille tabs that kept falling off made for perhaps not the best working conditions. I hoped nevertheless that they would find the final product worthy of their esteemed pages.

The memoir was a success. Letters came in from around the state, the most gushing of which were published in the newspaper over the days that followed. Sarah knocked on my door soon after, announcing that the editor himself had dropped by the house with something that might make me very happy. Indeed, I was floored by Mr. Harrison's kindness. On behalf of everyone at the paper, he presented me with a used computer preloaded with software for the blind. Little Luke, who was eight then and computer-savvy, taught me how to use this gift, and within a matter of months I was contributing regularly to various periodicals distributed in the area. From this print exposure came my first invitations to speak before the public. My wife's inherent Christian strength of spirit was aroused by what she saw happening before her eyes. The love, empathy, and compassion she witnessed flowing toward her husband from these strangers, common workaday people who listened intently to what insights I was able to give them, overwhelmed dear Sarah. That Mr. Harrison offered to assist us financially, lift the burden of her having to work for the contractor, so she could devote more time to helping answer every request to address this crowd or that, constituted another blessing on our household. I, who had come to abide misfortune, was now in the pulpit of Everyman, as it were. *Many are called but few are chosen,* the Bible tells us, and I—an unfledged beggar by the waters of Siloam—was chosen.

Sarah was never more attentive, never more heedful than during the heady times that followed. Invite followed invite, obliging us to be away from home for days, even weeks, at a time. When my wife told me that we'd begun to charge sponsors a nominal fee to offset expenses of travel, lodging, meals, not to mention the live-in housekeeper who also looked after Luke and Becca, I didn't object, though deep down I would have preferred offering my inspirational views without money attached. Harrison advised her on the best ways to proceed, and acted on my behalf as an agent, placing my lectures in various journals and anthologies. "Building the rep," as he put it. They were right, of course, telling me that if we wanted to get my message out there, we needed assistance, and who better than the listeners and readers themselves to assist? The venture was worthy, we all knew. There were many who wanted, needed, to hear my story of hardship and hope. I told Sarah that, if she didn't mind, she should be the one who managed the practicalities with Harrison's help. Back in the halcyon days before the world went dark, I wore the financial pants in the house. Given that now I couldn't tell a one-dollar check from another of a thousand made our positions clear. Sarah agreed with all my requests. Both my muse and protector, she was brilliant in her role.

What possible point would there be in reproducing a transcript of the speeches I made? Often I was introduced by a local priest or minister. My wife would then lead me to the podium. Applause. I launched straightaway into my backstory, guided my auditors from the shadowy valley of pain and grief to the mountain of renewal and joy. Self-pity was just that: a *pit* from which we must rise and shine. I told them about my New Year's Eve revelation, mentioning how I had come to believe that the marvelous scent of sage and roses in the bedroom that night was an auspicious sign from God, the soul-struck breath of my guardian angel. My favorite concluding exhortation was *Don't be afraid of miracles.* Applause. Then a few questions and answers. Do you think that God will restore your sight one day? was the perennial query I could count on being asked. My response was, in this life or the next, I believe He will let me see my wife and children again, for *He's a good and generous God.*

A reception would follow during which the voices around me brimmed with appreciative respect that made me understand just how attached each member of the human family is to another. My calling as a missionary of faith suited me well, and as the years elapsed, the uneasy peace I'd made with my blindness deepened. Never would I have touched so many lives had I not been stricken. I like to think that I was always a good man, but so many have proclaimed there's a genuine spark of greatness in me that at times I have to believe there may be.

Home, now, from nine long weeks on the road, after a restless night in my bed in the study—Sarah and I agreed to sleep in separate quarters after such long trips on the circuit because when I was particularly fatigued I tossed and turned—I awoke feeling not quite myself. True, I had been working harder than ever. Our schedule had been nonstop for months, so perhaps this explained my sensation of unbalance. Along with prayer, music has always been my remedy for any illness, and so it was I'd put on Schubert's Opus 78 for piano, whose divine opening chords would, I was sure, bring me around. Martita, the housekeeper, served my spicy cinnamon tea and tended my fire. Not wanting to bother her—and besides, the monumental Richter seemed to be working his magic—I said nothing about my disposition.

Some minutes after she closed my door, abrupt pain erupted in my temples. Beset by wild dizziness, by violent nausea, by spasms that stabbed like long needles through my skull, I shrieked, though no noise left my throat. Gasping, I rolled from my chair onto the floor, hitting my head as I did. I tried to call out for Sarah but couldn't. Then, as suddenly as the pain began it was replaced by numbness. I could hear the piano music very distantly, as if it were coming from the far end of a long tunnel. Light engulfed my eyes—a cascade, a flood, a torrent of *unblinding light*. As I grabbed at the arms of my chair to stand, I found myself staring into what appeared to be flames dancing behind the grate of the potbellied stove. My eyes agonizingly darted around the room and there, in this dim place on whose walls firelight flickered—more like Plato's cave than a Christian's den—were all the things I'd come to know only by touch. My table, my books, my computer, my cot, my chair. No embellishments, nothing on the walls, all very minimal, even dreary to my naïve eyes. But of course, I thought. Why decorate? Why wallpaper a blind man's cell? Standing now, a bit shaky, admiring my wife's wise Christian expediency, I walked around placing my hands on everything, still not quite sure what was happening. My vision was blurry, but with each new moment I became more reassured this wasn't a dream, a taunting nightmare. The radical pain having largely subsided, I remained a little numb, whether from excitement or physiological impulse, I didn't know or care. I wanted to climb to the roof and cry out to the world that my miracle had finally come. My feet carried me to the door that led to the main house, and I who rarely left my sanctum—why should I have?—opened it.

Bright white light poured through the living room windows, crisp sun reflected off the snow. But for the ticking of a clock, in Franz Schubert's wake, the house was silent. I took a few tentative steps and gazed, blinking hard while heavily tearing, in wonder. What had happened to our simple home? If you will, I couldn't believe my eyes. The walls were gilded and the windows dressed with billowing chiffon sashes. In an alcove stood a gargantuan breakfront on whose glassed shelves were countless porcelain figurines. I stumbled ahead toward facing sofas and stuffed chairs upholstered in striped silks of chartreuse and gold. Here was a commode with a marble top and a vase of orchids above the marquetry. There were two reclining brass deer on a prayer rug by the hearth. An antique grandfather clock clad in luminous mahogany stood haughty in a corner. Oriental carpets of red, blue, yellow, and green lay atop the white wall-to-wall. Fine old portraits of men and women dressed in the garb of another century hung everywhere, staring out at me from canvases black as lacquer. A chandelier centered it all, its prisms reflecting hundreds of tiny rainbows on the ceiling, which was done up with decorative plaster moldings. Though I examined each piece of furniture, horrified and fascinated, and though what I saw was as tangible as truth itself, my heart sank, because I knew this couldn't be so. I pinched myself, closed my eyes, reopened them. But the room didn't change. If anything, it became more lavish as my sore eyes adjusted to the light.

A familiar sound came from upstairs. It seemed to be Harrison, softly whistling to himself some random tune, as he often did when he accompanied us on the road. I thought to call out his name, tell him the astonishing news, ask him to come down, fall to his knees with me and pray, *Lord God, thanks for this deliverance,* but didn't. Who knows how or wherefrom inner voices speak to us, or in what mysterious ways they confide to us involuntary prophecies that save us from harm, disillusion, even doom? The whistling stopped and when it did, I took a couple of steps back, bumping into a side table and knocking a crystal lamp to the floor. I was startled to hear Harrison say, "Bunny?" And hearing him ask the question again, this time in a deeper, softer, more melodiously concerned voice, I looked around for a place to hide, an Adam's fig leaf as it were, suddenly frightened, frightened even beyond the terror of finding myself among the sighted, standing there agog, a dumb novitiate, a stranger in my own house. He glided down the carpeted stairs, silent as a proverbial ghost, and seemed relieved to find me, half crouching behind one of the big plush sofas.

"You all right?" asked Harrison.

Instinctively, I stared forward and said I was. "What did I break?" I wanted to know.

Out of the corner of my eye I saw him inspecting the damage, dressed to the nines in a deep blue silk robe, the same color I remembered Sarah's irises as being. His hair, which I'd always pictured black and short, was silver and stylishly long. His unshaven face was taut and handsome. Averting my eyes when he glanced at me, I noticed that he, like Sarah, had a little mole, though his was on the cheek. What bothered me most was that his robe was open in the front. If my wife or children were to walk into the room just then, what an eyeful they'd get. Think how embarrassed everyone would be.

Taking me by the arm, he sat me down by the gold wall in a chair appointed with fine overstuffed upholstery. "Stay right here," he calmly requested, his voice sweet but the look on his suntanned face as annoyed as a pet owner scolding a naughty puppy. I could have sworn he cursed under his breath as he left, but at that moment I didn't trust my ears any more than my eyes. At least while he retreated toward the kitchen he tied his dressing gown. I had caught a subtle glimpse of what hung there, haloed by white hair. It was nothing anyone should want to see, let alone someone who'd been denied the privilege of seeing anything whatever for a decade.

Other astonishments soon appeared. The more I saw, the more I understood it was important, somehow, that those around me thought I saw nothing. Conspicuous among my discoveries was how wrong I'd pictured everyone and everything. I who had begun truly to believe my fervent homilies, urging my followers to keep the faith first by trusting themselves, their convictions, their own views—*be thee blind or seeing with lucid eyes*—now began to understand how utterly I'd erred. If that morning returned to me my sight, the rest of the day brought my insights, as I have come to think of them.

Harrison in his baronial robe waltzing through our kinky *nouveau riche* living room was merely the first verse in my New Apocrypha. Martita, who came to clean up the broken lamp, was someone whose voice, again, I recognized but whose appearance struck me as incongruous with the life I'd believed my family was leading. Not that she, poor Cayman immigrant and clearly a good if very illegal girl, behaved in any way that could be perceived as unchristian. No, it was that they had her in a black uniform with white starched trim and in a state of what might well be deemed quasi-penal subservience. Harrison wondered if I wouldn't like to go back to my room, said I looked exhausted, Lord knows no one would blame me for wanting a little more rest, given the grueling schedule I had just endured. Again I asked what I'd broken and he answered it was nothing, just a glass one of the kids had left on an end table, not to worry. The maid crossed herself and, having finished cleaning, left the room.

"Where's Sarah?" My hands were shaking although I anchored them between my thighs.

"Out," he said, "shopping."

When I inquired when she was expected back, he muttered something and, excusing himself, flew upstairs, ever silently, no doubt to change into some clothes.

Time passed—twenty-three minutes to be exact, now that I could watch the clock—then Sarah unlocked the grand front door. Making her way to the kitchen, she failed to notice her husband seated in an unwonted corner, escapee from his holy cage. The years had not been kind. My once-wholesome Sarah had acquired, I must admit, a gaunt sophistication. Though elegant and drily beautiful, her face was as if invaded by knives—angular, hewn, deblooded. It was all I could do to maintain on my own face the blankest possible expression. This was only the beginning. What I saw next I wouldn't wish on the Prince of Darkness himself. Harrison floated back downstairs, gathered my wife in his arms and kissed her, put his forefinger to his lips, and pointed in my direction. I would like to believe she might have fainted, standing there in the arms of this man, staring at her blind husband not thirty feet away. To the contrary, she sweetly called my name, breaking from Harrison's embrace, and asked me the same question he had, patting my head, offering to help me get back to my room. I needed more rest, she cooed. After all, we had less than a week before we were committed to going to Louisville for the Christian Recovery Convention, at which I was to be one of the headliners. Bed did seem a desirable destination at that moment.

"Yes, bed," I answered, and allowed her to take me by the arm, as she had countless times over the last decade, and lead me into my monk's cell. I fell asleep immediately.

Seeing the world, I had not yet come to know how to reckon it. That was, I always felt, God's distinct purview, His task. Yet in the days that followed, seeing what I saw was judgment enough and though Job was my cherished Old Testament hero, I would prove to be no Job. Seeing, like my original blinding, was an unexpected trauma, a crossroads. The more I reflect upon what has happened, whether from a vantage of darkness or light, the more I see life as an investigation into just this: How much pain can we tolerate before we either turn ourselves humbly over to our God, that His will be done, or turn on the sadistic Bastard with every fiber of our being? Just how He found the fortitude, tenacity, and nerve to look down on me from on high these ten long suffering years, knowing all the while that every word of encouragement I offered to the far-flung members of His miscellaneous flock was fouled by the adultery and avarice of those who pretended to sustain His wretched servant, I cannot pretend to know. The myriad ways of the Almighty are, it has been often recorded, mysterious. We mere mortals who fail to know our own hearts can't begin to fathom what motivates His. Not that my poor wife's weakness of the flesh, her infidelity, and materialist lust are in any way the fault of the Precious Savior. Nor that my benefactor and proponent, Harrison, without whose support I might never have found my audience, all those hungry souls who have dined—I hope nutritiously—at my inspirational banquets, was guided by the hand, if not the hoof, of the Lamb. As I lay in the equally dark but somehow less blurry shadows of my new world, as deeply dejected as I ever was when I first lost my sight, I decided to follow my instincts and see what there was to see. My life became a blindman's bluff.

Sarah checked in on me later that same day, concerned why I'd been stumbling around in the living room. "You feeling all right?" she wanted to know.

"Fine, just fine," I assured her, and, testing the waters, asked if I couldn't sleep upstairs with her tonight. We generally had separate bedrooms on the road, and so often slept apart at home. Surely, I reasoned, the Lord would want a wife to abide some snoring now and then, if only for the sake of Old Testament conjugal duty.

Though I stared at the wall behind her, the look of dismay that shrouded her face, like Beelzebub's specter, was unmistakable. Her voice smilingly assured me that we needed to take it easy during this week off, while the frown on her lips mutely bespoke another message. I wanted to say, How could I have been so blind to your true feelings all this time? but kept my own counsel and meekly agreed. That seemed to brighten her mood. Her face relaxed as she brushed back her frosted hair and asked what kind of soup I wanted Martita to bring me for lunch. "Barley," I said, and watched my estranged wife's hips pitch softly back and forth as she left the sanctum.

The children were my only hope. My wonderful babies, my joys, bounty of my loins. They, I assured myself, had not veered from the path of righteousness like their mother. Persisting with my charade the next morning, I once more entered the main house. Rather than loiter in the garish living room, I joined Martita in the kitchen, which was also extensively renovated—shiny chrome, glass, and granite everywhere, and a tile-work splashback depicting urns choked with flowers and saccharine French farm scenes. Though she was at first surprised by my appearing in her domain, Martita helped me to a chair at the long table and got me my morning tea. It was quite early, I saw by the wall clock, too early for Sarah, but maybe not for the kids, who, I assumed, would come down first, on their way to class. Becca was in her last year of high school, and Luke, a junior. As Martita busied herself, chatting amiably about this and that, I furtively studied her, wondering just how much she knew about the goings-on around here. Her black hair combed into a chignon, her handsome, concise form moving lithely in her uniform, her dark eyes, her pretty hands—she cut a finer figure than I had imagined. Some obvious questions came to mind to ask her, but I thought the better of it. Ease up, I reminded myself. As St. Paul advised in his Epistle to the Hebrews, *Let us run with patience the race that is set before us.*

Luke entered the kitchen first. That is, a young man whom Martita referred to as Luke. Rather than coming downstairs, however, to have his breakfast, he ducked in through the back door, having apparently spent the night elsewhere. Abstracted, with eyes glazed, he noticed me as he opened the refrigerator door and drank long and hard from an orange juice carton, but said nothing. His hair was every bit as orange as the juice he consumed, and rose in numerous spikes off the top of his head. His mascara was smudged—little Luke wore mascara? Great chunks of silver graced each of his fingers. He was skinny as a broomstick and looked the warlock part he affected. I sat in stunned silence, maintaining my own vacant, glazed-over stare, which matched my son's. I didn't know they made boots that big.

"What's *he* doing here?" Luke asked Martita.

I interrupted, "How are you this morning, Luke?"

"Awright, I guess," he answered.

"You're up with the roosters," I pressed, at the same time wondering if he oughtn't be nervous that the coffin lids were all supposed to be down by this time, and then saw him give Martita a look that could only be described as threatening.

"Whatever," he said, taking a fat green apple from the bowl of fruit on the table and politely excusing himself with a sneer.

After he left the kitchen, I said, "Luke's a fine young man, isn't he."

If both Sarah and Luke had gone the way of Judas, and Harrison with them, it seemed improbable Rebecca had managed to resist the tide of treachery. For having *betrayed my credulous innocence with vizor'd falsehood, and base forgery,* as blind Milton himself once wrote, *the pillared firmament is rottenness, and the earth's base is built on stubble.* I fled to my cave.

A pestilence had swept through my household, like the very dogday locusts that had prophesied the onset of my blindness that summer night a decade ago. I lay on my cot, hands over my forehead and face, unable to move, loath to think, as sweat broke out across the length of my body and a range of black emotions chased through me. Above all, I wanted never to leave my room again. They could bring me my filthy barley soup and vile cinnamon tea whenever they found time between the commission of sins, and to hell with the rest of it. Indeed, when Sarah ventured by later, reeking of sage and roses, and found me prostrate, she let out a little cry of fear. Perhaps I should be ashamed to admit it, but that cry was like sweet music to me—even better than the opening strains of Stravinsky's *Apollon Musagète*, though it sounded more like Honegger's Symphony No. 2, the *molto moderato*, so very crushingly ominous, as performed by von Karajan and the Berliner Philharmoniker. Not because I was deluded enough to think it meant she was concerned, as such, for my sake, or that my heart melted with sudden forgiveness. No, no— rather because it gave rise to my plan. Whereas before I couldn't see her face if she voiced distress on my behalf, now I did, and Sarah's look was that of a caretaker grown weary of her role, disgusted, in fact, by it. Humanitarian that I long strove to be, and that many had seen fit to call me, I reluctantly sympathized with her. I understood her failings and well knew how many persons of good intent and a hopeful heart nevertheless plant the earnest seeds of their goodness and optimism in the yielding muck of ambition. Look at Harrison. He probably hadn't had designs on my wife, my home, my finances, my very self, when he first got me into print and onto a podium. How do I know? Because by the same reasoning one might say that I never intended for him to succeed so assiduously in ruining me, even as he saved the souls of thousands by helping me to save my own. Having noted that, inspiration took hold of me and would not give way to any alternative from that day forward, until it had fulfilled itself like the competent beast it was.

The plan began simply. I didn't feel up to Louisville. We would have to cancel.

Sarah thought we should all pray for guidance, and so we went through the gesture of prayer. I still didn't feel like going. Harrison suggested that a doctor ought to be brought in to look me over. Louisville was, after all, "awfully darned important to the further- ance of the crusade"—the Christian Recovery Convention was, if I didn't mind his saying so, the Holy Grail of such gatherings, the motivational orator's Valhalla. It was a dream come true for me, for Sarah, and everyone who believed in my message of hope.

"A doctor won't find anything wrong with me," I said, staring right through him.

"What then?" he asked, after underscoring again the importance of keeping this engagement, reminding me it was the kickoff to our big tour through the South, saying something about another book deal in the works.

I appreciated how much work Sarah and he had put into Louis- ville, the tour, all the rest, but couldn't do it. The problem was this. Somehow I had lost my calling. Sarah's face drained of all color as she looked at Harrison, who was also pale.

"You still believe in God, of course," my wife whispered.

I told her I supposed I did, it wasn't that.

"Well, what is it, man?" Harrison asked, noiselessly taking my wife's hand in his.

"Not sure," I said. My message of hope seemed stale, banal, for some reason, and the more I thought about it, the more I'd come to believe it was one better repudiated than preached. Likewise, God seemed more complicated than I'd believed Him to be. I didn't understand Him or His ways, certainly not well enough to speak His cause before others whom, by the way, I also did not understand.

Sarah withdrew her hand, stepped toward me, placed it on my head, which made me wince a little, and she said, "You're tired, dear, is all . . . your audiences need you, your family needs you, all of us need you to go to Louisville and shine the light of truth into the darkest corners of people's souls and help them find their way back into the sun."

Sarah, it would appear, had been listening to my patent drivel these past years so perfectly was she able to quote me to myself. God in heaven, I almost laughed, but the idea had nothing to do with gaiety. Instead, allow me to admit, it ran more along the lines of Paul's Epistle to the Romans 12:19. Look it up for yourself.

Over the days that followed my initial confession of apostasy came many wearying pleas and petitions from my wife, my manager, even the children. My prediction regarding Rebecca was not wrong. She had become what the kids call a Goth. The dyed black hair, the black fingernails, the black dress and black boots even bigger than Luke's, if that were possible, and a girlfriend in tow dressed in the same uniform. Becca, I should say, did seem the least egregious of the lot of heretics my family had become. She at any rate didn't seem to care as much as the others whether the income from my missionary work continued or not. She styled herself, I'm guessing, as a bit of an anarchist, though we all know anarchy is best proselytized by the disaffected well-to-do. Be that as it may, Rebecca was no more able to budge me from my den than the others, and Louisville soon came and went, absent its blind featured speaker. Harrison told me we received hundreds of cards and letters from well-wishers.

Which brought me to the second phase of the plan. The revenue stream must be stopped. This was not as simple as merely dropping off the lecture circuit since, clearly, Harrison had invested wisely and, despite myself, money still flowed in with those letters.

An anonymous tip to the Internal Revenue Service informing them that my family and closest advisor were bilking our religious foundation of tens of thousands of dollars, maybe more, for personal gain, rather than funding programs for the blind and other disabled, got the job done. It all went rather quickly. The lien on our home and bank accounts, the removal of the furniture and frippery in the living room and everywhere else in the house—yes, things moved irrevocably, decisively. Sarah spent a lot of time crying, I can report. When she wasn't doing that she was arguing with Harrison. Luke simply disappeared from the scene. And Rebecca, I gathered, was spending more time over at her girlfriend's place. Harrison's indictment for fraud and income tax evasion was bittersweet for me though my residual sentimentality toward him—the former him, I should say, the man who did help me in the beginning—faded away to nothing when I learned how much we had earned over those fruitful years, and how much he had stolen from his gullible mistress. They broke up. And once my attorney—a former devotee who volunteered his time—cleared me of any collaboration in my handlers' schemes, I filed for divorce from the lovely Sarah, who, seeing there was nothing to salvage, didn't contest the action. The foundation was dismantled. The media was ruthless. An insightful if scathing article about my "amazing fall from grace" was published in the very newspaper that gave me my computer and printed my own first efforts. Fond memories. Now I was left with the house and enough money to live modestly, having such comforts as society thinks are due a poor blind fellow who'd been bruised a bit in the school of hard knocks.

While I sometimes feel a numbness in the pit of my stomach when pondering the arc of my life, I still have my Sviatoslav Richter disc of Schubert's Sonata in G Major to comfort me. I still indulge in fantasizing how my daughter Emma, had she lived, would have saved me from my hapless enemies if not myself. But the past has passed. The sole question that remains is whether or not to feign a sudden miraculous recovery of my sight after Martita becomes my new bride. God knows there's much to be said for blindness, especially when one can see. Either way, I'm sure she and I will be quite happy living here together once we get this gilt off the walls.

THE UNINNOCENT

I N OUR INNOCENCE, we burned candles. We got them from a nearby church, and because my sister believed what we were doing was holy, she said it was fair to take them. Churches, Sister said, were not in the business of making money off children. "Alms for the poor," said she. "Suffer the little ones to come before me and unto them I shall make many gifts." My sister enjoyed creating scripture. She had an impressive collection of hymnals, though neither of us could sing. And, as I say, many candles. I worried about her logic and thefts sometimes, but made it a point never to contradict her. She was older than I, and anyway, what was a hymnal but paper and ink? What was a candle but so much wax and string?

The yellow tongues at the ends of their tapers would flutter when the wind flowed off the lake, and we'd look at each other, down there in the old boathouse, our eyes wide, our mouths agape. And yes, when the flames made shadows all over the rustic wooden walls, where the canoes lay on their shelves and oars were lined up like rifles in a gun case, we would know that *he* was there. We weren't, to say the least, objective in these exercises, these private séances. It didn't occur to either my sister or me that the flickering of the candle flames might have been caused by our own expectant breath. The wind, we knew, could have nothing to do with it. No, it was him. He had come back. He never failed us. After all, he was our Christmas brother.

He never spoke. Our task was to decide what his signs meant. Everything had deep meaning. If the smoke of the candles drifted in a certain direction, it was up to us to deduce what such a thing portended. If a bat flew out of the boathouse, if a flock of chorusing birds lit in a tree overhead, if a mouse danced along the length of the wall, by our reckoning there were valuable ramifications. We took it upon ourselves to determine what the signs were, and interpret. This must, I know, sound indiscriminate and childish.

An instance. Down by the lake. Blind old dear Bob Coconut, the dog, stiffened in the legs, lying in the long grass. The air blue. Autumn. The water was cold, and red and brown leaves clotted the surface of the lake near the shore, like an oil slick. Angela and I had a sign that day. We'd found a dead ovenbird that'd flown into the kitchen window, and we knew what that meant. Out in the boat, we got our friend Butter calmed down enough so that he would let us tie him up like we always liked to do, and tickled him, and warned him if he laughed we would throw him overboard. The blue air was turning toward purple as the sun moved down into the trees and evening was on us. We'd been so hard at our game we hadn't noticed how quickly the hours passed.

Butter wasn't having a very good time. Nice boy with his round face and wide-open pale-gray eyes. He couldn't complain, of course, because those were the rules, and because my sister had wrapped her muffler around his mouth. "Don't worry, little guy," Angela told him. "We're taking you home now." And he squirmed a bit before falling back into the bottom of the boat to breathe. "Don't you cry," she finished, "or Angie will have to hurt."

I was slowly rowing us in. Butter's parents would soon be worried. The evening star was up, a tiny eye of foil, winking. And then I saw him, our brother. He was standing on the lake. He was a milky swirl. His feet were in the mist that had come up out of the water into the warm and cool atmosphere. My sister put her palms over Butter's eyes so that he couldn't see. She thought he had been through enough, and she didn't want him to be so scared that he'd never come out to play with us again. Moreover, she felt that nobody deserved to see our brother but us. Butter sobbed in the bottom of the boat. Angela and I cried too, while the evening star got brighter and brighter.

Butter was drawn into all this because one of the candles went out at just the moment he walked into the boathouse when we were praying for the ovenbird's soul. Too bad for Butter, my sister told me later. And true, it was too bad, because from that moment on, all Butter's problems became a matter of fate. Nothing we did, said Angela, was because we decided to do it. Our Christmas brother—who was one with fate—told us what to do and we did as we were told.

Looking back, I must admit to some surprise at how unparented we were. My father's persistent absences were difficult to fathom, and what I've since been able to fathom is difficult to articulate, for the shame of what I think I understand. He worked hard to support us. He had a long daily commute from our rural home into the city. He was a tall, meek, square-headed, decent sort of man. And I've become unshakable in my conviction that he was a dedicated philanderer. I have no proof, and I never confronted him. My deduction is the nasty product of all those days and nights of fatherlessness coupled with my sure memory of his wandering, unprincipled eyes.

As for Mother, she was transformed into a cipher, a drifting and listless creature, by the Christmas brother's death. We never knew her any other way, though Father told us she used to be a happy girl. She took it all to be her fault. She was the one who slipped on the ice. No one pushed her. The miscarriage that followed her accident was quite probably the end of her life, too, along with that of the blackened holiday fetus. Angela and I—who came along later—were unexpected, were not even afterthoughts. Mother carried us, birthed us, but gave us to understand we would never be our brother. Nothing would ever replace him. Much as I loved him, sometimes he made me want to do bad things.

In our innocence, sometimes we were compelled to go to extremes to get our brother to come to us. We felt forced to do things we weren't proud of, yet never lost our faith in him even when, in our mad desire to tempt him home, we hurt things that didn't deserve hurt.

We always feared Christmas. We couldn't understand that other world, that parallel world where he resided, we couldn't see why Christmas made him so reluctant a guest. Here, we thought, was the one time of year when families should celebrate together, reunite and rejoice.

Angela was the one who decided to hurt Bob Coconut. I didn't make the connection between the dog and our brother, but Angela told me to trust her and I did. This was during Christmas, of course. My father and I had brought in the tree we'd sawed down at the tree farm. A prickly, nasty blue spruce. Ornaments, twinkling lights, cookies, the train set, cards hung over pendant string from end to end on the mantel. Bob Coconut lay on a rug before the fire, and twitched pleasantly under the influence of his dreams.

"You think Coco remembers when he could see?" Angela asked me.

I didn't know, but I thought so.

"Coco?" she whispered in his old ear. "Oh, *Co*-co."

"Let him sleep," I said.

"I bet Coco could see him if he wanted to. Dogs have those abilities, you know. They can hear things we can't hear. And they can smell better than we can. I bet he can see right into that other world, can't you, Coco dear?"

"Doubt it," I said.

"Hey, I've got an idea," she said.

I don't want to write down what my sister did to him. I wasn't surprised, though, that it failed to work. Our brother was farther away from us than ever, after that. From then on, I decided to trust nothing my sister said or did. Instead, I began to observe her.

Two Angela stories.

First Angela story. There was a period when she thought she was our brother, after he stopped appearing to us. "He's in me now," she announced one night. She liked possessing him, liked being possessed. On occasion, she allowed me to pose questions. "What is it like being dead?" I asked. "You'll know soon enough," he answered through his medium. "Do you love me?" I asked. "I love you fine, but I love Angela better," she said, her eyelids closing to narrow slits, the corners of her mouth lifted into a satisfied smile.

Then she found out one day that she wasn't our brother. Something mysterious happened to her, and Mother told her she was a woman. And so it was time for her to start wearing dresses. I got to shave her legs. My sister even photographed me while I shaved them, telling me it was good for both of us, a sacrifice. She wouldn't let me shave the hair under her arms, though. She said this was because she couldn't take a picture of me doing it. I would be too close to her. That is what she said. The real reason she wouldn't let me do it, I think, was that part of her still believed she was our brother. She could walk around with her glistening and smooth white legs in the sun beneath the pleat of her billowy skirt, a young woman with strong calves and hard thighs, and we could admire her lush femininity, but we could never release her from her masculine possessiveness.

Second Angela story. Once there was a parade in the little upstate town where we lived. I don't remember what holiday it was. There were a couple of makeshift floats. There were marching bands from county schools. I remember because it was the day my sister ran away from home. She was eighteen. She managed to vanish—"like a ghost," said our mother—and was not heard from for many years. She was a missing person. Some people thought she was dead. I knew better; I knew she was truly missing.

In our innocence, we grew up. Tonight is his birthday, or would have been. He'll always seem older than me, no matter how many years I keep on going. Angela is married and lives in New Hampshire now, her personal cold complementing its heavy winters. She has been married twice. She's been around, as she likes to phrase it. She has three children—she may be cold, but she's not frigid—and mentioned in a recent letter that she wants another.

I never understood this marrying business, and I can't imagine what it must be like to raise children. The dog I own here in the city reminds me of old Bob Coconut. He's far too lively and large for this apartment, but he is an amiable companion. When he curls up by the fireplace—the landlord won't let me burn a fire in the hearth, so I make do with a gouache painting of flames I made on cardboard—I think of those times, of the complexities and strangeness of a child's world. We were isolated. We didn't know what we were doing; we didn't realize how splendidly we were able to do what we wanted. All that is gone now. Is it schizophrenic of me to say that I regret the loss and couldn't care less?

Here is Christmas night again. Christmas Eve I spent with my friends. We ate dinner down in Chinatown. It was a noisy evening there, the streets teeming with revelers. Tonight, it is silent. I've thought about phoning Mother, even considered giving Angela a call. Not fond of Mother's new husband, and knowing Angela to be a chore, I have decided against communication. Were Bob Coconut here, I might light a candle for old times' sake. There is a cathedral around the corner, where I could snag one. I miss my ghost; he'd have made a decent brother, despite how our mother would have raised him, smothering him with a flood of feeling, drinking his love like a vampire. Yes, I miss my Christmas brother. He would have been a felicity in my olding life. He'd have been able to tell me why I'm all alone.

Outside the window, snow is making a feeble attempt to fall. The streetlights that form halos of its transient passage are cheery. A whole world tries its best to rise to the dignity and joy of the occasion. I wish the world happiness, and everyone in it peace. I do. I'll always regret what happened to Butter. We were uninnocent, but the very isolation that in some ways damned us has also acted as our benefactor and protector. I suppose I'm grateful no one has ever found out how it happened, or will.

TSUNAMI

E SCAPISM, AS LOVELL PUT IT, Lovell my husband with the most butt-backward name ever a good mother gave a bad son. "You're just looking for some kind of false peace by going groggy on me, girl," he said. "Just hoping that in some lame dream of yours, love is gonna get returned to you from a place none of us can ever return love from." As if Lovell ever knew a single thing about peace, false or otherwise. Not to mention love, or as he liked to call it, *lovelling*.

This was the year when the Soviets crossed over into somewhere, and there was bloodshed also in Haiti, as well as many deaths in Beirut, I don't remember which year but do remember that mine was not the only life in chaos. Selby was born before things began to go straight downhill, a shining star in an otherwise totally black sky. Just how many people, you might wonder, can one soul lose in a season? Well, nearly everybody that mattered, at least in my measly world. And what does a person do after all the funerals, the burials, the cremations, the memorial services, the condolence cards and caskets, the sad recreations we living must engage in when Daddy Death comes knocking? The answer was, for me, to watch the news and sleep.

One afternoon, that year of the mass graves of innocents uncovered in Croatia, I did what I always warned him I might do. I moved in with my best—well, my only friend, Joanna. Her husband, Kurt, and the posse (baby Ralphie, pretty Wilma Jean, and Nelly, who is stone deaf and dumb and yet bright as a new dime) took me and Selby and my other boy, Guy, into their home, without so much as asking why or wherefore. They expected it, must have. Lovell wasn't popular with them, though they were stoical about my decision when I asked Lovell to marry me on account of Guy. I didn't know exactly what I was doing that afternoon (raining hard and cold and gray) when I packed my bags and left the man, but grateful is nowhere near strong enough a word for how I felt that night at Joanna's, despite her cats, who stopped me up, and the scare of Lovell calling Kurt again and again demanding to know what was going on. He didn't understand my note, wanted to speak with me in person for clarification. Was coming over right now to get his wife and kids back.

Kurt told Lovell to chill, which just made the man more angry. The only reason my husband didn't make good on his threat was he got too toasted to drag himself the three blocks to Joanna's house. She and I stayed up late watching the news that night, Kurt and the kids all having gone to bed finally, and I remember there was something about an arson fire in a mosque, or a temple. Hate crime. Some worshippers died.

This story doesn't get better, so if you wanted to stop here I certainly wouldn't blame you. I can even tell you what happens so you won't have to bother. When Lovell got himself undrunk and did show up a couple days later, I killed him with the loaded handgun I found in Kurt's bedside table. It was easy, firing the gun.

I'd never held one in my hand before. Had a light heft to it and the kick wasn't as bad as they make it out to be on television. I was probably as surprised as Lovell that I actually pulled the trigger, but there it was to pull, and so I did. Neither Joanna nor Kurt was at home when this happened. The infants were napping, and the other kids were either out back playing or at school. Except Nelly, who wandered into the kitchen, where Lovell was lying in a growing red pond on the linoleum. She even helped me clean up the mess. Since I shot him first in the throat, and only afterward in the heart to be sure he was out of here, Lovell didn't make much noise, not that Nelly would have known either way. Selby slept through it all and so did infant Ralph, bless them.

Let me go back, if you are still with me here. Give some background framework, as Lovell, who was a paralegal (half a lawyer, just like he was half a man), might have put it. My parents and their parents before them, and I, were all born and raised in Tarr Creek. Population few, due northwest some hundred foothill miles of Cheyenne here in Wyoming. Grandfather was a doctor, Grandma Eileen was a nurse, and though their marriage was beneficial to the community at large (he was an awfully good physician, and she was an accomplished nurse), it was clear to anyone who ever encountered them that they were one very unhappy couple. My father played slide trombone in the Tarr Creek marching band and was some kind of hotshot back in his heyday, because his father, besides being the town sawbones, was also mayor, school superintendent, and on the board of directors of the First National Bank of Tarr Creek, which had branches in Laramie and Rawlins. Like me, my folks were brought up right, strict, clean, Methodist. My dad was a little spoiled, and sure of himself when he courted and married my mother, whose aspirations were lofty, as she wanted to be a grand opera singer on the stages of New York. To this day, and until all eternity because she died first in that year of the many deaths, she never managed to get even a quarter mile east of

Kansas City, though she did have a beautiful singing voice. Like a meadowlark. Her ashes are in an attractive cloisonné yard-sale urn on the living room mantel.

I was a lonely only. Lorraine is my name. My parents tried to have other kids, but it wasn't to be. Other than when my father had his heart attack and died on my seventh birthday, I don't think it would have been possible for anybody to have had a duller childhood than I did. Sunday school, Brownie Scouts, 4-H, Homemakers of America. Sometimes we went to the rodeo in Casper, or attended the Cheyenne Days festivities. Beyond that, there was just a lot of walking around in fields or under big cottonwoods or along the canal full of brown, muddy, laggard water, waiting more or less in vain for something to happen. I don't know why, but I barely remember a thing about my youth, at least on a day-to-day basis. It was that deadly dull. I did have a best friend, Cecily, who was almost my opposite, lovely as could be with a sunny attitude toward life, but after her family moved to Sedona, Arizona, I didn't bother making friends with anybody else at the time. Didn't seem much point in it if all they were going to do was move away. I was your average student, maybe a whisker above average, but all in all an ordinary person. The one thing that set me apart from other girls back then was that I sometimes had, for want of a better word, spells. My grandpa Hubert diagnosed them as fugues, which my mother said was a kind of music and so got into a row with him about it, but whatever they were, they made a noise in my head that sounded like a swarm of riled hornets. One minute I'd be walking the horse path along the canal and the next thing I knew I'd be downtown at the dime store, not having a clue as to how I got from one place to the other. Time fell out underneath me somehow. As often as not I couldn't do anything more than go to bed until things got back to normal. Some neighbor accused me of killing their yappy dog during one of these fugues, but that was in fact a filthy lie. They were just taking advantage of my malady to cover up the sins of others a bit closer to home. Their own boy did the butchering and they were trying to foist the blame elsewhere.

What Lovell saw in me was anybody's guess. People commented on it. How could such a handsome buck waste his time with that plain-Jane dullard Lorraine? She must be putting out, they whispered, where the nice Tarr Creek girls would not. Another theory circulated. Maybe my grandfather's money had something to do with his initial attraction. The one time I brought it up, he convinced me that wasn't the case, and besides, he knew I was never going to see a penny (another pretty story). Not that I'm ugly, just that I'm no prom queen. Dirty-blonde hair, celery-green eyes, hipless-slim, narrow shoulders. My hands were so thin I could fit them into a tall water glass.

Anyway, he saw something he liked, because he asked me out the same day we met. Lovell had a motorcycle, which gave him an edge over other Tarr Creek guys in those days, and he loved picking me up and cruising over to Iron Mountain or Horse Willow. I must fess up, in all fairness, I loved it too. The back of his head smelled like heaven in the wild, rushing warm wind, like pure baby scent. He was all swagger and braggart, and until I got pregnant with Guy, and Lovell was forced to marry me (shanghaied to the justice of peace, as he kindly put it), he seemed like one of those type people who would stay forever fresh and young. Life went out of his eyes when he sold the chopper and got the job, and the rest is history. The Lovell I once loved became the Lovell I learned was better to hate. Or at least fear. Love'll set you free, he said once, early on. What a poet. A regular Robert Frost.

There was a monsoon hit Thailand or Burma the year it happened, several thousand in the lowlands drowned, and I remember something about the poison-gas slaughter of Kurds in Iraq or Syria over there. After Selby was born a few years along in our model marriage, and I experienced similar hormone problems with my body that my mother did when she bore me, I did put on some weight, just like Lovell accused me of doing. And yes, I passed a good deal of time sleeping and watching the late-night news. So sue me, I told him when his complaining became too much. This was when my fugues, which I'd thought were long since cured, came back visiting and the hornets nested in my head from time to time. I figured it was stress, except for those few moments when the trapdoor fell out from under me and I'd find myself not doing the laundry or preparing meatloaf as I had been doing just a moment before, but instead walking home from the park after having had a perfectly pleasant conversation about sunflowers, say, with some man at the bus stop I'd never met before and wouldn't meet again. Sometimes I'd be in front of the set and then in a pew in church. Now I'd be making the bed then I would be sitting in somebody's parked car a quarter mile away from home. Like that. Nothing violent or terribly scary. Just confusing.

I never mentioned any of this to Lovell. He would only use it against me whenever we were having a disagreement. I could just imagine him stating that I didn't deserve an opinion about anything since I'm mental. Unable to completely keep it to myself, I did share with Joanna, who suggested that maybe I was having some kind of postpartum blues, which I thought about but it doesn't explain why this had been happening to me long before I had kids. I don't know. Grandfather Hubert had retired by then and I never liked the doctor who replaced him down at the clinic (my sons were midwifed), so I didn't bother with getting, as they say, help.

Help. All of us, each and every one, could use a little help, especially in a year they shipped so many starving refugees out of Mogadishu, or out of somewhere, to some fly-infested borderland between one country run by a tyrant and another by a dictator. If we didn't need help, there would be no need for God, even though he was the one responsible for getting us all into this jam in the first place.

You have to wonder what kind of vacation the Guy in the Sky was taking on the morning Lovell's mother, Dolores, died, just for instance. All of us who bothered to pay attention to her habits knew that Dolores's fate was to perish as the result of lung, or throat, or mouth cancer. She was a four-packs-a-day woman, and we warned her about this. "Honey, please stop, please at least cut down." No one could ever have guessed that my widowed mother-in-law, with whom, by the way, I had a friendship that included playing pinochle together, baking pies (she was a coconut cream addict, while my vice was rhubarb), and even once driving all the way down to Denver to go to a real classical music concert, would breathe her last after having been bludgeoned with a tire iron, according to the police. Lovell, who I had always thought had a distant relation-ship with his mom, surprisingly went to pieces. He wept in my lap and on my shoulder. He sobbed through the night. Bawled, actually. Bawled like a gumming baby. He was beside himself in a way I never thought he could be capable of. Lovell, who had been such a cool acre before he sold his Harley and had to enter the real world, was reduced to a fountain of warm tears. We made love that night. I believe that was the last time. No, definitely the last time. I didn't come and I believe he faked his. Either way, both of us were motherless now, I recall thinking.

Being so horrendous, her murder made the morning news. I sat with the children, who didn't understand much of what was going on. "Why is Poppy crying? Where are the Eggos, we want Eggos! Can we change the channel, please, please?" Lovell too watched the newscasters bring the story to life on the set. Here was her image on the screen, the Dolores I'd known and loved almost more, I swear, than I'd loved my own mother. Her win-ning white-as-coconut-meat smile, her casual long, windblown dark hair so beautifully streaked with silver, her careful cardigan. This was a real loss not just to our family, but the community at large. The newspeople, who of course had never met Dolores, were surprisingly right in their eulogies and kind words. Sitting on the sofa, I glanced every now and then at Lovell, prone as a cadaver in his navy-blue, wide-wale corduroy recliner. Looking at Lovell alive on his chair and looking at Dolores dead and gone on the television was like looking into the opposite ends of another universe where there was no news, there was nothing but mayhem and peace in harmony with each other. I watched him watch her on the television and I watched me watch him watching her in the mirror next to the set, and I was a changed person. Even more changed than I was the night before.

How to explain. His fingers, Lovell's fingers, at the ends of his hairy hands at the ends of his favorite frayed shirt bothered me. I was someone who'd gently kissed those fingers in years past. But they troubled me now because Dolores had died in an awful kind of way, and here was her pathetic son with his twitching fingers, my husband the great God-almighty Lovell, who had already hired a lawyer to handle "public relations" (there were none, as it turned out), act as media spokesman for the family of the deceased. One of the other peckerheads in his scofflaw firm, anxious to grab some Ben Franklins for doing nothing. The police questioned next of kin first, as they always do in these types of cases. Needless to say, everyone's story checked out. Lovell was at work, as a whole gaggle of legal-eagle hicks was prepared to corroborate. I was babysitting Kurt and Joanna's kids that day, as it was their wedding anniversary, and they drove up to the mountains to have a romantic picnic. None of her neighbors was without a verifiable excuse, and even one of them said he witnessed a man leaving her house by the rear entrance at just about the time of the crime. To this day, poor Dolores's case goes unsolved, which I think is ridiculous.

The distance Lovell and I felt was marked not by yelling or harsh words. We just went silent on each other. I don't think Guy and Selby so much as knew anything was amiss between their parents. Sure, Pop didn't seem to come home after work as soon or often as he used to, and there were many mornings when Lovell had left for a supposed early breakfast meeting with a client, or to deposit retainer checks, or some other rigamarole, without seeing the boys. But they honestly didn't seem to mind, and I was, I'll freely admit, proud of them for that. One way or another they weren't ultimately going to grow up with a father around anyhow, and so I did my best to bolster this manly indifference they'd begun to show by showering them with small gifts and perks, stuff like flapjacks with chocolate ice cream for breakfast, toys they wanted, the indulgence of letting them stay up late with me to watch the news about this earthquake in Mexico City or that one in Turkey, or to hear about how the polar ice caps are melting faster than you can boil water in a pan. It was a way of building their wayward father out of their lives, I suppose. I didn't give it much thought at the time. It's not like I had any kind of game plan, so to say. As for Lovell, when he stayed out all night long only to show up unshaven and sheepish the next morning, the sole question I'd have asked him, had I bothered to speak with the man, would have been, "Why so silent, mister? Don't you think I'm aware you're putting Dolores's death to good use in the arms of any number of town sluts? Don't you realize that I'm beyond caring which whores you've taken up lovelling with?"

Only because his best friend landed paralyzed in an irreversible coma as a result of losing control of his motorcycle and crashing into a bridge abutment over at Sandy Platte did Lovell come crawling home, looking to make up with me, give things another chance. I'm not a coldhearted woman. Forgiveness resides in this heart of mine. Besides, I was always fond of Rodney, too. Before I got pregnant, I used to enjoy sitting Saturday afternoons with the two of them in Rodney's garage while they worked on their Harleys. Motorcycle maintenance and the cooler full of beer and the top-forty transistor radio scritch-scratching away. I couldn't begin to guess how many times I saw them take those bikes apart and put them back together.

Even after Lovell had to let go of his hog in order to support his fledgling family, Rodney let Lovell take his out for the occasional spin. And now Rodney and his Black Bird, as he'd named it, were ruined beyond salvation. All the more sad since despite the many joyful hours Rodney and Lovell had spent fixing that treasured, sleek bike, the accident was blamed on a mechanical malfunction. The incident was only in the news for a day, which I thought was a shame given what a nice man Rodney had been. If I was a producer in broadcast news I'd have used Rodney's accident to do a report on how many young men in America own motorcycles and crash them, would have turned it into a human-interest news story, something to raise a higher consciousness about public safety. Well, it was not to be. Too many other tragedies vying for notice.

A suicide bomber in Malaysia killed thirteen the same week that the next in my tidal wave of deaths happened, even closer to home. This would have been about a month after Rodney was taken off life support and we buried him. If everything going on hadn't been so tragic, so relentlessly heart-wearying, I can imagine how it might seem weirdly comical for one looking in from the outside, like a bad horror movie directed by some psycho on steroids. But it wasn't funny. Her name was Angie. Angie Farber, a coworker of Lovell's. She was found in her bathtub with a garbage bag knotted hard around her head and a whole ton of sedatives in her system. Some famous author with a weird name I can't remember had done this sometime recently in New York City, and I was wondering if this wasn't where Angie got the idea. It sure seemed like a strange way to check out of Hotel Earth, nothing like the usual shotgun in the mouth or slit wrists. I didn't know Angie as well as Lovell did, but recall her around holidays being the typical life-of-the-party kind of girl. Trips to the drinks table, trips hand in hand with all the guys, Lovell included, as you might have guessed, to the doorway where the plastic mistletoe was thumbtacked overhead, many trips to the bathroom (not to pee, I didn't think), and even a couple of arm-in-arm traipses out into the snow to the parking lot. You get my drift. You have also surmised, to use a nice fat word a pundit pulled out of his bag of word tricks the other evening, that Angie was one of the women into whose bed Lovell took his grief over Dolores, and then again over Rodney. I didn't hate her when she was breathing the same air that you and I breathe, and I don't hate her even now that all the hard work her lonely heart and desperate lungs did in order for Angie to live her life—to make her bed and her coffee in the morning, to celebrate Christmas and Columbus and even Presidents' Day, to make the sweaty beast with two backs with Lovell—is over. To tell the truth, my feelings toward her are few. I'm less sorry for her now that she's taken her own life than I felt before when she was wasting time, going to hell in a handbasket with her dead-end job and ludicrous lover boy. I know this will sound callous of me, but in some ways I think Angie made the right decision.

Her suicide was what precipitated the big blowout with Lovell, but not necessarily for the reason you might be thinking. Because I'm a person who watches the news, and not merely watches it, but watches religiously, I am a person who is, and I can say this with all humility, somewhat informed. In other words, I'm not blind to things. I watch events unfold and I make my own considered decisions as to what forces are behind these events and where matters may wind up going, when all is said and done. It's like being a historian of the future. You make every effort to be objective about the data and then you chart in your mind's eye the possible ways life's drama has happened and is happening and shall happen. Let me cut to the chase.

I accused Lovell (behind closed doors, mind, in a quiet voice, long after the children were put to bed) of being somehow behind all these deaths. Oh boy, did he not like my theory. His reddening face and flailing hands and vehement denials—"Fuck you, bitch," of course, and all the regular crap men say when they're pushed to the wall—plainly suggested he did not agree. But it all added up too neatly for me not to begin to worry about the safety and health of my two small children and me. Why was it that these were all people connected to him? Why wouldn't he concoct some way of silencing Angie, his adulterous lover with those big, voluptuous lips and hips of hers and no doubt a gal who loved being spanked, Angie to whom he might have made some lame, drunken confession about Rodney, for instance, Rodney, who he was always quietly angry with for having the beautiful Black Bird when he had nothing but a rusted Dodge Dart, a scrawny wife who was in the process of getting fat, two kids who liked toaster waffles better than they ever liked him, and a nothing job that began nowhere and would end somewhere less than nowhere?

"If you're lame enough to think there's one pebble of truth in that bullshit," Lovell said, in a voice that deepened to a low, threatening growl, "then you better gather up your evidence and head right down to the police station before I get it in my head to kill somebody else I know."

"Maybe I might just."

"Might just what."

"Might just," I said, fixing him straight in the eye. (His face was so beautiful—why did he have to be so unbelievably handsome, cocky, and muscular, the greatest kisser of all time, not that I ever kissed anybody else, his eyes the color of molasses, and those strong hands of his, those hands that once upon a time knew their way around my body.)

"Listen. Before you go make a fool out of yourself, explain to me why I'd want to go and murder Dolores."

This one was harder to figure. Dolores had loved me as if she were my birth mother, loved me far more than she ever did her lackadaisical Lovell. How could a son commit such an atrocity toward his own mother, even out of jealousy? I knew this part of my accusation didn't make sense, so I kept my mouth shut, which only gave him an opening to blather on, and despite his mental feebleness he managed to make a point.

"By the way, Lorraine, while we're at it here. How come you're accusing me of doing something bad to people who wasn't murdered?" he asked, his voice now kind of high-pitched puling. "Roddy died driving too fast. Angie got it in her sick head to bring her own life to an end. What's up with you, Lorraine?"

I always hated it when he called me by my name. He never called me by my name when we got along. Only when he was scolding and screaming.

"Sounds like you know something I oughta know."

As if Lovell ever knew anything. "You might have tried to know a lot of things I know but you never had the guts or the energy," I told the ignorant son of a gun. "You never bothered to inform yourself about anything other than yourself, get any of the 'background framework' horsefloo you're always so busy gathering for your crooked firm's crooked clientele, and now you dare stand here and accuse me with no proof, no rhyme, no reason?"

This was the evening when I began screaming in his face about every single wrong, every slight, every sin my husband ever did or committed against me. Though it wasn't fun, it was the closest to an orgasm I'd had in a long time, if you'll pardon me for expressing myself plainly and truthfully. I reminded Lovell about the time he came over to my aging grandparents' for Good Friday supper, high as the moon on scotch, and treated them to an endless sermon about the magnificence of the Harley-Davidson organization, how a hog was quicker than the devil and purer than the Virgin Mary, and slurringly offered to take Nana Eileen for a ride across the wheat flats at a hundred twenty miles an hour (she declined, and I remember thinking this idea of his was more about the smallness of his peter, because in fact as handsome as he was, he did have a mighty little one, not to mention how long it took him to get up to maximum speed). About another time when he bravely kicked the television off its stand at two in the morning because I'd made the big-deal mistake of falling asleep on the sofa during the election coverage without having finished doing the dishes. The time that for no reason whatever he pulled up all the tomato plants Dolores and I had staked in the backyard, and stepped on the seedling pumpkins and zuchs for good measure, shouting his fool head off that I'd stolen his mother away from him, or some such untreated sewage of a falsehood. That once when he made my child Guy eat his chicken dumpling dinner, like a dog, on the back porch, put his plate down on the floor, having taken his spoon away from him, because the boy had made the mistake of refusing to oblige Lovell's need for Guy to eat with his mouth shut. As if my husband could ever shut his. The time he deigned to come to Easter sunrise service and got it in his head to put a penny in the tray as a way of insulting me and everyone in the pews around us. The time he slapped me across the face because in my protesting his always coming to the dinner table in summer with his shirt off, and him never hearing my complaint that only cavemen pigs would do such a thing, I decided to make the macaroni with my blouse and bra off and, having served everybody, sat down to eat just as jaybird naked from the middle up as he was. When he threw— so typical and what a clichéd cliché—my burnt pot roast out the kitchen window, right through the glass, by the way, in the dead of a January winter blizzard. The time when, the time when. And if you think I'm over the top, don't you dare. This was all Lovell's doing. Every bit of it. Every ounce.

I only packed a few things in my shoulder bag, didn't need even to bother except I'll admit I did it to make an impression on him, not that he could hardly have noticed, given how often he kept going back to his Cutty Sark bottle. I left my Dear John on the kitchen table, took Guy by the hand, and collected my little silent Selby into my arms, and without responding to any of his shouted questions from our front porch—"What the hell you think you're doing? How the hell do you think you're gonna get away with this? Where the hell you think you're going?"—I walked down the darkening rainy street straight to Joanna and Kurt's. You know the next part about my being forced to kill him a couple days later.

It's such an awful tragedy that so many people got drowned in what they call a tsunami over there near Japan I think it was, sometime in the middle of the afternoon. God might in His wisdom have at least had the mercy to create this killer wave in the middle of the night when everyone was asleep and wouldn't have known what was about to happen. Whole little seaside towns dragged into the ocean like that. Imagine a hundred-foot cliff of brine being your last vision on this earth. Now, there's a moment of pure helplessness for you. You showed respect toward your mama and papa-san, you ate the rice and fish they served up from the wok, you labored day in and out, you were a good religious person who meditated long and hard about things like Hiroshima because, just say, one of your distant cousins was melted there when we lit the bomb over their heads, none of them ever individually making it into the news, but having been a part of world history without wanting to be, you did your level best, just like so many of us have done. Then you looked up one day and here was a green wall of salty ocean whose monumental hand was about to grab you under. I related to you that night I left home, you dead ones, as I sat there with my friend Joanna, who, since it was four in the morning, was lightly snoring on the couch next to me. I thought about that scary word, *tsunami,* and how it sounded like Daddy Death's name, if he had one. The station ran the word across the crawler on the bottom of the screen so many times that I began to think it meant something special for me, personally.

It did, of course. It became the word I think of when I think of the year of the many deaths. There were a couple more after Lovell's, since I couldn't stand to leave my boys alone and destitute. I loved precious little Selby and my towhead Guy far too much for that. Their mommy had to do what she considered a necessary thing, but which in the eyes of this spotless world of ours would be considered, I sensed in my fuguing mind, heinous and unforgivable. But what do they know? Though I appreciate how hard the talking heads on the news try to do their best to help us analyze events—nearly all of them disasters of some sort—none of us, them included, I'm afraid, can finally understand. We can watch, we can listen and think about things like when a drunken oil tanker skipper runs his full boat into the rocks and causes thousands of fish and birds and other creatures to perish, or when some fanatic explodes his shoes in a jetliner over Ireland, or India, or the warlords in Colombia slit the throats of missionaries who turn out to be government spooks infiltrating their cartel instead of spreading the word of the Lord. But we can't ever really understand just how dark people's hearts truly are, how mysterious. Looking at Lovell lying there in his own personal blood tsunami, gasping his last, I realized he never even knew himself, so how could he possibly begin to know me, not to mention Selby or Guy, Angie or Rodney, Dolores or Eileen, anybody at all. I confess to not scoping the depths of my heart, not really. In my way I have tried, but it's just a jigsaw puzzle with too many pieces missing and too many pieces from other puzzles mixed in to ever ultimately get a clear picture. This was, however, the way God set things up from the beginning of time. We're born ignorant, we try to learn a few things but mostly fail, and then we get old, some of us, and forget whatever it was we managed to learn, and then when we die we go into a sphere about which we know exactly nothing. Dark before, dim during, black afterward. Hardly seems like a cycle of life, does it. Whole thing just makes me sleepier and sleepier.

I think I said to him, as he was lying inert on the floor, that I was sorry. I always liked that shirt he was wearing, a black-and-white-striped shirt I bought him years ago for his birthday. Who would have guessed it would wind up being the last shirt he ever put on and buttoned up? There was a time, I remember thinking as I kneeled beside him, just before Nelly came into the room, when we used to do the fun, stupid things young people in love seem obligated to do. When Lovell took me to the movies, back before we had to be husband and wife, it was nothing short of glory to slouch in the seats, our laps littered with buttered popcorn and our shoes stuck on the floor with smashed Milk Duds and spilled Pepsi, and without asking hold each other's hand and every so often trade tongues, as we used to say. The feel of his tight jeans under my palm back and forth on his thigh was like the day of creation itself. How I loved him then, my delicious Lovell. His smooth-shaven face wore a smile, a toothy one just a touch yellower than the faded yellow on my cheerleader uniform (our other color was, of course, red), but a smile still and all. He liked cheddar cheeseburgers with bacon and I ordered mine plain. He poured ketchup on his fries and I dipped mine in mayo. I loved his rabbit-fur hat, and sometimes when it was snowing unexpectedly hard in November and I'd forgotten to bring along a shawl, he put his hat on my head, and it came down almost over my eyes, but I loved it. It felt so warm and smelled so much like the best of Lovell. Again, let me be honest. When Guy was born and I used to nurse him, one time Lovell came into bed with us and suckled my other breast. It wasn't until about three months into Guy's life that Lovell started withdrawing. He probably deserves credit for having given it his best shot that year—nine months of my pregnancy, and those first few with the baby—because, looking back, I think it was all full-throttle agony for the man. False calm before the storms. But, Lovell, I give you credit for having tried.

Still, I knew there wasn't much time left after Nelly and I worked to wipe up the gore that Lovell left on Joanna and Kurt's linoleum. I phoned 911 to report the mishap and then directed Nelly to lock herself and her brothers in their bedroom until the ambulance came. She was so well brought up by Joanna. What a sweet little girl, I thought, as I watched her do as I told her to do. I wished Nelly nothing but joy in her life as I filled the downstairs tub with warm water and, having rummaged around in the sink cabinet, found some nice fragrant lavender bubble bath, the whole contents of which I poured in, and then it was Guy who I fetched in first from the backyard, Guy who gave me a quizzical look when I told him to listen to what Mommy said, to hurry up and take off his clothes and get into the bath, which he did reluctantly but with all good faith, and then slumbering Selby, who didn't give me any fight since he was napping and dreaming what I hoped were pretty dreams, so full of trust and whispered words was he before I gentled him under the rising tide of water that already enveloped his older brother beneath the graying foam. Remarkable how calmly and quietly this was accomplished. I was as proud of them as ever. I don't think I was crying. Peaceful was what I felt. Everything was crystal clear in my humming head. Still, it was all I could do to get myself back to the sofa and turn on the news and wait and hope I wouldn't fall asleep again before it was my story that got told, hoping they'd be fair to me.

———

THERE IS A SAMENESS to the days here that reminds me of my childhood. I mean to say that one day is not much different than any other, and that's fine with me, which is just as well since if I wanted things to be different I'd only be frustrating myself. Decisions here are not much made by Lorraine. The food is decent and the rooms are clean and the locks work. Lorraine can have visitors, but besides Cecily, who drove all the way from Arizona once to see me, nobody comes around. Which, again, is just as well. I have my memories. I have my meds. I have my health, more or less. I have my clothes. Got my paper and pencil. I have my bed to sleep in at night. My window to daydream by in the day. I got cracks in the plaster walls to trace with my finger making its way along their thin black rivers. I've got a lot, and I'm grateful for all of this. I wish Lovell would be kind enough to drop by one of these Sundays and bring the little ones with him to visit their mother. I'm not holding my breath, though. I think he's still mad at me for leaving home and, besides, I doubt his whore girlfriend Angie wants him coming around to chitchat with old Lorraine. She was always jealous of me, Angie was, that's what I believe. So, yes, I'm kind of alone now, but as I say, grateful. One thing would improve my life infinitely, though, and that is a television. Lorraine used to be so current with world events, so up on what was happening in this great big wild world of ours. It makes me a little sad to think how out of the loop she's become.

(MIS)LAID

WHAT WE HAVE HERE is a man who on a lovely September morning (touch of early autumn chill in the sweet New England air, some sugar maple leaves already turning red under a crisp blue sky) mislaid his mind. The man (Catholic heterosexual Caucasian bachelor with cocoa eyes, thinning brown hair combed over, athletic despite his narrow, even frail, frame) believed he knew why this was happening to him, yet his beliefs (not religious beliefs, but having to do with his mind no longer working after some four decades of functioning fine, insofar as he could tell) were evolvingly suspect. Where once he was sociable (neighbors often invited him to dinners, during which he told hilarious if familiar jokes and never failed to help clear dishes) and affectionate (his longtime girlfriend, while married to one of these very neighbors, was as devoted to him as a mother of three children could manage to be), now he was isolated, bitter. Whereas before he was dependable (had been with the same accounting firm for fifteen years, was the star shortstop on their interleague softball team, blessed with an infallible throwing arm and perfect aim), he now became not just unreliable, but entirely unpredictable. Never in his life having missed a day of work, he called in sick (head cold, he claimed) on the last Tuesday of the month, then drew the curtains in his modest house (two-bedroom Cape, dove-gray siding) and began what would by week's end come to be known as (aliased thus by local law enforcement) *the siege.*

During the first hours that slowly amassed into days, the man took no incoming calls (the phone did actually ring a few times on Wednesday) but started telephoning people who didn't understand or care about how or why his mind was suddenly wrong. These (outgoing) calls were repetitious, tedious, diffuse, and minimally articulate grievings punctuated by laughter (in turn sometimes punctuated by weeping). It didn't help that they were made to people whom he had never met and who hung up on him before he had a chance either to explain himself or apologize. Many of those who were treated to a minute (or so) of his ravings thought he must surely be drunk (stinking plastered), not knowing that he didn't drink (indeed was a teetotaler and vegetarian with a weakness for wheatgrass juice). By Thursday midafternoon his firearms quietly surfaced (no one would ever have guessed he owned such a cache of weapons, certainly not his lover, whom he took hostage that same evening when she dropped by, as she always did on Thursdays, to make love with him), and by early Friday morning *the siege* had begun (the frantic husband having notified the local cops of his wife's absence, and the man himself having also placed a call to the accounting firm with his list of demands). Once the standoff was in place (SWAT team and state troopers now on the scene), the news media showed up, satellite pillars towering over their vans looking like an ugly flotilla of squat, land-bound boats with sails furled. Throughout that long weekend, newscasters (whom the neighbors would soon enough invite into their living rooms for coffee and to elaborate their thoughts regarding the unfolding situation) began covering this (now renamed) *hostage crisis*. The man who mislaid his mind would himself watch them interviewed on his television and agree with most of what they had to say (he was always such a considerate neighbor, such a nice quiet man, et cetera), all of which he told his girlfriend (who didn't respond because the duct tape he used to mummify her head rendered her mute). Gentle wind rustled in the turning oaks and birches as a glorious moon (full, brightly persimmon) rose above the rooftops down the street.

Now, the girlfriend's husband (who for many years had hired the man's accounting firm to prepare his taxes) held on to a fervent belief that his wife was not, as the media alleged, her captor's lover, but was the victim of a random kidnapping (wrong place at the wrong time, he told his three children and anyone else who would listen). Because *this madman* (as the husband now referred to him) had no next of kin (inherited the house from his parents, deceased), the negotiator (brought in by the police to talk him out of harming his hostage) asked the woman's husband (who had liked the man, even considered him a friend before he turned into *a fucking psycho*) to think about making a personal appeal in the hopes of bringing this unfortunate misunderstanding (as it were) to a swift and nonviolent end. If handled properly, according to the (thick-shouldered yet somehow curiously dainty) trained professional, *suspect contact* with someone familiar and directly involved with the situation can (on occasion) change the hostile dynamics and help defuse said situation. When the husband (whose face was crimson and own fuse short on the best of days) asked if this meant he was supposed to *fucking beg* this *fucking psycho* to release his wife, the negotiator (flanked by stern men in bullet-proof vests) answered that yes, in essence, if he wanted his wife back (in one piece), a personal plea was the best way to proceed. This would have been on Sunday morning, this request from the authorities, who'd been for two days stymied by the intransigence, not to mention sporadic incoherence, of their perpetrator. Before patching the bereft (sullen, chain-smoking) husband through to the man (whose line was now restricted, thanks to local telephone company cooperation, such that incoming and outgoing calls were confined to contact between the principals), he (the husband) was briefed not to (under any circumstances) use incendiary language (*fucking psycho, madman*) with the armed and dangerous (alleged) offender holed up in the house. The news media, having by this time confirmed that the husband's wife had been seen on multiple occasions entering and exiting the modest gray home of the man who now held her inside (presumably against her will), made some requests of their own of the upset husband (interview solicitations as well as appeals for recent photographs of the woman), which he refused (using peppery language with them, too, *fucking vampires* that they were, et cetera). He (the husband) packed the three children off to stay with their loving grandmother (paternal) until the storm passed. Alone now in his own modest Cape (a very pale blue), the husband had to admit to himself (and to his God) that things weren't looking good, that it seemed increasingly possible (undeniable, in fact) that his *fucking wife* had hung the horns on him with this *fucking madman* and that he was from this moment forward going to look like (be) a *fucking laughingstock* (not just in town but in the eyes of a watchful nation). He took a leave of absence from the bank where he had worked without incident for a decade as assistant branch manager, and retained a lawyer (who agreed to represent him on contingency), and also withdrew behind the drawn curtains of his house. The magnificent autumn weather continued all the while to hold, various flitting warblers (some redstarts perched in a lilac, a yellow-throat in the honeysuckle) filling the air with song.

Yes (to be sure), there were signs of impending breakdown the week before Tuesday dawned and the man (who currently paced back and forth in his living room with a Browning BDA-380 clenched in both hands, listening to the dismal moans of his girl-friend, whom he had handcuffed to a radiator) mislaid his mind. On the Friday prior, for instance, he had arrived home from work and drawn a hot bath, then climbed into the water without having removed his clothes (his watch and loafers were ruined), an act that probably had something (everything) to do with the disagreement (brawl) he'd had with his girlfriend the night before. Rather than making love as they did every Thursday evening (a routine they had followed for nine years), the girlfriend announced (cheeks flushed, hazel eyes averted, one slim hand fidgeting with her wavy hennaed hair) that they *needed to talk.* This was, in the opinion of the man, not a promising prelude to the dark pleasure (their weekly two hours, during which time she supposedly attended a Bible studies group, ladies only) that stretched before them. Indeed, the last time his girlfriend intoned this *need to talk* was a year before when she presented him with an assortment of foil packets containing various condoms (lambskin, French ticklers, ribbed ultrathins), then told him that from now on their intercourse would have to be protected. He knew at once why his girlfriend wanted him to strap on these (goddamn) rubbers. Just as it had nothing to do with some fear of sexually transmitted diseases (both the man and his girlfriend were good about being tested during annual checkups with their mutual doctor), it had everything to do with her unwillingness to bear the man any more children and raise them under her husband's roof. Lovemaking with one of these (ridiculous) rubbers (the man told her that night the year before) was like trying to do brain surgery while wearing a thick pair of gardener's gloves (or some such meta-phor that got him nowhere). The girlfriend reminded him that not only was sex not brain surgery but (more to the point) that she had for all these years (at the man's insistence) required her husband to wear a condom whenever they copulated (a rare enough event in the wallpapered bedroom of the married couple, and thus such a rarer miracle yet the advent of three offspring whom the husband wrongly attributed to serendipitous leakage and fertile sperm), so if this was what she wanted it was only fair of him to comply. The man argued to no avail, as his girlfriend had excellent and ready responses to his every point. Yes, she agreed, he had always been good about giving her a (secret) monthly allowance to help with child support (which she used instead, for the most part, to build for herself a personal nest egg against the so-called rainy day, unbeknownst to either boyfriend or husband). And yes, he had been understanding and supportive of her desire to remain married to her husband (they had been sweethearts since grade school, and as devout Catholics didn't believe in divorce), and it was true he had not (very often, at least) expressed jealousy toward her husband or resentment about the children's ignorance of their true paternity or (even any real marked) rancor with regard to their (singular) circumstances. But at the end of the day none of this mattered because (at the end of the day), she said, she wanted *no more kids.* He acquiesced (having no viable option) and their Thursday evening rendezvouses continued through winter and spring much as they always had, the man not wanting to upset what seemed to him (sanely or not) a basically good situation and his girlfriend thinking (more or less) along similar lines. Given all this, then, why did she suddenly *need to talk* last Thursday?

Because she was pregnant. Three months along, according to the doctor who (himself an old-school Catholic) embraced the pope's call (this would be Pius II) for Catholics to conceive, thus to propagate large families so that the universal flock would be increased according to the (ironic, if not plausibly hypocritical) wishes of the Virgin Mary. Being an accountant (a good one, it should be acknowledged), the man (whose chalky face blanched as his mouth went dry) made some quick calculations and comprehended immediately the deeper meaning of his girlfriend's unexpected revelation. This was not *his* child, he breathed (lower lip quivering in a way she had never seen before, as if he'd been touched by an invisible taser mildly electrocuting him there) and waited for her to respond, suspecting she was going to tell him (as in fact she did) that she wasn't sure. He (however) was. As the man marched from the kitchen to the bedroom to the living room and back into the kitchen (where she sat, trying her best to *remain calm*), he recounted (at the top of his lungs and with awful precision) both his own itineraries, locations, and agendas for the month of June, and then hers. She had missed (as she did by joint agreement and without fuss each year) being available to him the first three Thursdays of that month (because her family made their annual trip to the Adirondacks to visit her parents), and in a (rare) disruption to their arrangement he himself managed to miss the last Thursday that June because one of his interleague softball games ran into extra innings (they lost). The woman sat listening to this (quite accurate) appraisal of things, feigning a certain interest in the logic of the man's assessment, nodding her head sometimes and other times shaking it (all the while warily observing that grotesque shuddering of his lower lip), knowing he wasn't wrong in concluding that (for once) the baby was not his. It was when the man fell silent, strode smoothly over to the kitchen table and quite unexpectedly slapped her (not hard, but it came as a shock), she told him (through a veil of warm tears) that he was right about everything. She'd felt sorry for her needy husband one night at her parents' (couldn't he understand such a simple thing) and, having left the condoms at home, figured nothing would come of it (rather). Granted, they'd only (discreetly and perfectly silent in the guest bedroom of her mother and father's old shake-shingled house) done it once but, as the adage goes, In for a penny, in for a pound (she didn't say as much that evening, though it occurred to her as she walked back home under a pretty waxing moon, wondering what she was going to do about this total mess she found herself in, drying her eyes on her jacket sleeve while elegant bats dropped in and out of the street-lamp light). They had agreed before she left (embracing tentatively after exchanging a few choice words about the unacceptable slap) to take a week to cool off and meet Thursday next to pursue a reconciliation.

Over the course of that protracted and galling weekend, the man found himself thinking (if thinking it was, given he was by then well into the process of mislaying his mind) at cross-purposes. Now he was calm (it doesn't matter), now hurt (how could she), now enraged (the time had come inevitably that everyone had to be taken off the ledger, zero-summed). He wished she would telephone him and (on a whim, for instance) propose that (perhaps, barring any plans he might have) he drop over for dinner with her husband and kids (vegetable lasagna night), so that he could accept her invitation or else slam down the phone in disgust (she didn't call). But no, he was banished now and there was no making up with her next Thursday (she should have at least called to see how he was faring, given he had done *nothing* wrong and she had done *everything* wrong), and this was why he filled his (father's old Waterman) fountain pen with black ink and took a sheet of paper and began to draw up his *list of demands,* not having (initially) a definite concept (clue) what his demands should be, but writing in the confident knowledge that (because of her mindless betrayal) what had been private would soon become (very) public (indeed). She'd get hers (he thought). That Monday, at work, he found himself studying the (seven) faces (three female, four male) of his (soon to be former) colleagues, wondering whether they fathomed the darkness that haunted their coworker's heart. They didn't (it seemed to the man), and this only angered him all the more, even though he had spent years (and a great deal of effort) keeping secret from them the source (his girlfriend and three bastard children) of what now infuriated him. He tidied his (already meticulous) desk the next day, knowing it would be his last, then walked straight home, pausing (briefly) to throw a rock (small but with cruelly perfect aim) at a mockingbird perched in an elm tree.

When the telephone rang (fast-forward to late Sunday night on day three of the *hostage crisis*), the man (startled from his quiet reverie about how his life was falling to pieces faster than autumn leaves) inadvertently squeezed the trigger of his Browning BDA-380, causing his (hitherto inert) girlfriend to scream, however muffled she was by the duct tape (which she'd managed to chew through in order to breathe better), while also causing the sharp-shooters and other peace officers outside the house (illuminated by klieg lights) to move into *high alert*. The man himself screamed before picking up the phone (after a good dozen rings) and asked, What do you goddamn want? as the acrid bouquet of discharged smoke settled in the living room and the fresh (impressively large) hole in his hardwood floor gaped at his feet. He recognized (to his dismay) the voice as that of his girlfriend's husband. What I want is to know what you want, answered the husband (reasonably enough), containing his fury with great effort. Brief silence, then more from the husband. What (he said) I don't want to do is cause trouble here (words scripted by the negotiator), I just want to know if my wife is all right. A (lengthy and sinister) silence ensued before the man assured his neighbor, this *totally retarded* former friend, client, and husband of his gagged and handcuffed, pregnant (by now very ex-) girlfriend, that she was doing really great. What was that gunfire all about? pressed the husband (again reading the scribbled prompt written in the negotiator's notepad). As if snapping out of a daydream, the man told the husband to pass the (goddamn) phone to somebody who had some (goddamn) authority here. What was being done (for instance) about his *list of demands*? The cuckold (just before the negotiator snatched the phone out of his hand and two troopers gently if firmly escorted him away from the *staging area*) told the man (dramatically, very audibly) that he didn't give *a rat's ass* whether he killed his *fucking wife* or not, and that he hoped (sincerely) that he put a bullet through his own *fucking brain* (if he had one) while he was at it. Screw you, thought the man, who now was confronted with a very different voice (the negotiator said hello to him, winningly), making the man think (wisely) that here (most definitely) was someone (he asked for authority and got it) more frightening (or else appalling) than even the (goddamn) husband, because he was cool and deliberate and sober (unafraid of the dark, anybody's dark), all of which suddenly shocked (as the expression goes) the man back to (as it were, fleeting) reality.

This negotiator (knowing what was of primary interest to his perp) asked first how the man was doing, did he have enough to eat, did the woman (never *hostage*) have enough to eat, or have other (uh) needs (prescription medicines). The woman, the man said (curiously sheepish given the imbalance of power at play here, the world being in *his* hands), was *doing better than ever* (disdain intended), though he realized for the first time since he took his girlfriend hostage that neither he nor she had slept or eaten (much, old tofu salvaged from the fridge before the electricity was cut off, washed down with tap rather than customary bottled water, which he'd shared with his captive, duct tape temporarily removed, who accepted his largesse with reluctance) and (thus) his (already mislaid) mind was not as (razor) sharp as it (undoubtedly) ought to be under the (developing) circumstances.

That (*doing better than ever*) sounded (not so) encouraging to the negotiator who (in his most concerned voice) wanted to address the man's demands. There seemed to be five of them, all of which would be taken with (utmost) seriousness (to be sure). It was just that the message (you see) that he had left earlier on the phone machine at the accountants' office was a little garbled (utterly unintelligible) and so in order to accommodate his needs (in the most immediate and efficient manner), it would be useful for the man to (now) repeat these ultimatums. The man cleared his throat and (wanting to cooperate fully, given things were going his way, it decidedly seemed) articulated his *list of demands.*

First off was a private jet (fully fueled) with an experienced (unarmed) pilot prepared to fly the man and his girlfriend to the destination of his choice (the man made this first demand despite the fact that he had never been on a plane in his life, was in fact terrified of flying, and had concocted the idea from having seen numerous action films that featured *hostage situations*). Further, he demanded that the sum of one million dollars (unmarked bills, twenties and fifties, once more inspired by those selfsame movies) be delivered to him (leather attaché) in exchange for his (written) guarantee to release the girlfriend once his destination (Cuba, he was thinking, certain—not quite—he wouldn't be extradited if, as he'd additionally mused, he donated most of the ransom money to Cuban baseball for the purchase of new gloves, uniforms, et cetera) had been reached. And furthermore, he demanded (lest he not summon the courage to board the jet and fly to Cuba) that he be granted legal immunity for his (unsavory to some, but surely not felonious to him) actions, since (logically) none of this was *his goddamn fault* but rather the fault of his (treacherous goddamn) girlfriend, not to mention her (goddamn all-of-a-sudden lover boy) husband (plus also that he had, solely *because of them,* mislaid his mind). And moreover, what he demanded was an apology (in front of television cameras, preferably in prime time) from all his fellow employees at the accounting firm, for each and every thing they ever did to make him unhappy (not fathoming, for instance, *the darkness that haunted their coworker's heart* on Tuesday last, damn them all to hell). Finally, the man demanded (noticing as he spoke that the negotiator had been very quiet, which he mistakenly attributed to attentiveness and even conscientiousness, perhaps to the fact that the negotiator must surely be taking notes, if not scrambling his qualified staff of sergeants and lieutenants, or whomever, even as they lived and breathed, to make arrangements for the flight and ransom money) that his children be made aware of the fact that their father was not their father, but that their *real father* (and here, more instantaneous than the crack of a bat against a ball, or a slap in the face, the bullet from the husband's handgun broke the living-room window glass, tore neatly through the drawn curtains, and entered the man's cranium, dropping him in an abrupt heap on the hardwood floor, killing him immediately and without recourse)—

At this juncture the husband's wife screamed again, this time unremittingly until the peace officers (having placed the husband under arrest, quite incensed and not a little chagrined that, while focusing on raiding the house through the kitchen door in back, they had failed to notice the husband, who had walked home after the officers removed him from the *staging area,* and there had a *nice stiff one* while he loaded his own handgun, no Browning BDA-380 but sufficient to the task, and marched back, keeping himself more or less hidden in neighborhood shrubbery, and aimed at the living-room window, not caring one way or another whether he happened to hit the *fucking psycho* or his *fucking wife,* just hoping he succeeded in murdering one of the *fucking goddamn fucks*) entered the house (firearms unnecessarily drawn) to discover the (dead) man on the hardwood floor (still clutching one of his dozen or so guns, the others having been neatly laid out on the plaid sofa and matching wingback chair) and the woman by the radiator (who stopped screaming once they uncuffed her and removed the duct tape), and (after searching the rest of the modest house) radioed the negotiator and commanding officer (both smoking unfiltered cigarettes in the *staging area*) that the crime scene was secured. The woman's husband gave himself up without a struggle and was led off (himself now in handcuffs) to be driven downtown for booking (where he called his startled lawyer, whose practice was mostly in estate tax). That he expressed (in front of several witnesses at the precinct house before his aforementioned attorney arrived) delight (not to mention astonishment) upon hearing he had somehow managed (sheer luck) to slay the *fucking psycho* would not help his case in the months (and years) to come (found guilty of first degree murder by a thoughtful *jury of his peers*). The man's corpse was (after being photographed from many angles) removed (body bag), and the media vans (pros aboard) thereafter left (this particular crisis being *a wrap*), as did the SWAT contingent and many officers (two detectives and a forensic expert remained behind *collecting evidence* such as it was), and soon the neighborhood settled back to (some semblance of) normalcy before a harsh early frost (this would be toward the end of the month) hastened the (magnificent) autumn foliage even as it killed chrysanthemums in flower beds up and down the street, while geese flew in (loud and traditional) formation across the (cobalt) sky overhead. As for the ex-wife of the (imprisoned) husband (and girlfriend of the deceased), she sold both (the dove-gray and very pale blue) Capes (having inherited the former from her ex-boyfriend, who had attentively included their offspring in his will, and the latter in her divorce settlement) and moved (with all four of her children) into a larger house (different neighborhood, as might be presumed). During her (understandably somewhat lengthy) period of mourning and recovery (from the trauma she was forced to endure) she relied on the (combined) comforts afforded her by her doctor (who determined which pharmaceuticals would help her through her difficult days, and nights) and priest (whose dulcet voice, not unlike that of the doctor, was so soothing to her in the shadowy solace of the confessional), each of whom (generous to a fault) took her (as it were) under their mortal (and immortal) wings.

ALL THE THINGS THAT ARE WRONG WITH ME

A s you know, we were each told to write an honest essay about the things that are wrong with us, and this one is mine. Having read over my charming masterpiece, I wouldn't wish the life it sketches on my worst enemy, of which I have more than my share. We were instructed by our therapist, Bruce—I doubt that's his real name—to explore what each of us considers our worst personal failings, and if possible *identify the genesis*, as Bruce put it, *of these vices*, taking care not to allow ourselves to *vent animosity toward others in the group* or toward those who had been the bane of our lives over the years. I can't have been alone in considering this a damn tough assignment, but I have done my best. Looking back, the hardest part of fulfilling the task at hand was to limit the essay to only seven things wrong with me. My original list, probably like yours, ran into the hundreds. Narrowing it down was a frustrating job, but I suspect this was the idea. *Reverse psychology*, they used to call it, *the counterintuitive approach*. By processing just seven of our faults, one each day of the week, we'd recognize that these were merely the tip of the iceberg in the overall scheme of faults, and also discover, by thinking about it so thoroughly, some glimpses of the possible good that lurked in each of our rotten hearts. I'm sure this has been a learning experience for the rest of you, too.

By way of introduction, my father was Bill. My mother is Irene. My sister was Christy and my other sister is Jocelyn. My one grandmother is Honey and my two grandfathers are Wilfred and Paul. My dead grandmother I never met, her name was Nancy, though my family rarely spoke about her because they say she wasn't nice and made a calculated marriage with my grandfather Paul, who is a heart specialist and the one success story in our otherwise pathetic gang. There is an uncle named Hamp, which is short for Hampton, and he is a crabby old drummer in a dated lounge act heard every Monday and Thursday down in Staten Island somewhere. I had an Aunt Janice and Uncle Arnie at one point, but they disavowed me, as have my cousin Bill and another cousin I never met, whose name is Claudia to the best of my knowledge. To clarify, Christy is dead and her widower is serving three consecutive life sentences for the murder of her half-wit boyfriend, Bill—yes, a ton of Bills in my life—Bill's stepmother, Addie, and my older sister herself. Hanged them in the garage. For the record, if you're taking notes, my name is John.

My father, first. We never got along and the fault must lie with me, because he was such a stellar human being, just ask him yourself. He tried hard to be the perfect dad, but I couldn't get with the program. There are so many examples of my ingratitude in the face of his flawless parenting that I could write the whole essay on this alone. An early recollection involves a Boy Scout jamboree where I learned to make cornstalk fiddles, tie a double knot known as the Flemish Loop, and sharpen my hatchet with a whetstone. It was during this summer weekend in the Poconos when some of us scouts and our fathers signed up for a taxidermy seminar. A deceased dude named Captain Thomas Brown wrote in some manual that *boys ought to be instructed in the art of stuffing birds and mammals at an early age,* and so on his high authority we were urged to start then and there. First we were told how to kill specimens in the best ways—pithing or poisoning instead of buckshot pellets, which turned the corpse into a mess. We then learned about skinning, defeathering, defurring, unfleshing, dismembering, and denuding the carcasses of chipmunks, skunks, moles, and other helpless wilderness beasts. As it happened, the taxidermist scoutmaster gave me and my approving father a great horned owl to stuff together. Seems a local farmer had been plagued by the bird's hungry junkets to the chicken coop—it had been cleanly shot and donated to the scouts for the purpose of stuffing. Urged on by my manly father, while gorge rose like lava in my throat, I mopped blood from the pretty plumage, then separated its skin from the body with my quivering fingers. Dad didn't help much other than to egg me on whenever I balked. As instructed, I dusted his guts—the owl's—with cornmeal to soak up the other fluids besides blood, and scooped the eyes, then painted their sockets with toxic soap and used the other junk they gave us—the camphor, salt of tartar, powdered lime, wooden dowels and heavy wire. With penknife and threaded needle and lots of glue I created a monstrosity that long weekend, a parody of an owl, as you might have guessed. My father blamed me and I blamed both him and the Boy Scouts, and not only did I never go to any camp again, but I shredded my scouting manual and used it to line my hamster cage. We never discussed the matter afterward, and though my deep hatred of the man began before this incident and matured in its wake, the failure of our father–son outing was like arsenic in an already poisonous relationship. I still have the poor owl, most of whose dusty feathers have fallen out. His beak is black and I put marbles in the eye holes, which gives him a bit of a crazed look on top of the refrigerator where he's perched. After this jamboree scene I became, to the old man's horror, a vegetarian.

Only legumes and grains have touched my lips, the latter, as with many of you here today, most often in liquid form. As for my dear father, he ate pork, fish, fowl, venison, veal, lamb, and beef right up to the afternoon he died of a massive coronary when we were alone in the house. If only he'd made it more clear to me what ailed him as he lay there thrashing on the kitchen floor, I might have been able to help him. His death, you could say, and don't think some haven't, was my fault—a natural extension of my guilty inadequacy as a son—if you were to ignore his repulsive dietary habits and lifelong bad temper, which gave him the high blood pressure in the first place. We buried him in his old Explorers uniform.

I don't hate my mother the way I hated my father, but I can't claim I ever brought the slightest ray of happiness into her life, either. She nearly died in childbirth, as she liked telling me over and over again, especially on birthdays, both mine and hers. Good old Irene with her blue hair and eyes, a head taller than her husband, back when he was among the standing, didn't like any of her brats, as far as I could tell. When they found Christy and the others in the garage, I swear her torrents of tears had less to do with having lost her eldest daughter than with the fact that another source of income had just got hung out to dry, old Bill having dropped dead on us just the year before. But maybe I'm being too hard on her, another fault of mine. She has always shown a mother's leniency toward me when it came to my menagerie of stray cats and mongrel dogs and birds with broken wings, and for that I owe her a debt of gratitude. Given how directionless my hours after school had become, once the Scouts and I parted company, and knowing from experience how poorly I got along with other goons my own age, my mother saw the interest I took in feeding, grooming, and playing with the homeless pets found in alleys, back lots, and in the fields beyond the way-crummy town where we lived, and thought it might be a good thing for me. Might keep me, as she put it, *out of the detention house*. The fact that it landed me *in* the detention house is a cruel irony I choose not to address right now, but, as I say, I was grateful for her forbearance, which I used at every possible turn to my own advantage. To a fault, I confess. What I mean to say is, the more strays and hurt animals I brought home with me—most lived in our basement, freely coming and going by way of a broken window—the more I wanted.

Some of you undoubtedly are the type of delinquents who got your start by hanging the neighbors' kittens on a clothesline. Well, that wasn't my game. Instead, when I couldn't help abandoned animals, I took in pets from houses on the other end of town, usually during the day when their so-called owners were away working, or going to school like I was supposed to do. Irene must have known what I was up to but kept her mouth shut, figuring she hadn't many other options left since the idea was, as I mentioned before, encouraged by her, and since I was on probation. She must also have suspected that all the dog chow and kitty litter, the birdcages and rabbit pellets, not to mention catnip toys and rawhide bones and so forth, cost more money than I earned on my paper route, which I did less for the dough and more to scout new mates for the menagerie. So when cranky Hamp, who was living with us, complained that cash was missing from his wallet, as did Grandmother Honey several blocks away, my mother's indulgence was put to the test. Despite all the tenderness I showed my animals, the way I went about maintaining my personal free-range kennel must have agonized the old gal, and so another strike against me.

My little sister, Jocelyn, and I were thrown together almost from infancy, as Christy was a decade my senior, while I was only a year older than Josie. We were virtual Siamese twins until the big guy, who found us putting on an imaginary tea party in her room, both of us dressed in her Sunday clothes and made up with lipstick borrowed from Irene's drawer in the master bath, lowered the boom on me. That was when he decided the Little League and

Cub Scouts and crap like that were the necessary antidote. I don't like nor do I excel at sports any more than I liked or excelled at anything the scouting organization had to offer. Our virile father, worried that his only son showed signs of orienting down a sexual avenue that would have been disgraceful in his macho eyes, missed altogether my more deviant direction, navigated for many years by my uncurbed little sister and me. If I'm sounding glib it's because, as any of you rubes who has walked the same path knows, I'm embarrassed by how good and natural our pre-pubescent marriage was. We said wedding vows one summer day in the downstairs den, and sometimes even now, all these years later, I think it's a pity Jocelyn met her fiancé, Michael, a TV-handsome young lawyer, but my love for her, which is also my failing, remains strong. I should add, it continues to give me profound, even grim, pleasure that the big bad wolf never found out. He perished on the kitchen floor sure in his soul that his only begotten son was a eunuch or worse. But, as you now know, he was mistaken. Old Irene never knew about us, either, and while Christy had her suspicions, she is no longer among us and in any case might have approved, since how much more out there could you get than Christy?

I would like to take a moment here to protest that all these confessions are beginning to make me sound like some kind of wicked, even pukey, human being, which I know I'm not. But don't take my word for it. Just ask any of the dozens of animals whose lives I saved over the years. Ask my grandfather, Paul, who posted bail whenever such a kindness was needed, to keep me out of places he felt I didn't belong. He should know, if anyone does, where I do and do not belong, since he's a medical man of considerable stature. He commutes to Columbia Presbyterian from a Tudor in Riverdale and, as I say, ought to know the score. But all right. I know this is against the rules, so I'll get back to my list, as our therapist Bruce stipulated. Just that it seemed to me the picture was getting too skewed, but I suppose, as a couple of you have just said, that's the point.

So, having mentioned my grandfather, I guess this would be the best moment to describe how, after poor Christy met her death and the trial of my brother-in-law was going on, he took me and Jocelyn in for several months. My mother's father, his heart went out to Irene during those dark times, and he wanted to do whatever he could to help her through a tough stretch. Since his wife, the loathed Nancy, had died some years earlier, leaving the surgeon in his large pile of brick and slate with only an elderly housekeeper under the same roof, he even seemed to welcome the company. And we welcomed the unbridled days of complete freedom, which took us out into a neighborhood of wealth, luxury, splendor that neither of us had ever seen. We trespassed like crazy, skinny-dipped in people's private pools, trampled their fancy flower beds, rummaged around in their garages, never stealing anything really but maybe soaping a windshield now and then if the car seemed antique and valuable. We discovered the joy of television and watched junk with the sound off all night long, while our grandfather went to bed early, his work taking him back to the hospital before dawn every morning. We made friends with only one kid in the neighborhood, and here comes the confession. His name was Brewster, or something idiotic. This was before I started the menagerie, by the way. Brewster had the most beautiful little dog, whose penance it was to suffer her master's putting out cigarettes on her belly. Josie and I started smoking that summer, and this snot Brewster conceived the idea after trying and failing to smoke a fag with us. We laughed ourselves silly when his face flushed red and he half coughed his lungs out, and I imagine it was our scorn that prompted his sadism. One day, having noticed the bitch lying near us in the grass on her side was covered with tiny, round welts that weren't her tits, I asked fat Brewster what he thought the problem was with his dog. Proudly smirking, he told me what he'd been doing. It was like a dream, as if his screams and those of my sister were televised with the volume low, when without the least thought I climbed on top of him and, holding him as still as I could, burned his cheek and forehead and chin and even one eyelid with my cigarette. He lived, the bastard, of course.

And so did I, though for my compassionate crime I was introduced for the first time to The System. A bad thing, I guess, all of it. My grandfather was unhappy, to say the least, about the outcome of his largesse and my mother was made only more despondent, though both saw my violent response to this prick's sickness as the natural outgrowth of the tragedy that had visited the margins of my life. For what it's worth, Brewster landed himself in therapy and the pup was removed to a shelter. Without a moment's hesitation I would do what I did to him again, even though I admit, once more, that it's one of the things wrong with me.

Maybe I should allow myself a lesser fault, a breather, as it were. My toenails are thick, brittle, apricot-colored, and split. They are extremely ugly perched on the ends of my toes, which are as long as most people's fingers. Let me show you. See how each nail is deeply ridged and as amber as any petrified resin out of your basic Jurassic Park. My father, who instructed me in all the mysteries of personal grooming, taught me to trim them in the shape of a V, like so, and they have served over the years, when needed, as weapons. Even dear Josie has a scar on her left cheek, the result of a friendly wrestling match under the front porch when we were five and six years of age, respectively. My toenails themselves and the injuries they have brought to others constitute a fault that should be considered more serious than the smiles on your faces suggest. Which brings me to a more unpleasant entry in my catalog.

As you know, my love of people—Jocelyn excepted—borders on nil, while my love for animals is almost without limit. So after they released me from juvie hall into my mother's custody, I scored that paper route, as mentioned, and one by one started taking in a slew of stray calicos and tabbies, half-breed mutts that mixed all kinds of things from dachshund to mastiff, not to mention pigeons, robins, sparrows, the occasional escaped parakeet, gerbils, rabbits, mice, possums, snakes, lizards, even a blind raccoon. Of course, the place did begin to stink a little. Hamp complained the most. Irene, having no sense of smell, and Josie being Josie, they didn't seem to notice. But Hamp wasn't wrong. Nobody, even I, could have kept up with the activities in our basement and backyard. All I did was care for my precious darlings, which is how I came to think of them, nor am I ashamed to admit it, even though I see some of you find it humorous. The rest of the time I tried to cop enough dough to cover the expenses. Josie tried to help me out, but her dashing beau, Michael, didn't like my asylum any more than he liked me.

As you must have figured out on your own, some years had come and gone between my release from juvie and Jocelyn's accepting this Michael's offer of marriage. It would be about ten of them, during which time I was only busted once on a minor infraction, thanks to some do-gooder from the Department of Health, who showed up at our door with a warrant and a bad attitude. Irene and Hamp happened to be out, so Josie and I virgiled this dude on an inspection of the cellar and backyard. Needless to say, he didn't like what he saw, even though, coincidentally, I'd tidied the litter boxes and various cages just the day before. When Mr. Clean wrote out his summons, he advised me that I would have to erect a fence around the backyard in order to avoid future visits. The neighbors, who never spoke to our family at any rate, were planning on bringing an action against us, he kindly informed me, and even treated me to the cliché about good fences making good neighbors. By this time I had a job over at the mall working at the mega pet store, so paying the couple hundred bucks fine was doable. Less so was his smiling directive to reduce the number of *domiciled animals*, as he called my beloved buddies, in the next thirty days, by about half. Smiling even more broadly, he offered *governmental assistance with the necessary removal,* after laying out for me the law regarding domestic pets housed in suburban environs, and other shit like that, but seeing I had a choice in the matter, I told him I'd take care of it myself. I would later find out that he didn't have the authority to dismantle my dream right on the spot because, living as we did at the edge of the edge of town, our domicile could be considered rural, and different restrictions apply to rural precincts, et cetera, et cetera. Still, the son of a gun didn't depart without confiscating Mindy, my African gray parrot, since of course I couldn't produce the necessary papers to prove I owned her legally, which you can bet your own damn rural domicile I did not.

If you're thinking this story is all fine and dandy, but where is John's fault in it, why does he relate it as something wrong with him, I share your concern. As you will see, one man's good is the next man's evil. The fence I erected was twice as tall and I hope a hundred times uglier than my neighbors had bargained for, but since no zoning restrictions prevented its construction—ours was no gated community with fancy covenants—up she went pronto. The dogs, the woodchuck, and the fox got to work right away digging tunnels, bless their hearts. The menagerie knew, just as its Noah did, that the wall was only for show, and not meant to keep anyone from the usual appointed rounds, mostly done under the light of the moon. In the meantime, I persuaded Honey, which is to say I paid her, to let me keep some animals in her detached garage for a week, guaranteeing her I'd take care of everything, she wouldn't even know they were there and neither would anyone else. Amazingly, everything went off without a hitch. The DOH lunkhead was satisfied, Honey made a couple dollars, the neighbors were stifled, Irene and Hamp turned a blind eye on the whole business, and all my kids were back home just days after we were reluctantly given a clean bill of health. As our therapist Bruce told me last year, it was probably my success with this scheme that pumped up my confidence and led to the mess that followed it just as naturally as piss follows beer.

It all developed so slowly that none of us noticed, certainly not me. Hamp croaked somewhere in here, and Irene moved in with Honey long about the same time Josie met her beau and moved in with him. Christy's husband was sent up to the big house for good. I, pretty much left to my own devices, painted the windows black and kept adding members to the family. Like any connoisseur, my tastes developed and became more refined. Not content with alley cats and mongrels, garden snakes and hamsters—though I loved these with the same love I showed all my chums—I began confiscating from hither and thither more exotic creatures. Where's hither and thither? Since it's all public knowledge now, there's no point being coy, so I'll fess up to some nocturnal wanderings of my own back then, to the homes of pet-store patrons who had purchased the more intriguing animals, the store itself naturally, and to a small, understaffed zoo one state over. I brought home some pretty snazzy friends. A lynx I named Lucy. A mink named Ned. Some peacocks. The mutts were joined by a sweaty old shar-pei named Chairman Mao and a Rhodesian ridgeback—Buster, I called him. A huge Maine coon and a sleek Russian blue joined my cattery. My mynah bird could recite the first sentence of the Gettysburg Address, a feat his tutor who stands before you is proud of to this day. Listen, can any of you asshats recite the first sentence of the Gettysburg Address? If not, stow the mirth. Finally, I outdid myself by spiriting away a baby mountain lion from the zoo one night, nearly getting killed in the effort. Were I an addict, this would have marked my bottom. Who knows, maybe I had become an addict, another thing wrong with me I hadn't even counted on confessing today. I named her Kitty.

This mountain lion, though I kept her in the biggest chain-link cage in the backyard and fed her an endless stream of food, broke out more than once and made a banquet from the menagerie. Gone were the peacocks, gone my Maine coon. Let me admit it: I was in over my head. She was growing faster than I'd ever seen a feline—or any other animal, for that matter—grow, and I came to the conclusion that I had to release her but quick, before things got completely out of hand. She would do fine in the mountains of northern Jersey, I told Josie, who spent less time with me than ever because she couldn't stand the stench, she said, and the blackened windows depressed her. She had agreed to help me with the transfer and even nabbed some sedatives from the pharmacy where she worked in order to calm the cat so it could sleep in the trunk during the drive. All my plans, all my hopes of rebalancing the upset menagerie were dashed when, the day before we were to make the run, Kitty got loose again but instead of going after her terrified mates in the habitat, she scaled the fence to maraud our neighborhood in search of something more interesting to eat. It wasn't her fault she ran into some kid a few blocks away and removed him from his swing-set even as she wrenched off the better part of his plump little arm in the process. Kitty was only following nature's mandates, just as the cops, who took me into custody and charged me with an impressive list of offenses including reckless endangerment, were merely following the mandates set out by lawmakers who know more about these matters than I seem to. The kid lived, but poor Kitty was destroyed for no good reason. Just because my grandfather came to my rescue again, not with bail this time but a crackhead lawyer and some wiggy psychiatrist who steered me here so I could hang out with all you bozos, doesn't mean that my menagerie was a crazy idea. Far from it—I think I was well on my way to creating a small piece of heaven there. That I couldn't pull it off is just one more of the things that are wrong with me.

NONE OF YOU HAS APPRECIATED my confession, I can tell, including Bruce over there, our good therapist. My words have not inspired you, nor have you benefited from listening to my sad stories. Now while I won't *vent animosity toward others in the group,* I am going to ask your indulgence when I confess that our therapist's assignment to *identify the genesis of these vices* may be beyond my capability. Can the mirror look at itself? I have tried like crazy to figure out why I've done the things people say I have done wrong, but in every instance I come up with the same answers, ones that seem pure and simple to me, but which over the years haven't con-vinced one solitary soul of my true innocent nature. I love animals and refuse to eat them, therefore I'm a lunatic? My brilliant father couldn't eat their butchered carcasses fast enough, but when old mincemeat gets his just desserts it's my fault he croaked? Fat snot Brewster burns holes in his puppy and needs quick punishment, which I implement, and who is labeled the criminal? Having no family to speak of, I invent one with my little sister, and therefore I'm a pervert. My neighbors want a wall, I build a wall and devote myself to taking care of God's helpless creatures, and for my troubles I am laughed at, then investigated, fined, ostracized, and abandoned by everyone. And the business about that mountain lion mangling the little boy? I already confessed to being out of my depth with Kitty. The tragedy was in the timing—I was, after all, about to correct the situation. Bottom line is, analyzing everything as best I can using common sense, all the things that are supposedly wrong with me are not, at the end of the day, my fault. I realize I've said right along that they are my fault, but—as Bruce hoped—I have glimpsed the good that lurks in my rotten heart. I doubt I even belong here with all you fricking spazmos.

Let me finish up by saying I'm very aware I covered only six things wrong with me, not seven as we were directed. I also know that for each of these there must be countless deeper pitch-black defects backgrounding them, but at the risk of cheating—which would be yet another fault in itself—I'm going to skip my last failing, because I see our time has run out. Too bad, since it was a good one, as failings go, and had to do with my aunt Janice and uncle Arnie, whom I love as the cobra loves the mongoose.

THE ENIGMA OF
GROVER'S MILL

I T HAS SLIPPED BACK into obscurity now, like a sun that rose
out of nowhere in freakish glory before disappearing once more
behind stone-gray clouds. But for a brief moment, Grover's Mill
was the most famous town in the country. For it was in this quiet
New Jersey farmland hamlet where I was born that the Martians
landed on Halloween eve 1938 to unleash a surprise takeover of
Earth with killing machines on tripod stilts.

Our family was no different than others gathered around their
Philco radios, their Emersons and RCA Victors, their big Zenith
consoles, listening in horror as Orson Welles's popular Mercury
Theatre broadcast breaking news of the invasion from Mars.
Except that my parents and my father's parents and I, forced by the
Depression to live under one roof on a dead-end street off Cranbury
Road, found ourselves at the epicenter of the attack. Like many
in the audience, we had tuned in too late to hear any references
to H. G. Wells and didn't understand this was all meant to be a

dramatic sleight of hand. The horror-struck voices of eyewitness field reporters, the screams and state police sirens, the devastating sounds of extraterrestrial machines hurling hellfire heat rays, it was all so real that even in Grover's Mill we believed the world was about to end. My mother and grandmother rushed from room to room, whipping the curtains shut, turning off every light in the house, as news flashes of increasing desperation continued to stream in on our Philco Gothic cathedral. Seven thousand infantry, the grim newsman reported from the scene, were wiped out by the Martians in a matter of minutes. Pandemonium reigned. Fearing for their lives, people were fleeing, we were told, in cars, trucks, trains, and on foot up and down the Eastern Seaboard. The description of gigantic three-legged metal monsters wading across the Hudson toward Manhattan, like mere men might cross a shallow stream, was terrifying. Nor will I ever forget peeking between the drapes of our front-room window, my mother's trembling hand on my shoulder, as we looked for signs of these invaders from the Red Planet. The gunfire we heard outside was, in fact, very real, though it would later prove to be some panicked farmers shooting at a nearby water tower they'd mistaken for one of the Martian tripods.

As it turned out, the world didn't end on Halloween eve that year. But my father's life did, and so did mine in a way. His suicide would become a mark of solemn, mostly unspoken, shame for the Mecham family. Or, that is to say, for every other Mecham except me, his namesake son Wyatt, who felt only black despair. Not that I didn't understand their shame. Because who would want to admit that an otherwise sane, sober, solid man such as my dad—a decorated World War I veteran, forced by injuries and the stock market crash into early, straitened retirement—chose to sneak out the back door, leaving behind his family to the obscenity of alien violence, only to drown himself in Grover's Mill Pond with boxes of nails crammed into the pockets of his trousers and coat?

I was not quite eight when my dad died, but I have keen memories of him, memories as sharp as paper cuts. The pipe-tobacco perfume of his mustache when he tucked me into bed and kissed me good night. Watching him at the workbench in my grandfather's basement wood shop, where he taught me the craft of cabinetry—I write this sitting on a Windsor chair he turned on his own lathe. Nor did the prosthetic leg, which he himself fabricated after losing his real one to a grenade blast, slow him down when we used to walk into town on some errand or another.

Above all, we loved haunting the pond near our house together, fishing from the same bank where he had once seen Woodrow Wilson casting for bass with Walter Grover, whose family our town is named after. When the fish weren't biting we'd take a walk around its edges, him gimping along with me close beside, drawing strength from the many beautiful hemlocks, huge willow oaks, and mockernut hickory trees that grew along the shore. Sometimes we'd stop and pick flowers together, a damaged soldier and his fond son, to bring home a bouquet of wild herbs for my mother, a clutch of asters or tawny daylilies. It seems to me even now that Grover's Mill Pond was so much a part of my father that when he felt the world was coming to an end, his only recourse was to go embrace its watery soul, become one with it. And like him, I grew up understanding that the pond—at thirty-seven acres really a small lake—lay at the heart of my personal universe from as far back as my conception on its very shores.

In hindsight, it's clear that although after his discharge from the army my father was awarded a sack of medals, he was too deeply scarred by what he had witnessed on the fields of France to be consoled by some shiny coins dangling from pretty ribbons. Soft visions of mustard gas, of men with bayonets lurching at mirror images of themselves, of tank treads churning fallen soldiers into foxhole mud—these visited him often in shrieking nightmares that woke the whole household when I was growing up. So when

Halloween eve came around, I guess my poor father had seen enough war that he couldn't face the big one, the unwinnable one, the one against the Martians.

The police found his wooden leg on a grassy beach where he presumably entered the water. At least he'd had the wherewithal to realize that keeping it on would have worked against his purpose that night. I still own it, my most cherished heirloom. And while I've heard it said drowning is the least painful way to die, the lungs filling with water just as if it were simply wet, heavy air, who would really know? In my father's case, it was the only conceivably meaningful death, so there's a dash of solace in that. And I'll take a dash of solace over a dash of salt on an open wound any day.

My mother would wind up in the pond, too. After Orson Welles had his little joke on America, and Grover's Mill in particular, and my family in point of fact, my mother, Mildred, changed, spiraled downward. Her dark hazel eyes behind those horn-rim glasses she always wore grew misty and vacant as Christmas approached. She would be in the middle of doing something, baking bread, say, and the cawing of crows in a tree would distract her so that she'd head outside to see what the fuss was about, only to return an hour later having no memory of why she'd lit the oven and what this batter was doing in a bowl on the kitchen counter. Our bedrooms were separated only by a door, and I could hear her talking to herself at all hours of the night. I cupped my ear to that door but never understood the meaning of anything she mumbled. *Native ear long nursery, peach. Tat sing, dat-tut-tat. Why the fall flow jigger?* Part of me wondered if she wasn't trying to communicate with the Martians.

What I did begin to understand, and quickly, was that I was in the midst of losing her as surely as I'd lost my father. She spent a lot of chilly evenings out in Van Nest Park studying the skies for saucers even though she, like the rest of the country, had been assured by the authorities, not to mention a contrite Welles himself, that the invasion was a hoax. I suppose my mother might have been looking for vindication of her husband's death, or else hoping against all odds that some real Martians would take her away to join him. I recall thinking, as I hid behind a big rhododendron bush one evening watching her pace back and forth across the long grass, glancing up, then shaking her head and staring at the ground, that she was becoming alien herself. On the other hand, to be fair, let me confess here that she and I both did believe we saw suspicious lights that infamous night, like moving and beaconing stars in the ghastly sky.

She started drinking. I imagine it didn't take much gin-mill hooch to send her, a wiry, nervous woman, off the edge. Drunk, she began saying things at the dinner table that upset my grandmother. Things like how she wished she'd never met my father and how she'd give anything to get away from Grover's Mill. How she hated its bleak bone-cold winters and furnace-muggy summers. How she couldn't stand being this tantalizingly close to Manhattan but not having one thin dime to go bathe in those bright big city lights.

Once when my grandmother Iris thought I wasn't listening, she confided to a visiting neighbor lady, "Mildred's gone and turned into Grover's very own *Mill Dread*. If it weren't for the boy, I'd set her out on her ear, for all that she's my own poor son's widow." I cringed at her soft, confident chuckle and crept away to stalk the pond's edge.

My grandfather took a kinder approach. He was no less a carpenter than my father had been. Indeed, father had taught son. Because my mother said she'd give anything to spend the upcoming springtime days rowing out to the middle of Grover's Mill Pond to watch the skies for activity, maybe take a picnic with her son, he indulgently refurbished my father's childhood rowboat for us to use. It was so beautiful, that boat. I could never get enough of leaning my head over its side and watching reflected sunlight dancing off the water, making its varnished belly glisten with different ever-changing shapes! And I must admit it made me feel proud to take my father's place at the oars, even if I risked being seen by some of the whispering kids at school who already deemed my parents lunatics. After winter faded away, we kept it tied up at the nearby dock of a friend of my grandfather's and went out on the water often.

For a time, my mom did seem to improve. Less midnight babble. Less astronomical observation. Her hooch still flowed like the Passaic, but not so much that she couldn't start doing a bit of bookkeeping at Grandpa's hardware store while I helped with shelving of paint cans, drill bits, saws, glue pots, and yes, even boxes of nails after school. Rowing and fresh spring-into-summer air brought a bit of healthy glow back to her cheeks. Life seemed on the upswing.

It was an afternoon in late September, the first autumn colors blushing in the red maples and sweetbay magnolias, and the rushes and deer-tongue grass swaying in breezes that hinted of cooler days to come, that we rowed out for what would prove to be the last time. We'd made liverwurst and onion sandwiches together back at the house, her favorite. Some peanut-buttered celery stalks, along with dill pickles and potato chips, were packed in the small wicker basket with a couple of bottles of cream soda. This was to be a real feast. Also an important moment for me, since I'd finally got up the nerve to tell her, now that she seemed enough recovered from my father's suicide to act more or less normal, that our mother-son outings were going to have to wind down, maybe even stop. Some kids at school had indeed seen us together on Grover's Mill Pond enough times that I was now officially getting razzed as a mama's boy. Time had come for both of us to grow up.

What happened next happened so fast I can scarcely picture it, quick as when a lightbulb blows out and the room goes instantly dark. We'd been talking about heaven knows what, a V of geese migrating south, how the pickles from Miller's were crisper than the ones from Malory's. Then I blurted it. My concern about being seen on the pond too often with my mommy, and how I was catching unholy flak for it at school. She pulled a hidden flask from her jacket pocket, unscrewed its cap, took a deep drink from it, and lit into me. Something about cowardice, something about me being my father's son, something about how alone she was in the world and that I couldn't possibly understand her pain. In the sorry wink of an eye, she was back to being her old unhappy self, wagging that silver flask in my face as she made her points.

My grabbing at it, slapping it away, was pure instinct. When it flew out of her hand and splashed in the greenish water, she just as unthinkingly stood up in the unsteady boat, snatched one of the oars, and tried to fish her flask back. I shouted at her to stop, that she was going to fall overboard, but before she could even turn her head to respond, the boat tipped over, throwing us and our wicker-basket banquet into the pond.

Our immediate impulse was to save each other. That much I recall with total clarity. But since I was the only one of us who could swim well enough to possibly get to shore with heavy, waterlogged clothes acting as a full-body drag anchor, I flailed her over to the capsized rowboat and shouted at her to hang on until I came back with help.

"I'm gonna drown, just like him," she gurgled, water running out of her mouth. Her face was as white as paint primer.

"No, you're not," I shouted. "Just stay put, you hear me?"

Wriggling out of my coat and frantically toeing my shoes off, I swam like mad, frozen with fear as well as the water's chill. With every kick and doggy-paddle stroke I made, the possibility that my mother was about to die in the same pond as my dad became more and more real. Half drowned myself, I lurched into some sedge, covered in mud, slime, and a slick of slimy, decomposing leaves that had fallen on the pond. By the time I managed to summon help, and some men hurried out to where the capsized rowboat serenely drifted, my mother had vanished into the murk. The frogmen, one of whom I recognized as having been on the same team that retrieved my drowned father not a year before, had her up to the surface in no time. But it was all too late. Her narrow, pale face was already bloated, her lips gone purple.

So began a time in the house off Cranbury Road that degenerated from bad to awful. My grandmother and I hardly knew what to do with each other when alone in the same room. I think she blamed her son's suicide on my mother, my mother's death on me somehow, and also blamed me for having been the reason my parents were forced to get married in the first place. Much as I couldn't admit to personal responsibility in that matter—after all, I had no say in their out-of-wedlock lovemaking under spicy-smelling sweet pepper bushes on the pond's bank—I understood how she could see me as a living symbol of her precious Wyatt's downfall. As for my grandfather, he was truly heartbroken, and shouldered much of the blame himself.

"If I hadn't got it in my head to fix up that boat—" he would mutter, then his words would trail off.

Grandmother Iris, who grew more brittle and crotchety by the day, could only agree with him. After my mother was buried in the cemetery next to my father, I was left by default in her care. Ours was a house of grief. But whereas my grandfather grieved for my mother and me, I got the sense that Grandmother grieved mostly for herself and the burden that I now had become. In school, we read about the ancient mariner and the albatross. I'd become an albatross, if no longer taunted for being a mama's boy. The crowd of punks who'd made that accusation now shunned me for a different reason. I was, they decided, an angel of death. Someone to be avoided like the plague. I had neither the will nor way to contradict them. At home in bed, listening to the ticking clock in my parents' empty bedroom, I found myself wondering if they weren't right.

People die in threes. So goes the old saying. Though seven years had passed between my parents' drownings, one intentional, the other not, death once more came lurking to round out the number. My grandpa had taken ill with a case of walking pneumonia at Thanksgiving and was hospitalized in nearby Princeton by early December. The snow was particularly heavy that year. Wind drifted shapely piles around the house and frost clung to the windows in fernlike patterns. Since my grandmother hated driving in bad weather, a man named Franklin, who responded to a help ad she placed in the local paper, drove us to the hospital every other day to visit. I couldn't help but notice that around Franklin my grandmother seemed to lighten up a little, which was a relief to me, since I could only imagine how, deep down, she must somehow have faulted me for her husband's illness. Franklin sometimes stayed for dinner after we returned from Princeton, recounting the places in the world he claimed he had visited—exotic locales like Morocco and Brazil and Fiji. What he was doing in these far-flung countries and how he could afford all his globehopping was unclear to me, but what did I care? Pretending politeness, I listened, at least in the beginning, even though I figured it was all a pack of lies. If from the very beginning I didn't trust his stories and overconfident manner, his presence nevertheless meant my grandmother and I weren't left alone at a painfully silent table. For that I was grateful.

As with my mother, my grandfather seemed to be improving daily, only to abruptly take a downward turn and die of complications between Christmas and New Year's. My grandmother's heartbreak over this, I must admit, startled me. She wept the most genuine tears I'd ever seen well from her steely eyes. For a time, I wondered if she wasn't going to end up in the hospital herself, so bereft was she. Neighbors dropped by with tuna casserole, cold fried chicken, and potato salad, which I lived on for breakfast, lunch, and dinner, noticing that she ate nary a morsel.

Franklin helped make arrangements with the crematorium and drove us over to the funeral home so we could pay our last respects before Grandfather was fed to the furnace. Though she abhorred her husband's final wish not to be laid to rest in the ground, where he would rot like old maggoty timber, my grandmother honored his instruction. We caravanned with several dozen of his friends and longtime customers to the dam end of the pond, where the ice was still unfrozen. On a gusty, blue-sky day in the dead of winter, the minister delivered yet another eulogy before my grandfather's ashes, gray as pumice, were scattered on the equally gray water. I couldn't help but think, as I burrowed my freezing face into my wool muffler, that at twenty-five dollars per eulogy, our family kept the minister so busy he might as well have been put on the hardware-store payroll.

Gallows humor, not very funny. But I didn't have much to laugh about, anyway. The wind made a swirling snow devil out at the far edge of the pond, where some kids were ice-skating, blissfully unaware of why a bunch of people in overcoats were huddled down at our end. We trudged away after the service, climbed in our cars, and slowly drove home.

Life at school didn't improve. The opposite. I should have been grateful that the punks had given up teasing me, but instead I felt ignored. What was worse, I was now pitied by many of my imbecile classmates. How I hated the sympathizing stares I got from students I hardly knew. Walking the hallway between classes became an ordeal both embarrassing and infuriating. My only recourse was to feign sickness as a way of getting out of school for stretches of time, at least until winter subsided. And when the weather warmed, I simply began ditching classes and hanging out by myself down at the pond. The school's student counselor dropped by one evening and spoke about my absences and failing grades with my grandmother and Franklin, who was by that evening, as he was most every evening now. I eavesdropped from an adjacent room and was relieved and angered by my grandmother's response, which was, in essence, "The boy's suffered a series of bad blows and ought to be allowed to work through his mourning as need be." I was relieved because this meant I was, as I understood, freed from adults lording over me, telling me what to do. Angered because I knew, even then, I didn't have the first idea how to mourn, and that I had been essentially abandoned to my own devices from that moment on.

At what point did I begin to suspect Franklin was trying to seduce my grandmother? I was young enough at the time—fifteen at the end of the Second World War—that anyone beyond their teens was an oldster to me, yet in retrospect I realize Franklin must have only been in his midforties. Though my grandmother was a decade or more his senior, she was still a handsome woman in her hawkish way. But no, I thought, shoving away this disgusting idea as one might a snapping, rabid dog. Don't be ridiculous. Franklin, fraud though he might be, was acting charitably toward a sonless widow and a luckless orphan stuck under the same roof, wasn't he?

I wasn't overly surprised when he moved into the house that spring as a boarder, occupying my parents' old room. My grandmother explained she could use the extra money to help pay down the mortgage, but I knew she could have gone on just fine without, living off the healthy proceeds of the sale of the hardware store. I had grim mixed feelings about the way things were developing. On one hand, as I say, I welcomed the buffer Franklin constituted between my grandmother and me. On the other, it took my breath away, angered and confused me, how proprietary he became. Not just toward my grandmother but the whole household. His authority was established with an almost businesslike swiftness, as if he had been born to the task. Impressive, too, was the ease with which he pushed back whenever I got it in my head to challenge him, even over the slightest thing.

When I commented, testing his patience one evening during dinner, that Franklin was more a last than a first name, he laughed softly, picked a fleck of tobacco that came loose from his hand-rolled cigarette with his thumb and pinkie finger, and said, "I've heard that one before. Benjamin Franklin and all."

"Well, why don't you let people just call you Frank? Wouldn't that be easier?"

"Would you want to call our recently deceased President Roosevelt, Frank Delano Roosevelt?"

"Why not? It's less of a mouthful," I countered. "Anyway, you're not the president."

He regarded me with a slow sidelong glance. "I like you, Wyatt. And respect you enough not to call you Wy. Franklin comes from the Middle English word for freeman—*Frankeleyn*. Frank means something else altogether. The Franks were a German tribe, named after a kind of spear they used back in the early times. When they moved from Germany to Gaul, that's how France got its name. I hate the Germans and can't stand Frenchmen. But I like the idea of being a freeman. So, Franklin it is," he said, and took another drag off his cigarette.

Increasingly, he liked to make smart little speeches like this while my grandmother now and then glanced over at me and nodded, as if to say, You might learn something if you keep your trap shut and listen.

I didn't hate him, not yet, but I couldn't figure Franklin out, either. He seemed never to have worked a day in his life, and it was unclear to me where he came from, what his background was, if he had family, how he knew so much, and how he managed always to have enough money to pay his room and board. The first person I ever heard use the word *enigma* was Franklin. And though he was talking about something else, politics or religion, when I asked him what it meant and he answered, "Anything that's baffling," I knew I'd never forget that word because it perfectly defined Franklin himself.

For instance, how could anybody dislike my grandfather's sweet old dog, Claude? I inherited him after my grandfather passed away. For a while, Claude became my best friend in the world. I could tell that he missed his master as much as I did, but he slipped into the habit of sleeping on the rug by my bed at night and accompanying me on my walks around the pond. A mangy mutt with a messy coat of blacks and browns and what looked like a smile perennially on his face, Claude—so named because he was prone to knocking things over, digging up the yard, a real *clod*, in other words—was a comfort to me, a pal in those months of grieving the loss of my one remaining male relative. As much affection as I directed toward Claude, Franklin showed him a hostile impatience.

"That dog should be kept outdoors," he told my grandmother at breakfast one day, after Claude had an overnight accident on the front-room rug.

"It's my fault," I argued. "I should have taken him out for a walk before I went to bed. He couldn't help it."

Franklin's condescending smile was directed toward my grandmother, as he went on, "He's pretty old not to be house-trained. By which I mean Claude, not Wyatt, of course. With your permission, I can build a doghouse for him."

"I don't know," my grandmother hesitated. "There's a foot of snow out there. I'm afraid he might freeze."

"Dogs are used to weather. He'll be fine."

Seeing that my grandmother was actually weighing Franklin's inhumane proposal, I slapped my hand on the table, making the silverware jump, and shouted, "No way is Claude going to be thrown out in the cold. He'll die out there. Grandma, I promise it won't happen again. He's a good boy."

When, a month later, Claude disappeared, never to be found, I knew Franklin was somehow behind it. I had no proof, however, and because we three had been all but snowbound together, the weather that winter being the worst anybody could remember, I couldn't figure when or how he would have managed to spirit Claude away without me or my grandmother noticing his absence. There were no telltale tracks in the snow, nothing beyond an empty food bowl, a coiled leash, and a couple of chewed-up rawhide bones to prove he had ever lived here. It was as if Claude had simply floated away, transported into the sky on flurries.

The spring following my grandfather's funeral, Franklin busied himself fixing rain gutters that had been damaged during a wet, heavy April blizzard, the last of that wretched season. He worked on repairing the front porch, wearing a jacket that had been my father's and a porkpie hat I recognized as my grandpa's. Closet-shopping regular part of the family he'd become, not that I had much say in the matter. I knew if I confronted my grandmother about the indecency of Franklin wearing these clothes, I'd get a sharp rebuke in response. Instead, resentment started to build in me like steam in a pressure cooker. I sensed he could tell, and that he got a perverse kick out of it.

One day he found me down at the pond fishing. Clearly, he'd been looking for me, because he said, "There you are."

I didn't look up from my line lying like a skinny snake on the water.

"There I am," I said.

My grandmother had recently accused me of being more and more alienated from those around me, and I hadn't bothered to argue with her. I was even more alienated than she knew. Had been in a couple of fights after school, on days I was forced to attend, and simply let the other guy win, if only to avoid having to talk about it later. I figured if I'd somehow pulled off a victory, I would have had to accept congratulations from kids I hated or else dealt with demands for a rematch. I wanted nothing to do with any of that malarkey. Instead I filched some cover-up powder from my mother's cosmetics kit to camouflage my black eye and bruises, though I wondered if it was possible, technically, to filch anything from my mom now that she was dead and gone.

"Catching anything?"

I squinted up at him, said, "Caught a pretty good-size stick an hour ago."

"Threw it back, I guess," he quipped, sitting next to me.

There was nothing to say so I left his line unanswered, just like my own line out in the water.

"Wyatt?" he went on, his voice pleasant as punch. "Iris wants me to paint the house."

Iris? My grandmother, Mrs. Mecham, you mean? I said nothing.

"And I was wondering if you'd like to help me. It'd go a lot faster with two of us working on it together. You game?"

I shrugged, uncomfortable with him sitting so close beside me. "I don't care."

"Great," he said, standing after grabbing me by the back of the neck and amiably shaking me side to side, like we were old buddies. I wrenched away, staring at the clouds on the pond. "We start first thing in the morning."

It would seem that Franklin had, maybe at my grandmother's behest, removed quite a stash of paint and primer, brushes and sandpaper, drop cloths and ladders, from the hardware store before its new owners took possession. He made me help him lug all this possibly stolen stuff from the cellar after breakfast.

As with most everything, Franklin possessed a remarkable knowledge about how to paint a house. We scraped away the old curling and chipped surface of each course of clapboard first, then sanded, primed, and brushed on two coats of yellow oil paint—a pale, jaundiced yellow that was my grandmother's preference—with white trim. Work went along steadily and in a few weeks the job was done.

Me, I was sick of the place by the time we finished, but Franklin and his Iris walked around it in the morning, afternoon, and then again before sunset, admiring its every angle. Whereas they couldn't have been more pleased with the outcome, I felt horrified and ashamed. We'd somehow robbed the house of its history and personality by making it look so different. It didn't dawn on me until after we'd folded the drop cloths, cleaned the brushes with turpentine, and put everything back in the cellar that what we had done was paint my parents and grandfather out of the picture. I realized too late that I preferred it the way it was before, comfortably the worse for wear, a pleasant dirty white instead of this cat-piss hue.

Even more, what came out of the experience for me had nothing to do with the project itself but with a growing curiosity about and deepening distaste for the project manager. The same way you can look an animal in the eye and know if it's sick or healthy, I studied Franklin over the course of those days together and began to form a strong opinion as to his character. I didn't let on as I observed him. I did as I was told, faking as respectful an obedience as I could.

When he said, "Climb up the ladder and see if you can't get a little more trim gloss on that eave," I climbed up the ladder and brushed more trim gloss on the eave. When he said, "Lunch break, Wyatt," I came down from wherever I was on the side of the house and sat in the violet shade with him and ate a ham sandwich, listening to him pontificate about how smelly the canals are in Venice in the summer, and how warm the mink hats they wear in St. Petersburg as the snow drifts down over Palace Square, and how in Varanasi, also known as Benares, one of the oldest cities in the world, says he, Indian seekers—"would-be freemen," he called them—bathe themselves in the chocolate-brown waters of the Ganges to find their way toward heaven, or some such. He was consumed by his stories and his own voice, while I watched a troop of black ants at my feet carry tiny morsels of ham and rye away toward some unknown underground destination.

As I listened and watched, my eyes narrowing to gain better focus, I began to believe, with the certainty of one who knows firsthand that death follows life, that there was something deeply disturbed about Franklin. Something unnatural, off. Was he just delusional, a suave but big fat outrageous liar? Just a user and a taker? Or was he on the lam, untrustworthy, hiding here in Grover's Mill from someone or something? Was he dangerous? Was he possibly *evil*?

"Did you wash yourself in the Ganges, too, then?" I asked, just to see what he would say, not caring really whether he did or didn't.

"I'm not a Hindu," he answered. "No point."

"So what'd you learn, seeing those poor saps dunk themselves in muddy water?"

Franklin sighed, looked away. "That human beings may be the lowest class of species in the universe. But let's change the subject. Your grandmother—"

"Iris, you mean?"

"—wouldn't appreciate me telling you such negative things, Wyatt. Besides, you're young. The world's mostly ahead for you. You'll have your own experiences and form your own conclusions about everything when you grow up."

"I don't need to get one day older to form my own conclusions," I said, hoping to provoke some telling response.

"No, really?" turning his slitted eyes on me.

I don't know why I felt the strongest urge to hit him in the face with one of my already clenched fists, but knew I'd be over-powered in a flash, so I said with as bitter and worldly a tone as I could muster, "Look, Frank—I mean, Franklin. I already know the world stinks. I don't need to go to Venice or any of your other fancy-ass places to figure that out. I'm not stupid any more than you're a Hindu."

Franklin thought about that, or pretended to, for a moment. Then said, mock-cheerful, "Lunch break's over, Einstein. Time to get back to painting."

Life pressed on over the next months. Franklin arranged for the three of us to go to Radio City Music Hall to see a show featuring the Rockettes, and while my grandmother was thrilled, I couldn't help but feel guilty about our grand adventure—he bought dinner at a ritzy restaurant, my first encounter with creamed herring—knowing it was something my mom would have given anything, but anything to do.

Being by now a total outcast, a shunned goat, at school, and not caring what others said about me, I started spending afternoons up at the cemetery, hanging out near my parents' side-by-side graves, before heading down to do my daily walk around Grover's Mill Pond. The role of mama's boy, or daddy's, was one at this point I relished rather than rejected, wishing the bullies could fairly taunt me with such labels again. What would I give if I could still fish the pond with my father, or row out to the middle for another picnic with my boozy mother. Answer is anything. But I didn't have any-thing to give, nothing anyway that would bring them back. And so I found myself hanging around as much at the cemetery as at the drowning pond, the ash-carpeted pond, because in both places I noticed my heart calmed and my chance at happiness improved. Or, not *happiness*—less miserableness.

The keeper of the graveyard, a pasty middle-aged fellow with gimlet teeth, unwashed hair, and a kindly, sad look in his eye, asked me one Tuesday, when there was no funeral to oversee or vandals to chase away, what I was doing there so often.

"Why you asking?" I asked him back. "Am I breaking a rule or something?"

"No," he said, shoving his hands into trouser pockets, shy, I thought, about talking to the living as opposed to the dead. "Just seems like a young fella like you ought to be having fun with your friends somewhere instead of haunting an old boneyard like this."

I shrugged.

Then he asked an unexpected question. "Well, seeing as you're here so much, how'd you like to pick up a little extra walk-around money?"

So it was I was hired to mow the lawn, sweep leaves and other leavings off the oblong marble markers, pick up trash—I couldn't believe all the junk, candy wrappers, discarded funeral programs, even a used condom—left behind by sloppy mourners and cemetery-goers. Ralph paid me in cash, and other than giving me my assignment for the day, didn't pull a Franklin on me by expecting me to listen to dumb speeches or answer a bunch of questions, so we got along pretty well. He had a daughter about my age named Mollie, who came with him to work sometimes, and because she seemed to share my outcast ways, we sat against one of the mausoleums and chatted during breaks or after work. Like me, Mollie had lost her mother. Not to death, but because she ran off with another man.

"She might as well be dead and drowned as your mom," Mollie said, shaking her head as she looked at me with unblinking, lovely brown eyes, dark as wet bark. "Don't hate me for saying so, but I sorta wish she *had* drowned. Least that way I could feel sorry for her."

"Yeah. I know," I said.

Because I didn't have any costly hobbies, and didn't care about going to the movies or buying burgers and malted milks—I would have treated Mollie, but she had no more interest than I did in these things—the money started adding up. I kept it hidden in the lining of a seersucker jacket I rarely wore, which was safely hung in the far back of my closet. My grandmother occasionally asked me what I'd been up to all day, and was perfectly satisfied with the hodgepodge of white lies I concocted for her benefit. As often as not, I even told her the partial truth—"I helped mow somebody's lawn," to which she said, "Good way to get some exercise," and the matter dropped. While I was pretty sure Franklin knew I was lying half the time, he let it ride. So long as I kept *our* lawn mowed.

It was right about then when Franklin announced his intention of painting and wallpapering the interior of the house, a project my grandmother embraced wholeheartedly, that I began to develop a project of my own. It began small, like a baby worm inside an apple. But as the days rolled by, it slowly formed itself at the core of my raw existence. Here I'd been earning money for no reason, but now I needed money if I was going to run away and start a new life somewhere else. I didn't know any other place besides Grover's Mill, but my home wasn't home anymore, it was being leached away from me. Now at least I had a plan, a reason to get out of bed in the morning. And if I wavered, a particularly disturbing encounter with Franklin solidified my goal.

This occurred when we were nearly finished stripping off the old wallpaper in the dining room, a stately leaf-and-floral pattern with Greek vases that I used to get lost in staring at when I was a kid, which was to be replaced by a more up-to-date geometric design. To me it was just more of the same business of erasing the past, but I had no will to get all hot under the collar over it. The two of them had gone into New York to pick the new paper in a showroom there, so it was a moot point.

Helping Franklin with this work during the mornings before heading off to my chores in the cemetery, where I could hang around with Mollie, left me little time for my loitering by the pond, and school was just a fading memory. I'd basically dropped out, without anybody making much of a fuss about it. I assured my grandmother I would finish high school later, after taking time off to regroup. Meantime, working both jobs—and let me say here, if I might, that I was a hard worker, despite any attitude issues I had regarding Franklin—left me a worn-out rag at the end of the day. It was everything I could do to get some supper into my belly, do the dishes, and slip past Iris and Franklin as they listened to some variety program on the radio, to head upstairs and to bed. A fast masturbation into one of my socks, and I was quickly in dreamland.

One night, I'd gone down the hall to take a pee. After I lay down again, for whatever reason, I was having a hard time getting back to sleep. I tossed and turned, punched my pillow, adjusted my blanket, then finally had just started to drift off when I heard someone turn the knob on my door and softly glide into my room. Far too startled, not to mention frightened, to speak or scream or even move, I lay there listening, and waited. Some long minutes passed, my heart up in my throat, and I did hear shuffling, very soft, across the rug, and the delicate, awful sound of breathing. I could swear I heard the intruder reach down and lift something up from the floor and—I can't say for sure because my ears were so full of the shush of my pounding heart—inhale. The next sound was not as indistinct. A floorboard creaked, only somewhat muffled by the braided rug. The silence that followed was, as the cliché goes, deafening—and it went on for such an excruciatingly long stretch of time that I began to wonder if I hadn't dreamed the intrusion. I continued my vigil with a corpselike stillness, and after a time I heard the faintest thud—not a thud, more like a *poof* of air—followed by another unnatural silence, and then the expertly turned handle again, though oddly no footfalls from my bedside back to the door. Mortified, I didn't move a muscle, barely breathed, hoping against hope that there would be no further activity. As the room began to lighten, the sun not yet risen outside but the sky pinkening the sheers in my window, I recovered my wits and began trying to sort out what in the world I'd experienced.

Franklin, who considered himself a bit of a chef, was making Irish oatmeal and Belgian waffles in the kitchen that morning, whistling, as I walked in and poured myself a glass of milk.

"Where's my grandmother?" I asked.

"When I came down, she wasn't up yet so I checked in on her and she's a tad under the weather this morning. Would you mind taking that up to her?" pointing at a tray set out with a soft-boiled egg, toast spread with marmalade, orange juice. The unnecessary touch of flowers in a cream pitcher nauseated me, I must confess.

"Breakfast in bed," I said, and proceeded to do as he told me.

Not that I suspected for a moment my grandmother had been the person who visited my bedroom during the night, but seeing her in bed, white as if she'd been soaked in bleach, feeble from flu, confirmed it hadn't been her. I placed the tray on her side table, asked if there was anything else I could do.

"No, Wyatt. I just need to sleep, is all. I'll try to eat some of that later."

Back downstairs in the kitchen, I certainly wasn't going to give Franklin the pleasure of hearing me ask if he happened to notice any burglars in the house last night. Best, I knew, just to leave him thinking I was dumb as a brick. One thing that continued to bother me as the day wore on was how my intruder, surely Franklin, had managed to exit the room without having made a single hint of sound. He'd deftly stolen into the room. Stood over me silent as death for a long time. But then it was as if he'd simply floated to the door when he made his escape. How did he do that? I took to leaning one of my schoolbooks—which I secretly read on evenings when I had enough energy—against the inside of my bedroom door before going to bed. This way, I figured I'd know if he had snuck in again in the middle of the night. I kept my father's wooden leg beside me under my blanket too, with which I planned to bash in his skull if the chance arose. But every morning I saw that the book was still there, so I gathered he had lost interest or decided it wasn't worth the risk.

As work in the rooms continued, the wariness and hostility I felt toward Franklin only grew, despite his apparent decision not to trespass further on my privacy when I was sleeping. Grandmother's health improved, in no small measure because of Franklin's doting, but rather than making me glad this only irked me. One could reasonably argue I had no right to feel competitive with him, but any natural instinct—granted, piddling—I had about being a good grandson was crowded off the stage by Franklin. He was like a land-going octopus with tentacles wrapped around nearly every part of my life. When she was sick, confined to her room, my grandmother had instructed me to do whatever Franklin said, that until she was up and out of bed, he was head of the house. The only problem was, this edict remained in effect even now that she was back to her old cold self. I found myself living with a strange new father now, one with whom I didn't share a drop of blood in my veins and toward whom never a kind thought ran through my mind. Had my real father been alive to see what was happening here, or so I fantasized, he'd have beaten Franklin to within an inch of his life and then dragged him—one leg powering the way—down to the pond to finish the job. Sweet dream, but just a dream.

The only time I felt free from the so-called freeman these days was when I was with Mollie. Much the same way the rich like hobnobbing with other rich people, loners are drawn to loners. Mollie and I were living proof of this. One might think that with his wife having run off on him, Ralph would have been extra strict about letting Mollie out of his sight. But from the first he seemed to trust and like me, so my meandering off from the cemetery to the pond with his daughter, our spending every spare hour we had in each other's company, didn't bother him. I felt like we had his silent blessing, and while he was rough-edged, unshaven, and stained by melancholy, I thought of him sometimes as a surrogate father, though I never told him so. Besides Ralph, nobody knew a thing about me and Mollie, because nobody cared. It was the only part of my life I inhabited with perfect independence, and as such it was my greatest joy.

Once, as I was lying in the tall grass with Mollie, secluded from everyone and everything but a redtail hawk circling high overhead, she asked me, "How come you hate that man living in your house so much?"

"I never said I hated him," and kissed her again, hoping that would be the end of it. Franklin was the last person I wanted to talk about here with Mollie.

When she pulled her lips away to breathe, she said gently, "But you don't need to say it in words, Wyatt. Whenever he comes up, the look in your eyes says it all."

Mollie wasn't someone I wanted to lie to, so I told her, "Hey, he just gives me the creeps, all right? He treats me like I'm his slave or something, and my grandmother goes along with it all. I just need to get out of there, the sooner the better."

"What's he done to give you the creeps? You don't seem to be afraid of anything, from what I know."

I told her about the night in my bedroom, and how every time Franklin was near me he got too close. I told her how even the way he smoked his cigarettes had a wickedness to it, how his endless stories seemed like a madman's fictions, and that every favor he'd done for us seemed to have strings attached. "It's like he's a virus, taking over our lives and making us sick. I feel like I'm living in his house now, instead of the other way around."

The concept I'd been harboring, and the mounting hatred that fueled it, took a giant leap in a more dangerous direction when my sixteenth birthday rolled around. Franklin got it in his head that this was too important a milestone in my life not to celebrate it in grand style. I'd have preferred to eat pizza out of a box, but he would have none of that.

"We're throwing you a party," he announced a couple of weeks before the big day, knowing it was the last thing I wanted. "Oh, yes. Cake, candles, champagne, the works."

"I don't care if he is turning sixteen, Wyatt's still too young for champagne," my grandmother objected, if meekly.

"Bosh," was Franklin's response, not even bothering to look in her direction. He had her, by this time, utterly under his sway. She said nothing further.

When the question arose as to whom we might invite to this proposed party in the newly refurbished dining room, Franklin had a ready answer that floored me.

"Well, of course we'll ask over some of the neighbors who've known you for years. The McDermott clan, the Riordans. I guess there's nobody at school, but maybe the minister and his wife might like a nice slice of homemade cake and a glass of spiked punch," he said, ticking these off on his fingertips. "Oh, and you'll want to invite that girlfriend of yours, Mollie."

Grandmother Iris jolted wide awake suddenly, and said, "Why, I didn't know you had a girlfriend, Wyatt."

My arms crossed, astounded, fuming, I stared at Franklin, who calmly returned my gaze with one of shameless triumph.

"That's because I don't," I snapped.

"Well, however you want to label her," Franklin said, waving off my denial as if it were a casement fly. "I'm sure she'd love to come. You can bring her father, Ralph, along, if you think he owns a bar of soap to clean himself up with first. He can help chaperone you two lovebirds." These last bits about soap and lovebirds, meant for me alone, Franklin said under his breath.

Iris confirmed she'd missed it by adding something trite like, "By all means, let's invite the lucky young lady and her father. Wyatt, shame on you for keeping this a secret from your poor grandmother."

Looking back over the years, having had plenty of time to think about it, I've come to believe this was the instant when Franklin sealed both our fates. I couldn't have known it for a fact just then, as I excused myself, rose from the dinner table, and fled the house to walk to the pond in growing twilight. But what I did know, with blinding clarity, was that I had not been hallucinating on several recent instances at the cemetery when I thought I'd seen somebody, or something, lurking in the grove of oak trees near the McKearin family plot, or prowling in the weeping branches of the huge willow that hunched over the Wylers near a brook whose waters emptied into Grover's Mill Pond. And this somebody or something was clearly spying on me, hoping not to be seen.

I hadn't wanted to admit it to myself, in part because a reasonable voice inside assured me it was a madness not unlike my mother's, but in that moment I also knew for certain that on one particular occasion, when I saw Franklin's shadow cast on the fresh-mowed graveyard lawn, it had not two legs but three. I might have dismissed this out of hand had not Mollie too seen the shadow that afternoon, and agreed that the person hiding behind the big Dutch elm did seem to have three legs.

"Optical delusion," she later judged it, making a little pun to try to leaven things.

I wasn't so sure.

Down by the pond that evening after Franklin had revealed himself as a menace, a true nemesis of mine, I tramped slowly around the pond—my pond, on which I'd always been able to rely. Bile pumped through my heart as I tried to breathe in and out to calm myself, but the stagnant air only stung my throat. Franklin had done everything he could to usurp the roles of my father, my mother, my grandfather, and now had in essence declared himself my babysitter, my watchman, my warden. What was clear to me, clear as the shimmering full moon that floated on the face of the water, was that if I simply used Ralph's wages as I'd intended—to run away, whether with Mollie beside me or not—Franklin would track me down. He seemed to know every inch of the world like the back of his bullying hand. Had me convinced there was nowhere I could hide but that he'd rout me out, like the woodpeckers in Van Nest Park rout out bugs secreted in tree trunks. No, I couldn't afford to delude myself on that front. And if my hunch was right, that he was one of the invaders left behind after the Halloween eve attack half my lifetime ago— one who somehow escaped death, immune to the microbes that exterminated the others—then it would be all the easier for him to seek and find me. They have their extraterrestrial sensory powers, after all.

There are four ways a person can die. Natural causes, accidental, suicide, and murder. And while I don't like to think of myself as someone drawn to death, by that time I had firsthand knowledge—and, in these waters, firsthand experience—of all of the ways to heaven or hell but one. It fell to me, I believed deep down, to complete the cycle. What did I have to lose? Mollie would still love me, I was sure. She would understand. So much for the aphorism about death coming in threes.

My father owned a service revolver that I inherited upon his death, along with his war medals, his gold watch, and other mementos. I stored these in his locked steel box, the key to which I kept hidden along with my stash of money in the back of my closet. There were also half a dozen bullets in the safebox, and though they were pretty old, all I needed was for one of them to work.

Suffice it to say, I didn't invite Mollie or her father to my birthday party. Why should I subject them to Franklin's humiliations? And after what had happened to Claude, I couldn't risk it. Instead, I left the house, which smelled admittedly wonderful with a chocolate cake baking in the oven, and met Mollie as usual in the cemetery. Knowing it was my sixteenth birthday, Ralph had given me the day off, and since Franklin was caught up with his party preparations, I knew she and I could while away our hours in private. I had already hidden the revolver, loaded and ready, wrapped in a camouflaging green T-shirt of mine under a juniper bush by the pond's edge. So my day was free and clear.

I had asked Mollie not to buy me a present. Better, I told her, to save her money. She did, however, produce a small rectangular box wrapped in shiny paper, which she presented to me with an excited smile.

"It's not much," she said.

"No, it's beautiful."

"You haven't even opened it up yet, silly."

"I mean just everything. The shiny paper, the ribbon, you."

"Stop," she said, with a blushing frown. "Open it."

Inside was a pocket-sized field manual on the trees and wild shrubs of the Northeast. I was thrilled, but said, "Hey, you promised you wouldn't spend any money."

"Don't worry, I got it cheap at the thrift shop. Besides, I know how much you love to be outdoors, so I figured you might want to know what everything's called," she said. "For your next birthday, I'm thinking about a bird book, or maybe one with all the insects."

"It's the best present anybody ever gave me," I said, and we shared a long, yearning kiss.

Mollie and I spent the next hour lying side by side in a hidden clearing, marveling at the names we read together—flowering dogwood, staghorn sumac, sourgum—and the color illustrations beside each description. In my life I had never felt so deliciously sheltered from the world, alone and yet so complete and contented, and when I set aside the book and began kissing Mollie again it was the most natural possible act for us to make love, and so we did, each of us losing our virginity that afternoon as the sun crawled down the sky.

The ache I felt when saying good-bye to her, moving just as naturally though nowhere near as blissfully into my next important inevitability of the day, was painful, to say the least. I had no idea whether I'd ever see Mollie again. The chances were good that Franklin wouldn't be fooled by my ruse, that he'd overpower and possibly do to me exactly what I planned to do to him.

The party was supposed to begin at six. Glancing at my father's watch, which I'd worn today in his honor, I saw that it was already five thirty. As I walked to the place where I'd hidden the revolver, my afterglow of happiness and euphoria began to dim just like the cloudy sky itself, moving toward sunset and the end of the autumn day. Franklin and Iris, I imagined, were getting pretty anxious by now. "That kid will be late to his own funeral," I could hear my grandmother rue with a cluck of her tongue. Franklin's comments would not be as colloquial or forgiving. I pictured him pacing from room to room, steaming mad. I could almost hear him from here at the pond swearing I was the most ungrateful little punk he'd ever met in the four decades and seven continents of his experience.

My guess that he'd angrily throw on his jacket—my father's, that is—and march in a snit down to the pond to find me was dead accurate. Loitering in full view, pretending to be sulking, brooding on the shore, I waited for him to come, service revolver shoved into my coat pocket. There was a breeze over the water, rippling it like a melted washboard. A flight of starlings, black tatters blown along, swarmed above. Soon enough, here came Franklin, a determined look on his vile face, his jaw set, his hands thrust into his trouser pockets. I saw he was wearing a colorful cravat, one of my grandfather's.

"What's the big idea, birthday boy?"

I didn't say a word. Just wanted to let my silence draw him closer, like he was a kite and I was reeling him in on an invisible string.

Predictably, he just kept talking, scolding me as he neared where I stood. "Don't you have an ounce of respect for others? Your little harlot Mollie and the rest are probably already back at the house waiting for Mr. Boohoo. Well, this game of yours is going to end. I know places far away from here where delinquents like you can be sent for rewiring. Get you a brand-new personality. Tomorrow—" and I pulled out the revolver when he was two strides away and pulled the trigger, putting a slug right into his heart. He dropped before me without so much as a groan, eyes widening, on his knees in an attitude that looked for all the world like someone shocked into prayer, and I shot him once more, this time in his face.

Methodically following my plan, I removed my clothes and swam his limp body out toward the middle of the pond, where I sank him as well as the revolver. Back on shore, I dried myself off quickly with the shirt I'd used to wrap the gun, dressed, and walked back home, numb and amazed.

"Oh, there he is," Grandmother Iris cried out.

Franklin had been mostly right about the guests having already arrived, though of course he'd been mistaken about Mollie and her father. I accepted a glass of punch from the adult bowl, the one with champagne added to the cranberry juice, and did my best to engage in conversation with the neighbors.

When Iris asked, "Where's Franklin?" I answered, "How should I know?" though I could hear my voice quaking. Not from guilt, but something more akin to excitement. I couldn't believe I had summoned the courage to carry through with my plan. To say one is proud of taking a life is fundamentally unethical, morally wrong—I know, I know. But Franklin had become, for me, a saboteur, a guerrilla, an enemy combatant, and taking him out of the picture seemed more an act of domestic warfare than anything else. I held to the belief that my father would have approved.

"He went out looking for you, you know," she went on, a raspy reproach underlying her words.

My charade didn't last long. After several more trips to the punch bowl, I decided, woozily, to confess to the minister what I'd done. My grandmother was by then beside herself worrying about Franklin and I thought there was no point in dragging out my little pantomime. From my perspective, I had rid myself and the world of a scourge. A scourge that threatened not just me but every one of us. I had, in the end, nothing to hide.

Problem was, when I confessed that Franklin wasn't here because I'd killed him, and that he was dead in the pond along with the revolver I assassinated him with, the minister scoffed. "I'm well aware that you have your issues with Franklin, Wyatt, but I think the alcohol is speaking here, and not you."

"No, ith's true—" I slurred.

"I know things have been tough for you, my son. Losing your mother and father, your grandfather. All tragic indeed. But blaming bad things that happen to us on others is not the Christian way," as he put a large, warm, consoling hand on my swaying shoulder.

Tongue foundering from the champagne, continuing to insist I was guilty of murder, I felt my legs wobble and fold beneath me. The minister, helped by a neighbor, carried me upstairs to my bedroom, where I promptly passed out.

By next morning, Franklin still having not returned, my grandmother reported him missing to the police. At first she neglected to repeat my drunken claim that I'd killed him, assuming as the minister and others within earshot had that I was expressing an immature desire rather than an absolute fact. But after a few more days, having sobered up, of my continuing to insist, adding that I was quite certain Franklin wasn't of this world, she finally broke down and reported me. In her shoes, I might well have done the same.

The officers, themselves doubtful, especially in light of the more unusual aspects of my theories about Franklin, allowed me to walk them down to the place where I had hidden my weapon and committed my crime. No one had heard gunshots the night he disappeared, fortunately or unfortunately. Nor had anyone reported seeing anything unusual on Grover's Mill Pond that evening. Joined by a detective, the cops walked through the grass and down to the gently lapping water, seeing and saying nothing until one of them knelt down and picked up a spent bullet shell.

"What kind of a gun was it you said you used on the victim?" he asked, standing.

"I'm not exactly sure," realizing I might better have kept the revolver if I wanted to convince anyone of what I'd done.

That they found no traces of blood in the grass might have strengthened my case about Franklin's origins, I felt. Perhaps he didn't bleed because his kind didn't have actual blood running in their veins. And yet I could have sworn I saw his face erupt in a gushing geyser of red when my bullet hit its point-blank mark. On the other hand, I reasoned, maybe theirs is thinner and evaporates like so much mist under a hot sun.

What happened next confounds me to this day. They brought
in divers, yet again, and this time even dragged the pond with a
special boat they commissioned for the job, having taken me into
custody for my own protection, as they put it. And what did they
come up with? Nothing. No body, no revolver—just the usual
jettisoned tires, an old boot, a porcelain dolly missing its head,
fishing tackle, and part of a rusted nineteenth-century threshing
machine. My court-assigned lawyer got me free in no time, but
not before the tabloid papers had a field day with me. I still possess some of the newspaper clippings. *Murdered Martian Missing in
Grover's Mill. Boy, 16, Claims Revenge for Dad's Death at Martian
Hands. War of the Words in Jersey Missing Mars Man Case.*

Mollie and I were kept apart by my grandmother, who now
had taken a much harder line toward me, especially after the
discovery of the bullet casing, which, although it proved nothing
to the authorities, she understood as very damning. Citing me as
a troubled child, abnormally disturbed after my parents' deaths, a
juvenile delinquent and high school dropout, an unruly young
man given to thoughts of violence, potentially psychotic and a
danger to her and society, she moved to have me committed
to a state hospital for evaluation. I voluntarily agreed to this
because, for one, it got me away from her and, second, made
it possible for Mollie to visit me, as the facility was a relatively
short bus ride away. Third, though I didn't talk with anyone
about it, I felt safer sleeping in an institution designed to keep
some people in and other people out than I ever did back home
in my bedroom, knowing that Franklin had somehow managed
to escape my attempt to rid the world of him.

When half a year after Franklin's vanishing a large amount
of money was discovered missing from my grandmother's bank
account, it was clear I couldn't have taken it since I was essentially
under observation day and night. The authorities traced a money

transfer to a temporary account in Greece. I heard that an international police dragnet pursued the thief, but the trail was as cold as the far side of the moon. Mollie, whom I married while still in the hospital once we were both of legal age, tried to use Franklin's larceny to prove to me that I was mostly right, that Franklin *was* evil, a con man, the opposite of honest, direct, *frank*—but also that he was not some alien.

"Martians don't need money," she assured me with a wistful smile.

I nodded my head in agreement, hoping to mollify Mollie, knowing it was her fondest wish that I might come to my senses and sanity based on this information. Whatever I thought I had done the night of my sixteenth birthday, I had *not* done—this is what the few who cared about me wanted me to understand. The time had come for me to seek a discharge and take my place once more in society. So I renounced as delusional any lingering thoughts I had about Franklin—believe it or not, I never knew his last name; did he even have one?—though I held privately to the hypothesis that he was probably spirited out of the pond in a rescuing spacecraft rather than somehow disappearing that afternoon with the numbers to Iris's savings account, having had enough of us both.

When she died of cancer, not long after my release, Grandmother Iris willed the old house to me, there being no one else left to give it to. In her final years, I think she might have seen the light about who Franklin really was. Oh, I don't necessarily mean that she ever embraced my theory, which I cling to even now in judicious silence but sure as a spore clings to a moldy loaf of bread. Yet the fact that they never did find his body after so many days of dredging, so many man-hours of frogmen searching Grover's Mill Pond's muddy bed, surely must have left her uneasy. I would like to think that if he really didn't die of his gunshot wounds that night, and if he didn't drown when I swam his leaden body out into the pond as far as I could before I submerged him, filling his mouth and nostrils with the water meant to weigh him down like liquid concrete, if he did happen to best death a second time, then Iris might have been paid a visit by Franklin. An after-midnight visit to her bedroom, not unlike the one I experienced that time.

And if she had, and he came floating into the scene of her helpless, troubled slumber, inhaling, hovering, I'd like to think that maybe she felt a panic of second thoughts about this beast she allowed into our family house off Cranbury Road. I would like to think that if in naked terror in her bed, she reached to her bedside lamp and turned on the light, she might have seen him undisguised, monstrous and gloating, for what he was.

ELLIE'S IDEA

S HE AWOKE AFTER A NIGHT of delirious dreams into an idea so
fully formed it was as if she had spent her whole life thinking
about it. Sublime in its clarity, this idea was as sharp and scary as any
of the nettles that threatened to take over her neglected garden that
August. Her pillowcase was damp from the sweat of its inception.
So were the sheets knotted around her arms and legs. How was it
possible she had never thought of it before?

As with any idea that laid claim to the sublime, hers was
marvelous in its simplicity. *The truth shall set you free,* wrote Saint
John, and while she had never been much of a churchgoer—aside
from her wedding day, Eleanor Mead hadn't darkened a holy
door in years, raised as she was by an agnostic mother and atheist
stepfather—she presumed that such a universal truism would work
for a person of any faith, if not the faithless. The idea was this.
For every wrong she had ever done against others, every betrayal
ever made, every lie said, every evil committed, she would make

immediate amends. She would apologize to each person she had ever hurt, and she would mean it from the bottom of her heart. This was a crossroads in her life and it wasn't one she had been expecting, but she was going to face it with all the courage she could muster. By confessing and seeking forgiveness, her slate would be wiped clean and her mind freed of the guilt scrawled all over it. She could start anew with a conscience not quite as pure as a child's, but certainly clearer than it had been ever since she found herself alone like this. Sure, the idea was daunting. Who wants to admit to doing wrong? And not only admit it, but confess directly to the people who have been most hurt by such behavior. But her fear was no match for the confidence she felt this morning, the knowledge that this was the right thing to do. No going back.

Waking by herself still felt strange. Sunlight was pouring into the naked bedroom. She looked at the clock on the bedside table, but of course it wasn't there anymore. He had taken it with him. Hadn't that been a wedding present from a mutual friend and thus not his to take? It didn't matter, she thought. She wasn't going to think about him, not yet. The idea was what mattered. The idea would take care of all other ideas. And no, she wasn't going to binge. She wasn't going to purge. No matter what, she wouldn't indulge herself in her worst, most secret pleasure. Make some tea, she told herself, and get down to work.

She felt good about this, very good. The smile on her face was a welcome relief from the frown that had defined it for the last week. Her task was set and the outcome was to be nothing less than full redemption. Acts of unabashed humility, her apologies would permit people, her *victims,* as she now realized they'd been, to heal from the abuses suffered at her hands. How self-indulgent to have believed she'd always been a good woman. What a delusion, she whispered to herself, barely audibly, so arrogant. How could she have been blind to the obvious fact that she had never finally been good, not really good, toward anyone who crossed her path over the course of her thirty years on this confounding Earth? Her moment of enlightenment, brought on by a downward spiral of miserable days and nights of deep silence, had to happen eventually. Now the consequences of her misdeeds must be addressed. And they would be. Thank heavens, she thought, for nightmares.

Slipping into her favorite pair of baggy white painter's overalls and the wrinkled, unwashed white dress shirt her estranged husband had left behind in the laundry hamper when, without warning, he vacated their small rented house last week, Ellie, as most everyone called her, even looked the role of the rumpled saint. As she rolled up her sleeves she noticed the broken button on the left cuff she'd meant for months to replace. Guilty as charged. One more thing to apologize for, assuming he would be willing to speak with her. Hadn't Matthew asked her a number of times to do this one simple task, and she, whether from forgetfulness or resistance to housewifely chores, had never risen to the occasion? She left the shirt unwashed because it still smelled of him, who had otherwise been very thorough in removing his effects when she was away last week on a long-delayed visit to her parents and sister. Well, not a visit, as such, but rather because of an emergency that required her to go. Still, whether her rare trips to Ithaca were to visit or help out with a crisis, Ellie's homecomings were always fraught, as she and her sister never much saw eye to eye about anything anymore. About politics, culture, religion, about everything under the sun they'd become polar opposites in their thinking. And like the terrestrial poles themselves, they were now as icy cold toward one another as they once, long ago, had been equatorially warm and embracing. But both parents had been injured in an automobile accident—her stepfather had a dislocated shoulder, her mother, broken ribs—and she was needed to assist for a few days, lend a hand getting them set up at home after their release from the hospital. It would have been nice if Matthew had offered to come along. Ellie wasn't a good driver, didn't like to drive, and felt wary of getting behind the wheel in light of what had just happened. But he simply couldn't get away from work. So she had left on a Tuesday morning, stayed in her old bedroom with its view of Lake Cayuga for three nights, and returned downstate late Friday to find her life modified beyond recognition. As if it were a toy box whose trove of games and puzzles some discontented child had decided he'd outgrown and on an impulse dumped into the trash.

Hudson River haze crocheted its way through the ghost-white limbs of the big sycamore out back. The viburnum was full of red berries, and birds flitted about in its long, heavy branches. It was going to be a scorcher, one of those steam-bath days. She sat down at the table in front of the row of French windows in the kitchen and took a sip of chamomile. The room, she noticed, badly needed plaster and paint. She could have made those repairs herself but somehow never got around to it. Had negligence always been her gravest shortcoming? If so, it was a shortcoming followed by many others, no doubt. She began listing names on a yellow legal pad and beside each of them wrote down misdeeds as far back as she could remember. The only sounds in the room were the scratching of a mouse family that lived inside the wall by the hutch and that of her pencil moving across paper. Before the morning was over and the sun had risen past the peak of her roof, Ellie Mead had reduced her life to a brave catalogue of apologies-in-waiting.

Now, she had long since lost touch with many people and so her confessions to them would have to be made in the abstract. This was one of those moments when being religious would be useful. She could pray, as she had tentatively tried in times past, that the Lord pardon her for the whole lot of them, her torts and transgressions, and have done with it. But what redress, what satisfaction was there in whispering to some deity she wasn't convinced sat on high listening, judging, and portioning out forgiveness? What was prayer, as her stepfather stubbornly said so often when she was growing up, if not pitiful murmurings into the unsentimental void? Even if there were a God, it wasn't His place to absolve her any more than it was hers to absolve herself. Still, some dozen names in her ledger fell into this awkward category of the alive but unreachable. If she had a computer—he had usurped their laptop—she might be able to search them out on the Internet. Had she any money, she supposed she could have hired someone to track them down. But she hadn't, especially now that Matthew had abandoned her, leaving little more than a couple of months' rent in their shared account.

The dead presented a similar problem but were, ironically, more immediately accessible. Knowing that she had no conceivable alternative, she did mete out her responsibility with these people, these gone souls, by quietly addressing each one. Verbalized words for virtual ears. She knew she was only talking to herself and that there was no chance they heard her, but any and all catharsis was valuable. Besides, apologizing to ghosts was good practice for what she faced with the living, though she did have to wonder whether this wasn't a form of prayer.

One person in particular occupied her thoughts. Her confession to her birth father was short and simple. She was sorry she never met him. She had always hoped she had nothing to do with his having joined the military when he found out her mother was pregnant, but she knew it was a false hope. She was sorry her mere existence had frightened him away from her mother and from herself before she even took her first breath of air. She also hoped he hadn't put himself in harm's way on purpose when he was killed in a noncombat accident, slipping under the wheels of a cargo truck in Wiesbaden, Germany, only a week before the furlough that would have brought him home to join his wife, who was about to give birth to Ellie. The few photographs of him that her mother possessed showed Pvt. Jimmy Tremblay to be a sum of paradoxes, cocky yet scared, strong yet somehow vague, disciplined but with a chaotic glint in his tardy, honest eyes. She was remorseful she didn't understand him and never would. She hoped he would realize that she never had a choice in the matter. She told him she knew he wasn't listening, or couldn't, and for this, as well, she made her amends for being such a doubter.

Others among the dead also needed addressing, and she spoke to them in turn. Her best childhood friend, Denise Bye, as diabetic and obese as Ellie was bulimic and skinny, whom she tripped on the school playground, causing the girl to come crashing down face-first into macadam that scarred her cheek and broke off her left front tooth. Ellie still despised herself for that. She also hated herself for the time she persuaded classmates to finger-write the unclever quatrain

Mary Purcell
Go to hell!
Why choose her
The lousy loser!

on the dirty windows of the school bus, revenge for her having edged out Ellie for a role in some Thornton Wilder play, never noticing at the time the keen irony in the wording of her insult. Who was the loser then? Not Mary Purcell, nor, for that matter, Jonathan Saunders or Cheryl Lane or Slug Moore or the nice math teacher whose name she could not remember, a short, kind, sweating man who wore a different bow tie every day of the week—all gone to dust now, and while they presumably couldn't hear a word of Ellie's amends, she hoped there was some invisible mechanism in the universe that would convey her contrition to what spirit or soul was left of them.

The lost and the dead. At the end of the day, much the same difference. She knew they were, in essence, a detour, a means to delay, a way away from the more difficult work at hand. "I feel nothing but regret toward all of you," she said, as the mice scratched away. "I didn't treat you as any respectable person would. When I'm dead, if we're all gathered together like they say in the fairy tales and religious myths, I will tell you each I'm sorry face-to-face if we have faces, heart-to-heart if we have hearts."

Curious, how the idea of an afterlife left her not hopeful but bereft. She was surprised to find herself sitting at that table, staring at her trembling hands, tears welling not from joy or consternation or even sadness but some vague and growing dread. She wiped her dampened eyes on the sleeve of Matthew's shirt. Press ahead, she advised herself. The idea will protect you from the part of yourself that should always have been restrained from hurting others. The sun was strong through the windows and cast a checkerboard of shadows on the counter, the floor, the table, her hands, the list.

Three years had passed since the wedding—her first, his second—and aside from two frustrating miscarriages and the fact that his job kept him away from home more than either of them liked, Ellie believed their marriage was working. At least working as well as marriage—a touch-and-go institution at best, she had always been told, and now knew firsthand—could be said to work. She'd even made a point of asking him from time to time, We have a good marriage, don't we? You're happy with me, Matthew? I'm a good wife, aren't I?

He always answered her with an encouraging, Sure. Or, What are you talking about, of course we're doing fine. Or, Please don't do this to me, Eleanor.

His farewell note was riddlesome if succinct. *Sorry to do this but my life hurts and I need clear space to sort stuff out. Don't hold it against yourself like I know you will. Need to breathe so please don't follow me and don't worry. I love you.*

To telephone him at work would be to ignore his request. Even so, he was at the top of the column of people she had to contact today. Although he might fairly be categorized as among the lost, she needed to reach Matthew and make every apology necessary to persuade him to come home. After all, her shortcomings surely contributed to his abandoning their house and marriage. If he could just lay out for her how she could do better, she would try harder to live up to his expectations. Maybe she was missing something. Did he know she was willing to get treatment now? Had he figured out why she was, in the way she was, who she was? He did complain sometimes that he hadn't married Stick Woman. And now look. What happened to your tits, he'd asked her a month ago at the Savages' house, but he was pretty inebriated, actually very drunk and abusive like he sometimes got, when he offered that one up. Not that he was wrong. For a few years before the marriage she had been doing better, but not so much for the past couple. She dialed, looking at the serrated edges of her fingernails.

No answer. Maybe he had taken an early lunch, not that he wanted to hear from the likes of her anyway. Matthew had been pretty disgusted by her for months now. Nothing she did was right. When she tried again a quarter hour later, a man picked up the phone. "Who, may I ask, is calling?"

"Ellie, Matthew's wife. And you are?"

"Randall McGibben, Ellie." Scandal McGibben, Matthew called him for reasons she never quite understood. Matthew's supervisor at the savings and loan. "I'm very sorry about your parents."

"Thank you. I need to speak with Matthew. When will he be back?"

"Back from what?"

She paused before saying, "Well."

"You mean he's not with you upstate, something about your folks being in a car wreck, took the week off to help out? Maybe I misunderstood."

Ellie waited, knowing whatever answer she gave might work against her husband and therefore against the idea. Nothing was more important than the idea. "I'm sorry," she said. "I, I've made a mistake, really sorry—"

Poor woman must be distraught, he told himself. Maybe one of the parents was worse off than they had thought, or didn't make it. "Not a problem. Look, if he's available, you might let him know—"

"—and also, Mr. McGibben? I have been meaning to apologize to you."

Boy, did she sound frazzled, he thought, but then the few times he had met her, Christmas parties and a funeral, or a wedding, she had struck him as sweet but quirky, wound a little tight. Pretty, though, with her Annie Hall clothes and ragamuffin gold-blonde hair that looked like it was cut by a blind man who liked the sound of his scissors. All spiky and flying in different directions. Striking pale blue eyes. And thin as dental floss, wouldn't even touch a canapé. He had never been able to figure out whether Mead was the luckiest guy in the world or very much otherwise. She was talking now in a voice that was different, graver, more frayed than he remembered. If voices could look over shoulders.

"Last April, when Matthew had to take off a few days during your regional conference because he was really sick, you remember that?"

"He had laryngitis."

"I know it created a bit of hardship for you not having him there. Well, that was my fault. It was my thirtieth birthday and I—well, I talked him into taking those days off so we could go to Costa Rica. I'd always wanted to visit there and I guess he didn't have any more vacation time left in your fiscal year?"

He was listening.

"Because of our trip to Oaxaca. Anyway, that was not his fault, it was mine, and I'm very sorry for any inconvenience it may have caused you."

She thanked him for hearing her out and believed that he seemed to accept her apology, in a reticent sort of way. Before they hung up, he reiterated that he would appreciate hearing from Matthew as soon as he found a free moment, and Ellie agreed, her mood buoyed by this, her first confession and apology to a living, breathing person. Aware it was a facile, even childish thing to do, she drew a line through McGibben's name before making her next call.

Their best friends, Peter and Ava Savage, whom she hadn't heard from since she got back from Ithaca, would probably know where Matthew was. He had most likely spent the last week in their guest bedroom, a room in which Peter the month before, drunk and disoriented, had tried to convince Ellie that sleeping with him would resolve all the tensions between them and smooth the way toward a more complete and whatever-it-was-he-said relationship.

Ava answered with a cascade of outpouring sympathy that caught Ellie by surprise. "How could he leave you like that? I just don't understand. How are you holding up, baby?"

"Ava, have you seen him?"

"Of course, yes, sure. He was here earlier this week and you would have thought he'd killed you, the way he was going on about how guilty he feels."

"Is he there now? Could I speak to him?"

"Afraid not. When Peter got home, he and Matt had quite an argument, and they both stormed off in different directions. Neither one of them is here at the moment."

"Argument about what?"

A lull descended, not a long one but rather like a slow blink instead of a normal quick blink, and with all the import such a difference signifies. Ellie heard, as it were, the blink, but decided not to address it, and so—informed by the idea—moved forward, her chest tightening. That Ava knew where he was needed to be set aside.

"Avy, I have something important to tell you and I need for you to listen to me. I woke up this morning with this idea—"

"I hope it's a good idea."

"—and nothing's more important to me, so I hope you're in a forgiving mood."

Ellie was always such a naïf, Ava thought. Good intentions, good heart, virtuous as all get-out. But she had grown up in some kind of whacked idealistic family situation that kept her sidelined from reality and left her in a woeful state of utter innocence, an innocence that now and then seemed like stupidity. She never in a hundred lifetimes could have guessed what was really happening around her, poor thing. On the other hand, wasn't she enviable for that? Enviable because she wasn't so much ignorant—if ignorance was bliss, ignorance was not getting the job done when it came to Ellie—as she was one of life's pure and simple perpetual amateurs. Who could say it wasn't admirable, even, her consummate amateurism? The word means you do something only for the love of it. Few, thought Ava, are left with that graceful deficiency by her age.

"And I'm really sorry about that."

"About what?"

"We never did, you know, anything. I think he's held it against me."

Ava asked Ellie what she'd just said—had been distracted—and learned that Peter had cornered her when Ava and Matt drove to the store to get another bottle of wine after they ran out during one of their weekly dinner parties.

"But my point here, Avy, is to apologize to you. Because I thought about it, kissing him. I did think about it, and, well, okay, I, we did, a little."

"Ellie—"

"It should never have happened and I swear it will never happen ever again. Do you think you can see your way to forgiving me?"

"Of course I forgive you, honey. Things happen like that in life."

"Please have Matthew call me?"

"I'll tell him if I see him."

This confession was quite a lot harder to make than Ellie would have supposed. The buoyancy she'd felt before was gone. Even as she drew a line through the name Ava Savage, she took pause at the fact that her friend wasn't a little more upset by her admission. The meaning of the blink and of Avy's ready forgiveness could only have a very few explanations. But rather than attending to dawning suspicion, she thought it best to move ahead with the idea. Nothing much to be gained right now by contemplating people's responses. Avy had accepted the apology and that was that.

Never much of a drinker—Matthew wished she were, had more than once suggested it might loosen her up a little, in bed and out—Ellie thought to make an exception today, since this day was exceptional in its own right. Not without a little difficulty, she corkscrewed open a bottle of white wine—at least he'd left the fridge untouched—poured a healthy glassful, and placed another call, this time to her sister. Answering machine. She left a somewhat tortured message saying, in brief, that she needed to speak with her as soon as possible. "It's important," she finished, then hung up, had another drink of wine, which was fruitier than she liked but was nicely jazzing her mind toward pushing further with the idea.

Ross was next, the only man besides Matthew who had ever meant something to her, whom she had ever loved, to use that difficult word, but it was true, loved. Ross, the man she left for Matthew. Unless he had moved, she expected to find him in his loft studio in Williamsburg. Thought of as a second-tier painter by the several critics who had ever reviewed him, Ross was a man Ellie had always believed in. In his vision, his future.

More than once over the years she found herself wondering what he was doing, what the work looked like now, if he'd had anything exhibited outside of galleries owned by friends in Red Hook and DUMBO. She had sent him a birthday card last year behind Matthew's back—another thing she would have to confess to her husband, if she could find him—but heard nothing in response. A woman answered the phone after what must have been a dozen rings. Big run-down loft, it used to take Ellie quite a while to get to that same telephone, old black rotary thing Ross had found at a thrift store, back when she lived with him. She asked if Ross was there.

"He's busy right now."

"Painting?"

"Who is this?"

Ellie told her.

"Hold on," she was told by a dauntingly impatient, if familiar voice.

She could so easily picture the loft with its long gallery of dirty windows, its uneven wide-plank floor, its myriad pipes like circuitry on the ceiling, every feature a legacy of its working-class, industrial history. This had been Ellie's home for more years than she'd been with Matthew. How many hundreds of hours had she posed nude for Ross? Vain as it might be, she missed those canvases with her abstracted image centering a furious hail of thick, dark, layered oils, like some exploded satanic halo. Sometimes she felt that seeing herself through his dizzying view of her was a truer act than looking in a mirror.

"What is it?" That was him all over again, abrupt as a palette knife slapping Belgian linen.

"Ross, it's Ellie."

"I know *who* it is, *what* is it?"

"I'm calling to apologize for having left you for Matthew. I really did love you and I never wanted to hurt you but I, it was a confusing time for me and he had a career going and—"

"What, stop, are you crazy?"

"What's her problem?" the woman who had answered the phone asked in the background.

"And, listen, I need to apologize for not really being as good to you as you deserved."

"Ellie, look. I haven't heard from you for how long, and this is what you have to say?"

"You never got my card?"

"What, are you standing on a high ledge or something?"

"Tell her to jump," the other woman said.

"Shut up," Ross said, perhaps to both of them.

"Listen, this is important to me."

"It's always about you, isn't it."

She could hear the woman still talking in excited tones and just then she placed the voice. Of all things. "Is that Dante?" she asked. "Could I speak with her for a moment? I need to tell her something."

But Dante and Ross were now arguing with one another and her request was ignored, unheard, until Ross finally addressed Ellie again, his voice a taut snarl. "And tell that idiot husband of yours that if he so much as tries to get in touch with her again I'll kill him and paint an Expulsion from Eden with his blood."

Ross always leaned toward violence in the ways he expressed himself. At one point she must have found it alluring to live with a tortured soul who spoke from depths few ever plumb. Now his vitriol was more depressing than evocative. She had somehow managed to forget that side of him, one of the reasons she'd left. "You mean you've heard from Matthew?"

"Good-bye already, Ellie."

That didn't go so well. No, that one seemed to open wounds more than salve them. She took a deep breath and exhaled, shaking her head slowly as if blowing out invisible candles. With that gesture a memory surfaced, bringing a nostalgic smile to her face, of the time she baked Ross a big birthday cake and managed, pretty closely, to replicate one of his paintings on it using different-colored frostings. His response, rather than delight, had been one of outrage and insult. Ellie's smile flattened out. Lost years, those had been. Yet, she thought, shaking off the memory, hadn't she more or less accomplished what she set out to do today? One can only make the apology. What was more, she now knew where to send Dante (no last name, just Dante) a letter saying she was sorry for having been part of the reason her then-husband left her. What startling symmetry, that Matthew's former wife would be at Ross's place today. Life was more often like that than people acknowledged. Were there a God, he had a very dark sense of humor. Their quarreling sounded like lovers', she had to admit, the unbridled intensity of it being unlike any other kind of argument people shared—did one *share* an argument, like trading blows or insults, *trading* and *sharing* being terms that trembled with amicability?—and maybe they were lovers now. Two jilted people who through the agency of commiseration find in one another a promising new future? Possibly they were even married. Ellie felt a brief twinge of jealousy at this thought, but quickly put it aside. Today was not to be a selfish day, and jealousy is nothing if not a selfish emotion. What right did she have, anyway? This idea was about self-purification, not backsliding. Some apologies would not produce forgiveness. That was how things were.

Pull yourself together. She wrote Dante a handwritten letter and addressed it care of Ross in Williamsburg. Two more lines through two more names, knowing she would never hear back from either of them.

As the afternoon heat settled in the kitchen and as the now-warm chardonnay played more in her mind, an urgency began to take hold. She left messages on machines whenever she happened not to find someone at home or in their place of work. The idea was still a good idea. A sublime idea. The only idea. But she felt the pressure of it, its burden and weight, building behind her eyes. It would be best if her task were fulfilled as expeditiously as possible. No reason it couldn't be completed before she went to bed. A day of penance, like the day of the dead, except for the living. How long did baptisms take? A blessing, a brief submersion in holy water, and that was that. You were ready for entrance into heaven. Whatever heaven was and, for that matter, wasn't white the wrong color wine for a communion? It was. Anemic blood. No matter. Her quest for absolution mustn't devolve into the snake biting its own tale—tail, that is. Ellie was no Ouroboros, but a seeker of forgiveness.

She had borrowed a tiger-patterned silk scarf from Charlotte Nicosia that she never quite found it in her heart to give back. When her friend inquired, she'd allowed herself a white, or at least a beige, lie, saying she'd lost it. Of course, the whole misadventure was pointless since Ellie never wore it in public for fear of being exposed as the liar and thief she was. So she laid out the details of her subterfuge on the Nicosia family's voice mail, offered to return it, never suspecting that she had happened to tap into an old wound, as Charlotte herself had also stolen this siren of a scarf from her sister-in-law, under similar circumstances. Ellie would never know why Charlotte didn't return the call, but she was at least able to cross off one more name.

Once, when Matthew was away on bank business, on a night when she couldn't sleep, she had taken a long walk down to the river. This was in autumn, as she could remember the satisfying crunch of fallen leaves underfoot while strolling under the occasional cones of amber streetlights. Coming back up the hill, turning onto her block, she saw a group of boys vandalizing a neighbor's car. Halloween prank, she supposed. They saw her, she saw them, they ran. Next morning, when the police canvassed the neighborhood for witnesses, Ellie, not wanting to get involved, improvised that she had been asleep at the time. The children afterward, having never been caught, always gave her uncomfortable winks and smiles when she encountered them. She owed Carl Swansea an apology, and made it, setting the record straight for his wife, who asked her if she knew how to spell the boys' names. Afterward, she called the homes of the vandals and left messages apologizing that she could no longer keep their secret.

Then there was that time she kicked the neighbor's dog when he—Manny was his peculiar name, a rowdy terrier since deceased—snapped at her heels in the rain once when she cut through the Lytells' yard running home. She left a message on their machine apologizing for that and for the fact that, under circumstances not so very different from those surrounding Peter Savage's advances, she also kicked Arthur Lytell—kneed him, rather—last Christmas, in the Lytells' master bedroom, where she had gone to retrieve her and Matthew's overcoats for the walk home after the party. Though they had feigned an amicable neutrality in the months following the incident, Ellie knew things had changed somewhat, and she wanted to say she was sorry and hoped he understood she didn't mean to injure either him or his aging pet. And also hoped Mrs. Lytell didn't mind her saying so, but Arthur would have to appreciate the reason she never answered any of his private letters inviting her to meet him for a drink, to talk, *work things out,* as he put it, was because her husband would frown on such a meeting and she didn't want to make him unhappy. Lytell, *lie tell.* Another name, another line.

Her phone rang. An unexpected, jarring sound but also possibly promising. Someone was calling to forgive her, she thought, or better yet, maybe it was a reconciliatory Matthew. Instead, Randall

McGibben. Had she been able to let her husband know he needed to check in with the office? She improvised, doing her best to sound businesslike. "Not as yet." Could she give McGibben a contact number where Matthew could be reached immediately? Something had come up that required his attention, McGibben pressed, then, hearing nothing but terrified silence at the other end, said, "You don't have any idea where your husband is, do you?"

"Well, of course I do," knowing that such a mistruth was just what she had committed to avoid under the aegis of the idea.

"Are you sure you're speaking with me honestly, Mrs. Mead? Eleanor?"

"You can call me Ellie."

A pause, then doing his best to mask exasperation, "All right. Ellie."

Here was a turning point she had neither foreseen nor knew how to negotiate. She swallowed, took a breath, and said, "No, sir, Mr. McGibben. I'm lying. And I apologize for that. But I'm lying for a good reason."

"I'm sure you are. But you can appreciate my position and why I need to know what's happening here."

"Well, if I knew myself—I mean, if I myself knew—I would tell you. Do you accept my apology? It's important that you do."

"What? Sure. But we need to find him."

"He'll call as soon as he—are there any problems?"

"Well, Mrs. Mead, there may be. But I need to address them directly with Matthew."

Ellie hung up and focused on the list while distractedly meditating on what she possibly meant by *for a good reason*. She knew there was a good reason behind all this, but she could not identify what it was at that moment. Wasn't it possible she was trying to hurt others to make herself feel better? It was possible. Wasn't it possibly more possible she was doing all this to make her life, and the lives of all those around her, more truthful, more—she hated this word, but it was the one that came into her head—empowered. She was becoming powerful in the very meekness of her disclosures, she thought. But it wasn't about that. It was about the beauty of cleansing herself. Of purging a lifetime's deceit. It was about facing her demons. About making this day, this very hot day, evolve into meaning, meaningfulness, a passage from bad to better. She caught herself chewing on her fingernails—old, nasty habit.

It was about moving forward with the idea.

She dialed Will Jones down at the auto shop and apologized that Matthew hadn't been by to pay the repair bill for the transmission, brake, and body job done back in February. Yes, she was aware that a collection agency had been assigned to secure the overdue debt, had seen the mail, why else would she bother to call if not to say she was sorry for the trouble? No, she had not known that there had been a suit filed, a lien imposed. No, she didn't understand what all that quite meant, but she'd called for a different reason. But before she got to that, she mentioned her husband had gone off with his car and she didn't know where he was, and she wondered if he did. *Bastard absconded* was a little harsh, wasn't it, she asked before hanging up on him. Abrupt termination would have to suffice as a way of concluding some of these confessional apologies, at least with the argumentative and recalcitrant. She hadn't even had the chance to tell Will that the body work had to be done because she'd had a minor accident—black ice, a sturdy Norway spruce tree—and that the insurance company was reluctant to see transmission and brake problems as viable liabilities. Rather than tracing a line through his name, she bracketed him. Made her think about erasing Randall McGibben's name with its dark, excising line in order to rewrite and bracket it, too. Some of the business seemed too unfinished. But then, no, she realized her part was fulfilled. What she could do she had done and that was that.

After indulging herself in several minutes of doodling beside the name Will Jones, she stood up and more or less floated through the house, much as a specter might, looking to see if everything was as she—he—had left it. Nothing had changed. Why should it? The idea was still uncompleted, a work in progress. What she would give to eat something, anything, a lot of food, and then hover over the toilet, put her fingers down her throat to bring it all back up in its satisfying awfulness, as she had done countless times in the past. She considered going outside, taking a breather, a short jog down the street and back. But the memory of the vandals kept her from doing so. She didn't need to risk adding experiences to her life now; it was all about reducing, subtracting. Besides, no good would come of it. Indeed, she would be slowed down. Feeling a little guilty, she called Matthew's work line again but there was no answer this time. Without giving the potential consequences a thought, she telephoned Ross again, as well. She wanted to know just when and how Matthew had been in touch with Dante. After minutes of ringing, she hung up and tried to focus on refocusing. Just stay with it, stay with the program, she told herself.

She sat in the quiet, listening to the mouse family in the wall. Scratch, scratch. Their scraping sounded louder than before, more persistent. She always liked mice, felt they were cute and harmless, but Matthew insisted they had dangerous habits, could chew through electrical wiring and cause a fire. She would need to set a trap before bed tonight, although he was always the one to do it in times past, just as it was he who collected the remains and disposed of them at the far end of the backyard. But unless he returned, that responsibility would also fall to her, she realized as the phone rang.

Her sister. "What's the matter?" Lila said, her voice as rude as Dante's had been. She could tell that Ellie was trying not to cry. This was a side of her that never worked well with Lila.

"Nothing," Ellie lied, then confessed, "A lot."

"You sound awful."

"Matthew left me."

"I know."

"And I'm drinking."

"Brilliant. Matthew just left here, and I'm not drinking."

Lila excelled at comebacks. Ellie once kidded, years ago, that they should create a new gridiron position unique to Lila. Quarterback, halfback, fullback, comeback. She was not in a joking mood at the moment, though. It was more and more clear that Matthew had been seen and heard everywhere but the two places he was supposed to be. His mercurial absence then presence then absence was beginning to take its toll on the idea, retarding its progress. She told herself she must carry forth with her confessions and let her husband make his own journey, which would eventually lead him back, she hoped, to where he began, so he could see she was a new woman. Still, she couldn't help but ask, "What was he doing there?"

"He was here because he's not happy with his life."

"He drove four hours just to tell you that?"

"You are such a fool, Ellie."

She held the receiver away from her head, breathed, decided not to hang up, so brought it back to her mouth and ear, and said, "Matthew's not why I called you."

"So what then?"

"I want to tell you that I'm sorry for hating you as much as I do. I don't even feel you're my sister. It's never made sense to me that you are." She paused for a moment, expecting Lila to sally forth with some acid sarcasm or another, but she had, it seemed, been momentarily shocked into silence. "It's never made sense, and I have wished my whole adult life that you weren't my sister. And if you had to be my sister I wished you were my dead sister. That's how much I despise you, Lila. I'm not going to waste your time or mine hashing over all the reasons I feel this way, because you already know them. I just called to tell you that I apologize and

to let you know that while I intend to make an honest effort not to
hate you from here on out I apologize in advance if I don't succeed
in doing so."

Lila cleared her throat, then said, "That's it?"

"That's it."

"Then I'd like to clue you in on a few things, my dear."

"Not now," said Ellie, ending the conversation, if such it
was, by placing the phone on its cradle. She wondered, for a
sad instant, about Lila and Matthew. They had been together
a decade ago, briefly—a month or two—before Lila left him,
much the way she always left every man she had ever been with.
Abruptly and without explanation; not unlike how Matthew
himself had behaved just now toward his own wife. It had been
Lila who introduced him to both Dante and Ellie herself. For all
his dark-eyed, dark-haired good looks and his generally being a
decent, even urbane person, Matthew was as helpless as Lila was
shrewd.

As Ellie blotted out her sister's name, a refreshing surge of energy
rose within her. The sublimity of the idea that had brimmed with
such promise that morning once more took hold. She poured the
last of the wine into her glass. Half a dozen quick calls to honor
her regrets about small matters—an heirloom vase borrowed and
broken; a surprise party inadvertently divulged; the failure to visit
a friend after surgery; the missed appointment; the unintended
insult; the unkept promise—and the list was narrowed down to
a handful of victims. There was light at the end of this tunnel.
She could see it, the light, and was reminded of the light the
dying supposedly see when they are about to verge into death, an
iridescence of angels' wings, that primary light of truth itself. Ellie
wanted to walk to the light at the end of the idea. In spite of the
surprising number of indignant, even irate responses her apologies
had generated, she felt better about the idea now than at any point
during her long day. It was as virtuous an idea now as it had been

this morning. No, even better. Far better. She was frightened but had to stay faithful to the course she'd set.

When she awoke she was surrounded by thick, warm, muggy darkness. The phone was ringing but she couldn't find it. She reached out and patted the air in front of her. The jangling music of it was right here somewhere. Her head was splitting. Must have passed out, sitting at the table where she had spent the day and now into night. She found and then dropped the receiver, which made a hollow hard-plastic rattle as it hit the floor. Now someone, a man whose voice was small and distant, was saying, "Hello?"

"Hang on," she said, fumbling for the switch.

"Hello?"

The light was painfully bright. She picked up the phone. It was Matthew. What had she wanted to tell him earlier? she wondered as she listened. He wanted to see her, he said.

"When?"

"As soon as possible. Right now."

"I thought you were in Ithaca."

"Who told you that?"

"Lila."

"I was, but I'm here now."

"What do you want to talk about?"

"I've been thinking, is all," he said. "So what did Lila tell you?"

"That I'm a fool."

"That's why she called?"

"No, I called her."

"About what?"

Ellie didn't really want to revisit her conversation with her sister, and had no interest in hearing Matthew lie about his having gone there to rekindle a spent fire, or maybe even pursue the continuance of a flame that had glowed all these years in secret, so replied instead, "Ross tells me you were in touch with Dante."

"Did you call Scandal earlier today?"

"Actually, he answered your phone the first time, and the second time he called me."

"You spoke with him twice?" Matthew didn't sound like himself. The usual confidence was absent. There was something akin to a whimper in his voice that made her feel both sorry for him and annoyed somehow.

"Matthew, will you forgive me for asking you a question?"

"Ellie. Let's do this in person. I'd like to come by in an hour or so. All right by you?"

When they got off, she walked around the small house and opened every window. The place was like a steamy, plaster-walled sauna. She who so rarely perspired—wraiths don't—was damp and clammy. Her temples pulsed and heart raced unevenly. Almost midnight, according to the stove clock. Had there been some aspirin in the medicine cabinet, she would have taken a few. She remembered she had bought a pint of cooking sherry before being summoned to Ithaca, intending to use it in a French onion soup, Matthew's favorite, and went to the kitchen cabinet, half expecting it to be gone. She still had one more call to make and could use the succor. *In vino veritas.* Some ice in the glass and she was ready to complete the idea.

Her mother answered. Sounded sleepy.

"You have a couple minutes, Mom?"

"What time is it?"

"Late, but I need to talk."

"You don't sound right, Ellie. Are you sick?"

"How are you doing? The ribs?"

"Still hurts to breathe, especially at night, but we're coming along slowly. What's happening? Your sister called here earlier and said you were hysterical. Having problems with Matthew."

"He's on his way home right now. She's mistaken, as usual."

"I'm glad to hear that."

Ellie took a drink of sherry, hoping her mother couldn't hear the ice clicking. "I want to apologize to you."

"I don't understand."

"When I was young? You used to make such wonderful meals for us. Such a great cook, a chef, really. What other kids were eating *coq au vin* one night and paella the next? Well, as you probably've suspected over the years, I threw up a lot of that food in the toilet after dinner, saying I needed to go to the bathroom."

"Young women sometimes go through periods when—"

"I'm still bulimic, Mom, just have it under white-knuckle control. But that's not my point, my point is I'm sorry you put in all that effort for nothing."

"It wasn't for nothing, Ell. You're alive, aren't you, and basically healthy."

"Then, there's this. I have always loathed George. Yes, he's been a decent husband to you, at least I think he has, but I can't stand him any more than he can stand me. And I'm sorry about it. I apologize to you from the bottom of my heart, and even to him. I know it's immature of me, should get help, therapy, and all that stuff, but I miss my real father—"

"Ell, how can you miss him when you never met him? Dwelling in a past that happened is one thing, but to dwell in one that didn't exist?"

"And also, I think when you talk with Lila you'll find out I said I was sorry for hating her, too—"

"Please don't use that kind of language about your sister, Ellie."

"Half sister. George's daughter. I wish I'd never met her."

"You two used to get along so well."

"We grew up and apart. There are stories to tell. I'll write them down for you if you want. But that's not my purpose here in calling.

I just wanted to tell you that I'm very sorry about everything I've done to make your life harder than it needed to be. I've been a distant, wayward daughter at best. Will you forgive me?"

She could hear her mother weeping. Not what she intended.

"Please don't cry. It's bad for you. Your ribs."

"If I could change the past, Ellie, I would. Most people would. But we've got what we made for ourselves and each other. And asking for all the forgiveness in the world isn't going to change that."

"I disagree. I think it will. It has to."

"George's right here and he's saying he would like to speak with you."

"You haven't accepted my apology, though."

"I accept, I accept. Now would you have a word with your father?"

My *stepfather,* she thought, before realizing that this was almost it, this was the moment when the idea was very near completion. She said, "I need to speak first, though. Tell him that."

"Hello, Eleanor. I gather you're going through a rough patch—"

"George, I'm fine. Don't give me a second thought," she said, knowing she should ask him how his shoulder was, apologize for waking him up, express her regrets for never having been quite the daughter to him that his darling Lila always was. Instead, she said, "I thought it was important to tell you that I think I have found God."

"What?"

"Yes, I'm a religious person now, and wanted to apologize to you for that." The third lie she had told today, and offered in bad faith, at that, meant to wound. He said nothing; there was nothing for him to say. He'd never tendered much affection toward his stepdaughter on the rosiest of days, and wasn't going to let her get the upper hand on him now, either. The girl had always been a trial.

"That's fine, El—"

"No. You don't understand. I mean, I just *love* God. *Love him.* His purity, the sanctity of his creation. His omnipotence and transcendent wisdom. The love he feels for all his children. I'll tell you what, George. If I could have God's baby I would do it. He could come down from the clouds and have me right here on the kitchen table. You'll just have to forgive me for feeling sorry for you, George, because when the apocalypse comes and all of us are judged for having been good and loving toward others, or cold and distant—" But this time one of her victims hung up on her, and so she sat there, holding tight to her chest the glass of cooking sherry whose ice cubes had melted, in a state of mind that did after all come close to the ecstatic.

She sat unmoving, but moved. She knew that the consummation of the idea would create an aftermath of new wars and fresh truces, breakdowns and buildups, of coming-to-grips and losing-one's-grip, of advances and retreats, tears and laughter, and also, now, of one spirit—if Ellie had a spirit—who could just sit still. Sit at her plain wooden table in this stark kitchen with its French windows overlooking an unmown yard under the stars and waxing moon, knowing she was, for a single ephemeral moment in what she hoped would be a long life, but might not be, unsullied. Free from corruption. At peace with herself. She finished her wine with a complicated smile on her face even as the key turned in the front door.

Good, she thought. Now he can set the mousetrap.

THE ROAD TO NADĚJA

KNEW I LOVED LYDIA when I stole her ring. How she cherished that pretty object, cameo of a stag carved in bloodstone and set in gold. The stag's haunches had been rubbed to the palest pink—she always worried the face of the stone with those nervous fingers of hers. I wondered how many other fingers down the centuries had fondly touched that talisman, as I hid it in a small leather pouch and pulled the drawstrings tight. Then I thought, *Listen, ring, nobody owns you now.*

How Lydia cried! I was so harsh with the concierge at the seaside hotel, threatened to call the authorities, demanded that the maid be brought in so I could question her myself. Yes, I was enraged, my heart was burning, while next to it in the breast pocket of my jacket the ring raced and pulsed, like a little eel chasing its phosphorescent tail in the surf beyond our window.

This has always been the way with me. I take things. And the unhappiness Lydia felt for weeks after the disappearance of her ring made for some of the most exquisite joy I have ever known. She wept, she stormed, she despaired. She needed me, and I consoled her. It was the crowning gesture of a short courtship, my theft, and was, I believed in my heart of hearts, purifying for her. I never made the mistake of offering to get her another ring. That would have been crass. Nor did I patronize her with the sermon that toyed at my tongue, pled to be spoken as we made our way from Italy to Spain, the sermon about renunciation. Whenever a few days passed without any mention of the theft, I did allow myself subtly to reintroduce it into our conversation. "I wonder if we ought to hire somebody to snoop around the hotel where you lost your ring, and see if that maid is wearing it." Lydia thought this was a wonderful idea, and when I was sure she approved, watching the light of hope come back into her pale green eyes, I hesitated, brushed my hand over my lips, and shook my head no. "Why torture ourselves about it?"

Lydia's ring was not, of course, my first theft. Far from it. Indeed, the pouch in which I kept it was once the property of my grandfather. He used to house his antique fob watch in it, and though it had been the watch that motivated my theft—silver with a face white as a full moon—I liked the pouch as well. It has served as a faithful hiding place for other little objects over the years.

My activities as a taker have always been steeped in a purpose more meaningful than mere acquisition. Taking from those one knows is easy, from those one adores easier yet, in many ways more desirable, more evocative. What my friends and relatives once owned, what was precious to them, was so available to me as to almost force me into possessing it. In the act of assuming possession I was subtly transformed, and whatever had been the relationship between me and that person was transformed too. We were brought closer by the absence of their treasured object. By lifting Lydia's ring or Grandfather's timepiece I had created an opening, a gap through which I might better have access to their hearts. What time was it? "Seven thirty-three, Grampa," I'd answer, checking my own cheap wristwatch. It never failed to bring a gentle smile to his lips, and up into his lap I would go, and my dear grandfather would praise me, and my grandmother would say, "You're such a fine young boy."

Theft, in other words, has always been for me an act of fostering love.

When my grandfather passed on—this was how we had to put it in our family, "passed on," like there was somewhere to go—it was everything I could do to keep from giving in to the idea that the poor man ought to be buried with his fob watch. He never found it, and he'd looked long and hard. This was the first time I ever considered returning something I had taken. Being well advanced in my ways—no one in my immediate family and few among my friends hadn't given up something to my growing cache—it was a disconcerting moment, a moment of truth. I was twenty when he died, and still living in his house as I had done ever since the death of my mother and father.

My parents lost their lives on their way to a family gathering, all dressed to the nines in the wreckage, Christmas presents strewn everywhere so cheery and colorful that I, who was six at the time, couldn't resist opening one of them while I waited in the backseat of the car for the men to finish sawing through the cold, crimped metal to set me free. I have an intense and perfect memory of the wrapping paper on the box. A plum-cheeked, merry Santa, working in his shop surrounded by elves. A ledger that listed who was naughty and nice on his cluttered desk. The blue snow falling outside his windows, casting light through the room full of toys. Above all, that big bag of his, by the door, brimming with presents he was going to give to children around the world. The good children, that is. And I was a good child, I didn't cry when they finally got me out. I hugged the baby doll I'd found in the box tight to my chest and made sure it was warm, too, when they put a blanket over my shoulders. Glass was being broken behind me, and the saw was singing again. The man wouldn't let me look.

I moved in with my grandparents after the accident, and they were caring toward me. My grandfather continued to work past the age when most men retire, to help support me and send me through school; to make sure I was dressed as well as anyone and could participate in those activities in which boys, as they got older, liked to involve themselves. I loved going to the movies, I enjoyed reading comics, especially those where the superhero had a secret life, a dark side. I owned a .22-caliber rifle and went out into the woods with friends and shot small game—squirrels, skunks, even the occasional snapping turtle. After I took my grandfather's watch, it was I, as I've said, who would have to tell him what time it was. My grandmother was always after him to buy another, but he refused because he kept thinking he had misplaced it somewhere in the house.

"It'll turn up," he said. As right as my grandfather was about so many things in life, he was not right about that.

Parentless though it was, I can't say my childhood was bad. Still, I announced one morning, having helped myself to some of the brandy Grandmother kept in a breakfront for special occasions, my intentions to leave school, and to leave the country. I was restless and wanted to wander. There wasn't much my guardians could say. I knew that in March of the following year I would have access to my inheritance. So I packed my belongings, withdrew what savings I had in the bank, and kissed my grandmother good-bye. Grandfather's fob watch came with me.

Lydia and I met in Rimini, sitting adjacent to one another at an out-door café on a mild Adriatic summer afternoon—but I'd been over-come with an odd expectancy, as I walked through Paris earlier in the spring, that someone important was near me. I remember thinking this just when the police swept through the crowd of May Day rioters, clubs and shields above and before them. As I was running toward the cathedral, carried by the anger and panic of the antiwar mob, I swear I saw someone catch Lydia by the shoulder and pull her down right in front of me. I tripped over her and her assailant.

She has since said that nothing of the sort happened to her. Still, I wonder; when I later showed Lydia the scarf I'd snatched from this woman's neck during the melee—not, of course, revealing how I'd come to possess it—Lydia said, "That's strange." Turns out it was identical to a scarf she once treasured, this scarf I'd fondled in the darkness of Notre Dame, where so many of us lingered until the rioters were dispersed or arrested, the fires outside were extin-guished, and the island was restored to calm.

Now, the Tempio Malatestiano—without a doubt the greatest work of architecture to be found in the seaside town of Rimini—is cloaked in marble stripped from another cathedral on the same coast. Sigismondo Malatesta's masons, in need of materials to sheathe the brick facades and having no access to Tuscan quarries, sailed up the coast to the Byzantine port of Classe, where they raided the Sant'Apollinare for all its clean exterior stone. Half a millennium later, the Sant'Apollinare still stands naked on the sandy flats north of Ravenna, and the Tempio still wears its stolen emperor's clothes. Quiet sarcophagi, circled by harmless, lazy bees, line the temple's length outside, sheltered from the rain under its crumbling eaves.

She told me the story about the building's maker, did Lydia, standing under those very eaves. To her it was a parable of "greed and madness." It was "a rape still unavenged." I suggested that, to me, this was an appropriation, an example of Renaissance expediency in its purest form, and was not surprised when she stared at me with one of those quizzical looks I adored, and asked what was I talking about?

Was my ensuing silence too a kind of expediency? Or was I just being lazy like those black-and-yellow bees that one by one alighted to sleep on the warm marble lids of the ships of death that majestically flanked us where we conversed? What was I to say when, goaded by this silence, she launched into a diatribe about the evil souls of thieves? "I think we should bring back the punishments they used to have for burglars, where they cut off the hands of men who steal." Who was I to disagree?

We were married in March the next year. A day so overcast that a sky spangled with a hundred suns could not have pierced the green and black clouds that stretched out across the earth. (Green for her eyes, black for mine?) March was the month I was born, March will be the month I die. Aptly named, March. The month of deliberate movement, of marching into whatever might lie ahead.

Our wedding night was sentimental, affectionate. The wind that wrapped its damp arms around the room, once more in Rimini, in the very hotel we'd stayed at before, didn't dampen our spirits. It only invited us to wrap ourselves tighter in one another's arms, and we obliged, and I took nothing from Lydia that night but her intimacy.

The things I have stolen over the course of the years have always been, of necessity as well as of preference, small in size. Because I have archived the objects I've taken, it has been practical that they not occupy much space. Until recently, my life was not burdened by their secret presence in it. I have never so much as kept them under lock and key. My custodianship would, I knew, inevitably come to an end sometime. I'm not so dour a man that the theft of my cache would fail to strike an ironic note. The thief robbed; who wouldn't find comic justice in it? I mean to say, I am aware of the tenuousness of ownership—I know we cannot ultimately *own*. We're just caretakers in this life, isn't that the euphemism?—death being the only real landlord, the real holder of the *real* estate. If someone took my talismans away from me, I always thought until recently, "So be it"; the purpose, as I have said, was satisfied in their original removal.

Why then did I decide to do what I have done tonight? My answer: I was following my heart. In my experience, instructions from the heart are far more explicit and far less easy to follow than instructions from the intellect. The intellect can tell us what we ought to do, can speak to us with our own sham voice, can reason and cajole. The heart doesn't bother with such nonsense. In that regard it collaborates with death, where language stops cold—where the words "no more" or "not to be" or even "terror" are changed into sound waves that weave forever outward, unheard by ears, not responded to by voices.

Though sentimental, perhaps, Lydia was no fool. After the small extravagance of an overseas honeymoon, we settled where I'd grown up. I bought from my aging grandmother her house and furniture and established her in a comfortable room off the kitchen on the first floor. And while I would have been content to live frugally, and idly, on the interest earned by the balance of what my parents had left me, Lydia had grander plans. How animated she was as she described to me and Grandmother her dream of raising a family. Side by side on the front-room sofa we two sat as Lydia paced the kazak rug, and I would wince whenever my grandmother rolled her silvery, balding head forward and clicked her tongue with approval. What all this meant, of course, was that I was sent out to work.

I can't say I initially resented the responsibilities I began to incur on behalf of Lydia's dream. No; for a while I was content with my decision to be married, and was happy enough to have come back home after those years of wandering. What did worry me was that the novelty of marriage and the imperatives of responsibility began to pervert my own routine. Miss it as I might, my resolve to steal had abated. Days, months, seasons passed without my making a single addition to the cache, and I realized I'd lost what I discovered, in the full-blooded impudence of youth: the perfect way to people's hearts. Denied, I felt myself slowly atrophy into an indifferent worker, a sullen spouse, a distant grandson. However stifled I felt, however lethargic, I was not so blind as to remain unaware that my family and friends were treating me differently than they once had. I fought it, this feeling of isolation, and somewhat in desperation made the petty theft of a coffee mug from a fellow employee at the office. Waste of time. She merely brought in another.

In the meantime, Lydia and I failed at having children and decided to adopt. Daniel was the boy's name, a Eurasian child with a sweet smile and dreamy eyes. I would never have named him Daniel, for isn't a Daniel one who was meant to be fed to lions? But the choice was not mine.

Daniel became Lydia's universe. His needs were constant stars, his fears comets, and everything Lydia did was drawn now into his orbit. Daniel this, Daniel that, Daniel the other thing. If he had been the size of a voodoo doll, I might have considered adding him to the cache in order to win back the love of my wife. He was a black hole, Daniel.

Though I loved him and was a good father, my mind strayed. Lydia didn't notice what was happening; there was no way for her to continue to be aware of me in the same way she had been before. I withdrew into a helpless anger. Since I hadn't given her a wedding ring—no ring could match that bloodstone stag—I had no second chance to win my way back into her heart with a second disappearance.

She's been gone a long time now. So has Danny.

I made an experiment. It occurred to me to take things from people I didn't like. A neighbor down the road, a man toward whom I had always felt an unfounded aversion, relinquished to me (on an impulse one night when he was out of town) a brass mantel clock that I knew was a family heirloom. For good measure I selected a velvet blouse with a brilliant row of white buttons from his wife's closet, a blouse I'd seen her wear on special occasions. When I got these home—long after Grandmother had gone to bed—and set them out on the table to enjoy, I realized what folly the exercise had been. I felt nothing. The clock was ugly. I took the blouse to my face, breathed in, and remembered how ravishing my neighbor's wife looked when she wore it. I smelled the trace of perfume, and of perspiration. All very well, but none of the pleasure I sought was to be had from it. With disdain I added the objects to the collection, the cache, unfulfilled, but a man who knew himself somewhat better than before.

The cache. I took to visiting it more often than I had in the past. It was like a photograph album, but better, in that I was free to conjure the pictures as I pleased.

A steel-gray Fedora, this was an uncle's. I liked him all right. A pencil sketch of a lady's slipper orchid. A fountain pen, communication. A feather, flight. The carving of a seal, in soapstone, a memento from a friend's journey to Alaska. A rabbit's foot, a tarot deck. A cigar box tied with string. A shell, a stone, a tooth. A blue ribbon earned by a friend from grade school, whose face I can picture but whose name I've forgotten, a boy who won the race but lost to my need to possess the reward of the occasion. A tattered Green Lantern comic book. A mandolin, a handblown vase with clovers etched around the rim. A doll that wet when tapped on her back and tilted in a certain way—a possession that went all the way back to the fatal accident that wrested my parents away from me. My stuff, my cache, my museum, my booty, my precious trash. I pondered what it would have been like to add to it a clump of sod from my father's grave. A clump of dirt festering with weeds, their hopeful, stupid shoots nosing toward the sun, their tiny green buds opening like prayerful hands, the fools!

One doesn't give in to such impulses as mine without making, somewhere down the line, a sacrifice.

It is March again. Years later, but not enough of them to change my way of thinking. There may never be enough Marches to bring me to a change. Sure, I know about remission. I also know about relapse. Remission is a place you visit; relapse is home.

I had grown interminably tired. Tired of myself, tired of my fond obsession. Once ascetic, almost to a fault, I'd begun to drink. In the late afternoons at first, after work (yes, I kept my job, just to sustain the human contact), I became a sour anonymity whose fingers were reflected in the shiny surface of the bar as they reached for their solace. Later, I would start in the mornings before work; then continue quietly, furtively, through the course of the day. If my need to steal, when satisfied, had often in the past given rise to moments of unspeakable ecstasy, the exhaustion that now crept over me, coupled with a steady depression, brought me out to the field last night.

I had to do something. I was stalled. I found myself unable to so much as *think* of acquisition—my poor dead hobby—let alone carry out some meaningful theft. No, that life was over, gone, and in its place I'd erected a monumental Nothing in honor of its faded glories. My spirit had grown more numb than the stolen marble on Malatesta's temple, my flesh more indolent than the sleepy bees that lolled on its tombs.

What happened was I became paranoid about the cache. This was something new. What if, say, when my guard was down, I let some stranger in on my secret? Not given to confession, I nevertheless became certain I could slip up at some moment, especially if I kept going on like this. And since I saw no prospect of changing, I realized there was only one way to protect my past from my future, my future from my past.

The eye steady, the will steady. The field of last year's cotton stalks, all picked clean and standing dead as mummified soldiers, waiting to be tilled under before planting time. I had driven several hours north to get here. From a coastal port, doesn't matter which, to flatlands with nothing more to brag about than the heaviest humidity thereabouts and flying with pride the Confederate flag. No map, my headlights directed me. It had begun to rain, and large mothlike configurations of melting mist burst into view. All of it, the whole cache, I'd gathered into my duffel to bring with me, and when I pulled it out of the trunk the weight of the bundle surprised me—surely it had grown. I couldn't help but think, if someone were to see me dragging this impossible burden deep in the night, how much I must have looked like a murderer intent on burying his victim. Nothing so predictable as a corpse would he have found if he—joined perhaps by a phantom crowd of vigilantes, my victims among them, lighting their way with torches—stopped me from making this simple act of relinquishment.

New moon. Damp March after a warm winter. The night was black. The field was black. My hands were black. Or maybe it was that my hands had become a part of the field, this field I had visited once before, and that was why I couldn't see them. Who would have guessed they'd be so capable of doing what they did? Who'd have thought it could be so easy to take a lifetime's obsession and bury it, like you might some pumpkin seed, or a casket. Lydia's voice, it was as if I could hear it again, impassioned by the thought of a robber being punished by surrendering to society his sinning hands: "Go ahead," she said. "At least give us that much back. And stop acting like it's such a big deal." How did she know where I was, I thought, as I looked up into the watery sky. Ghosts, I guess, know these things.

The realms of strife, often so foggy, sometimes become crystal clear. I remembered a cousin, the best hunter of us all back when we were boys—I remembered his bowie knife, and the good times we had after I'd removed it from his pack. Always happy to loan him mine, he and I were boon companions for years. I groped around, found it deep in the duffel, pulled it out of its sheath. I am sure it would have glinted had there been more light. I ran my finger along its blade, and, yes, it seemed to be sharp as ever. I produced a bead of blood, just to see.

"Go ahead," that voice again proposed. "You don't deserve those hands." Lydia had been critical of me sometimes in the past, but never cruel. When I put the knife away, she said, and these were her last words: "You disgust me." Wish though I might to let my hands live in the field with the rest of my harvest, I knew I had never done anything to make myself worthy of such a sacrifice. Besides, if I cut off my left hand, how would I then cut off my right? The penance would always remain incomplete. Lydia, rinsed with rain, melted into oblivion.

Who knows where to stop? When is not in question; when happens to you. Where remains your choice.

There wasn't a house in sight and the road back was untraveled. Without remorse or farewell, I left the shallow grave, the muddy field, and the silent stretch of road behind. I was tired still, more tired than before. If I'd known my nighttime act, my slap in the face of whenness, would have succeeded in exhausting me even more than I'd been before, I wonder whether I would have gone to all the trouble. My resolution to rid myself of the cache had come from the simple notion that by having done with the dregs of a bad habit I might be freed to find my way—not forward, necessarily, but somewhere exhaustion could not flourish.

Yet here I was, in the company of these people. Brandy for old times' sake. A game of cards in a corner, laughter behind a curtain. Several men in uniform, furloughed perhaps. Others at tables, smoking and talking the night away. It was the woman tending bar who attracted my attention, however, young with skin the color of clean muslin, and deep black hair—like mine—and eyes—my own. More unlike Lydia she couldn't have been, except that she too had an uncommon name.

Naděja. It was Czech, a form of Nadja, or Nadia, she told me— almost rhymed with Lydia. She didn't seem to favor any one person in the place, and yet she had a way of making everyone feel special. This I admired. A real gift, to empathize like that. I saw that my hands were dirty, and washed them, and when I returned, I asked her what Naděja meant, and she said that the Russian form was Nadezhda, from the word meaning hope, "and hope is a virtue," she added, with a tender note of cynicism.

I stayed until everyone else had left. I had no idea what time it was, nor even where I was, or where I would pass the night. All I knew was that when Naděja removed her bracelet to wash the glasses, continuing to talk about where she grew up, her sisters and brothers, and the prominent events in her life, yes, the future once more became bright. As I listened to Naděja, the room—so simple, so homey—began to teem anew with life, and already I could feel the delicate warmth of her dearest treasure, brave against my palm.

LUSH

WHEN MARGOT DIED, A dark maw rose before me, a somber shaft into which I tramped, wanting never to return. If ever I'd felt empty during the seven fragile, drunken years we were married, I entered a consummate hollowness after she left me with my inheritance of bottles. Vodka was the legacy I embraced behind the drawn shades of our house, because vodka was the one thing I believed I truly understood about Margot, my nickname for Margaret, who hadn't a drop of French in her beyond a thousand sips of Château Margaux.

In the months that followed her death I became so saturated by my *cure*, as I called it—I liked renaming the world—that there was no more a dawn to my drinking day than a dusk. Pints, fifths, quarts, gallons, I worked my way through them all like cancer does flesh. Our kitchen counter, not to mention the linoleum floor, was crowded with glass vessels, some yet unsiphoned but most sucked down to a lullaby of disregard. When I managed to sleep, it was on that same linoleum, the sofa, the bathroom floor. Slumber was a rare guest that offered my sodden anatomy pause in the otherwise uninterrupted siege of boozing I wreaked upon myself. This bleak therapy, meant to tranquilize the memory of my alcoholic wife and maybe annihilate myself in the bargain, was so exhaustive that the few friends who still put up with me believed I was hot on her heels. Passingly successful in life, I'd be a permanent triumph in suicide. The way I chose to mourn her death, I would soon enough perish in a toxic seizure or else go as unceremoniously as she did. Maybe it was just as well she totaled our car beyond repair and I didn't get around to replacing it that ugly winter. Our savings and her life insurance policy set me up so that I didn't have to drive anywhere. Before they could fire me, I quit my job. The neighborhood bar was within walking distance, but I preferred the privacy of my home and, besides, rarely had the right legs for walking. The liquor store people took good care of me. Television was a solace. Groceries weren't of much concern since I had no appetite for food, but when I did get a craving for crackers, or frozen pizza, I knew the nearby convenience delivered to invalids and the elderly. Not forty, I was a crawling convalescent.

We never met before the day my life changed and hers ended. What a ruthless irony, that I was driving the florist van to the hospital to make deliveries of bouquets and huggy bears and Mylar balloons with the greeting Get Well Soon and that all this florist's freight of cheer was heaved onto the road, flowers everywhere shredded and smashed. I remember how we stared at each other, two women in the snow, how we found each other's gaze through the exploded glass of the wreckage and I remember the look of shock on her face, a look I understood without any words passing between us like she was saying I'm sorry I never meant for us to be lying here in the cold can you believe this is happening? and You gonna be okay over there you don't look that great but one of us should get up and find somebody to help us don't you think? while with all my strength I was trying to ask this woman trapped inside her demolished car the same questions. To this day I don't believe it was any more her fault than mine, though the autopsy proved she was way under the influence. Just we each caught a patch of ice at the same wrong moment and now here we were in the silence after the collision staring mute at each other across a chasm, a mortality gully, believing in our hearts that though we were badly fucked up bleeding on the new-fallen snow, we were both going to make it, were going to survive this, that yeah we'd have to go through some days and weeks of recovery but all would be well in this woman's life and in mine.

I think she smiled at me, blinking the blood out of her eyes, smiled encouragement at me since she could see I wasn't moving, was no more able than she to jump up and run to the nearest house for help. Looking back, I should have felt a lot colder than I did. It was blizzarding by the time the ambulance finally arrived. I remember looking over at her while the white blanketed us and this woman who in those few weird moments had become like a friend, maybe even a best friend, closed her eyes to rest her head on the pavement beside her overturned car, and thinking how very beautiful she must have been this morning when she got up and dressed for her day never once imagining it might end like this. Her coat was black caracul, her jeans were faded, which gave me the false impression she was a woman who was casual and even comfortable living her life, and she wore a pair of knitted mittens.

Like my wife, I never much liked not being high. It seemed to me a cruel waste of time not to be drinking. We'd gotten together on that premise in the first place, met for a drink, though at the time she had been dry for one brave month. That a lifelong romance would enter the scene—love at first sight, we both confessed later—was an unexpected blessing; perhaps less so her freefall off the wagon. She'd left the city the year before, moved a couple of hours north, telling herself she would take the riverside train down often to visit galleries, or go to museums, things she seldom got around to even when living right there in the midst of so much culture. New York, she said, exhausted her. She was too young for the silver that had begun to streak her chestnut hair, the oily skiffs under her large eyes, the fidgety hands, night sweats, the delicate flesh that shrank on its already slim frame. Nothing and nobody held her, so she took the chance and rusticated up the Hudson, convinced it would offer a healthy alternative to the habits she worried were consuming her. Clean air, birds, the changing seasons—these, Margaret hoped, would reawaken a lightness of heart, an enchantment with life that had come so easily when she was a girl, but got lost somehow. She would quit smoking. Would take long walks every day. Follow a dietary regime. Read one good book each week. Garden in summer and learn to cross-country in winter. Above all, she'd stop this overdrinking business. As she told her mother, she needed to drain the swamp.

Margot did in fact memorize the names of birds that came to her feeder. Junco, goldfinch, black-capped chickadee. She stopped with the cigarettes, and after a tough, edgy, migrainous two weeks of hacking, began to breathe more evenly and notice subtle scents in the rural air, the rich aroma of the soil around her tiny rented house after a rain shower, the salt smell of butter on her bread and the rye itself. *Middlemarch* and *Madame Bovary* she read with confused pleasure. She planted a small patch of zucchini, Swiss chard, basil. Through a mutual friend of all things—we had few friends—she set the date to meet me, just a guy who worked at a small law firm mostly involved with real estate closings, divorces, and wills. Despite the reasonable argument she'd admit she made with herself against such a slip, she bought cigarettes on her way to the tavern where we agreed to rendezvous, a cozy, dark, wainscoted cocktail lounge in the nice historic local inn. No doubt chastising herself while making a silent promise she'd again quit the next morning, she smiled as I lit her up and we entered on a dialogue that transformed our night, all our nights from that one forward.

She would later tell me that not only did she think I was smart and open and wryly funny—my deluded Margot—but were she asked to describe the face she would most love to look at for the rest of her life, mine was that face. She loved, she would later say, my brown hair, which lapsed over my forehead when I laughed, and how I combed it back with strong but delicate fingers, fingers of a pianist—Eros again at his confectionery, given a less musical man never existed. My hazel eyes, she said, sweetly sad perhaps. My furrowed brow and a mouth whose lips were maybe paler than those of any other man she'd met but sharply drawn. She even liked my name, James Chatham, and said it had an honest ring to it. How love colors everything.

When I ordered another tequila neat I wanted to know was she sure she wouldn't have something besides club soda. Well, she said, she hadn't been drinking much these days . . . but seeing me shrug in such an understanding, empathetic way, she thought why not. She'd have what I was having. Tomorrow would be a new day of abstinence. No smoking, no drinking; she'd been so good, she had earned tonight.

I remember asking her about herself, what coaxed her away from the city, a place I professed to love though I never got down there much, in fact deeply feared it. The need for fresh air, she told me, a fresh perspective. Her favorite museum? The Met, of course. How was it possible I'd never been to the Met? She'd love to go through the Met with me sometime. The Egyptian gallery. The wing with the dugout canoes, painted masks, and shields from New Guinea. Sure, another, she answered the bartender and told me about how this fellow Michael Rockefeller, former governor Nelson's son, assembled the New Guinea collection before he disappeared, murdered and eaten apparently by the very tribe in Irian Jaya he'd been observing. I told her I thought of studying anthropology when I was in college, but maybe it's better I never pursued it. No, she laughed, her face gone nicely numb with that third drink, a nostalgic warmth I could see rising through her like sap in a spring tree. She hadn't felt so radiantly alive since she moved here, she told me as much, taking the hand I offered her on the varnished rail. The bartender stood us a round as it was an otherwise slow evening.

Turns out we went to school together her husband and I, and though he's a year or two older I remember thinking he was such a nice guy, quiet and very gentle and unassuming, which he still is despite what people say about him and his dead wife being sots. Martin drinks and my father used to disappear into the likable haze of his evening preprandial as he called it but I never held that against either of them, everybody has problems and faults and things they like to do that other people don't. Like Kim Novak said about William Holden in that movie Picnic, *We don't love people because they're perfect. Look at how supportive Martin was after the accident, and I know that if Dad were around he'd have been there for me too. Hard to believe it had been only a week before Martin and I were going to move to the city, where he could really have a chance with his career and I could apprentice with a Fifth Avenue florist, become expert in modern techniques of arrangement, move beyond all these crummy nosegay-style economy vases and dumb carnations and daisy poms and Red Rovers. Give me fresh orchids and phallic calla lilies and bonsai a hundred years old! was what I thought when Martin first broached the subject last summer of moving, taking the leap, giving life our best shot. Even my mother was all for it, though naturally she mentioned we ought to go ahead and get married before leaving the old burgh for Emerald City. I told her we'd try living together first and then if it worked—white long-stemmed roses for everyone! The world was looking up.*

My mother knew his family, Margaret's husband's family. His father was prominent here she says, a member of the town council for many years, hardworking, a skilled stonemason, and when the season came around quite the deerslayer. They owned the blue Victorian downtown that had been in their family for years, everybody believed it was haunted and that bad luck befell them because the ship captain who built it for his wife and children was lost at sea in a whaler and their spirits still hovered at the upper-story windows looking out toward the river awaiting his return from Cape Horn. I don't know much about ghosts but I do know that the Chathams never had an easy time despite their Presbyterianism and their reputable roots in the community and a work ethic that seemed part of the very fabric of the family. My mother said that while James's dad liked working with his hands he had the wits to make a good surgeon or artist or anything else he'd have set his mind to, even served in the last year of the Second World War as an ambulance driver in Italy. James went to Albany and got his law degree but rather than clearing out of this little backwater of ours to make his killing in a city where the pockets run deeper, he set himself up with a local firm. After his parents died, his sister married and moved to Philadelphia, and they sold the big house. End of an era.

We awoke the next morning not knowing how we wound up at her place, but in truth we didn't care. Margaret offered me coffee, which I drank, reluctant to ask if she had any Irish Mist or brandy in the house, something that might keep the buzz on. That night she told me that after I'd dressed and gone off to work, she sat with her head in her hands looking up now and then to see what bird might be at the feeder, thanking God she'd left her unfinished pack of cigarettes at the tavern. Otherwise it would have been impossible not to have just one with her coffee. She almost made it to noon before getting in her car—the same one that would double as her temporary crypt those years later—and driving to the liquor store in town she had formerly passed, averting her gaze, many times since moving up here. Besides talking about anthropology, Flaubert, perennials, sailing the Hudson, which was an enthusiasm of mine, her work as a graphic designer, we engaged in an excited controversy about which were the best liqueurs, the most memorable wines, the craziest mixed drinks we'd ever tried. This was far and away a more candid almanac by which we might get to know each other, read one another's souls—a revelatory map of our personal geographies and histories, where we'd been and where we might be going.

The time I first tried retsina, *Hyméttos,* I remembered its name and the amazing bittersweet resinous stink of it, though I blacked out in Mykonos, then found myself robbed and more or less naked on the beach at Megáli Ámos. That once in her grandfather's house in Burlington, Vermont, when she was six or seven, Thanksgiving it was, she finished everybody's wineglasses, furtive in the kitchen after the dishes had been cleared and the family'd retired to the den to watch some game on the set. Yeah, yeah, I had one like that. The wedding trick all kids play, draining the flutes of flat bubbly the guests left behind, not giving a damn about the soggy butts you'd skim away first, if you happened to notice them. Her first Rob Roy. My brief infatuation with margaritas. Hers with Long Island iced tea. Pink squirrels, kamikazes, grasshoppers, Singapore slings, not to forget the sophomoric sophistication of dry vermouth on the rocks with a lemon twist—God in heaven, the hideous gaudy swill children are willing to irrigate themselves with, before we discover the mature world of manhattans or a dry Bombay martini.

Her intention at the liquor store was simply to stock a kitchen cabinet with some things for me to drink, when I came by next.

For her part, she had to stay dry now, having had her little holiday from abstinence. None of the bottles she bought, however,
remained capped or corked for long, partly because I dropped
over that same night, as excited to carry on with our dialogue
as she was, and partly because after I called in the afternoon
to tell her how much I loved our night together and asked if I
could see her, she needed something to calm her nerves. By the
time I arrived with a quaint bouquet of fresh tulips in hand,
Margaret was well along in her cups. I noticed, even though I'd
had a few stiff courage builders at a roadside on the way over
myself. We were too fatigued from the night before to match
the extravagant buoyancy of that first encounter, but this evening brought another kind of gift. Yes, we drank and drank,
the chardonnay first, then on to cognac, which had always been
one of Margaret's Achilles' heels, but even more than simply
wanting to drink, we wanted to drink together. Sworn solitary
boozers, forever before preferring that no one stand in judgment of our innocent habit, this was new for both of us. What
a breakthrough, we both thought to ourselves. Later, after our
love affair fully blossomed, in the depths one night of a liquory
confession, we'd disclose this fact and only fall more deeply
in love in the aftermath. We were seldom found apart the rest
of August and into autumn. I took my beer out into Margot's
narrow, shaded yard and helped her weed the unyielding garden.
She packed Rose's lime juice and Absolut in an ice chest to mix
gimlets out on the water, sailing the Hudson in my old catboat,
a single-masted wooden affair, my pride and joy. To toast her
first visit to my apartment over a gatehouse garage where I dry-
docked the sailboat, I brought out a sixteen-year-old Laphroaig,
which we finished as the harvest moon poured pale grenadine
light through the window. I tried to teach her how to pronounce
the name, an old Saxon carbuncle of a word. Lah-*fragge,* I said.
Accent's on the second syllable. But there aren't any syllables,

or else way too many, she laughed, then tried, Lap-fro-age? No, Lah-*fragge*, I said. *Lah-prfo-agge?*

They say your fate is hidden in your name and while that probably isn't true for everyone it happens to be so for me. My last name, Meredith, never meant much other than it sometimes caused some of us in my circle to laugh because Meredith was my best friend's first name, but I always liked my own first name, Ivy, because ivy is such a magical plant. Oh, the poison ivy jokes were inevitable but ivy is like a green flower and can grow in the shade and poor soil and climb trees and endure climates as different as those of Africa and the Azores, Japan and Russia, and can live, as Lord Byron wrote in one of his poems, for two thousand years—well, three hundred anyway, discounting poetic license. Birds like ivy for nesting in and butterflies lay their eggs there. The Greeks believed that ivy was a preventative for drunkenness and the best cure for a hangover. It's in Pliny, trust me.

So being Ivy it made some sense that I always wanted to be a florist and loved flowers from as far back as kindergarten when we planted a drift of yellow daffodils in the schoolyard. None of us kids believed in our hearts that the bleak little brown bulbs we'd buried in the October ground would survive the winter and burst into bloom next spring. When they did, that was it for me, and to this day a daffodil bulb is more bewitching and baffling than just about anything in this world. Fly to the big bright moon, map the human genome, do what you will, there is no greater miracle than a drab bulb stuck in the dirt and buried under winter snow that blossoms out of the mud year after year. I remember when I saw those daffodils bloom in the mucky grounds at school, I told my mother I wanted to plant ivy in our yard and so we did back by the toolshed and it grows there even now. I could see it from the window where I sat day in and out during the first months of my recovery. I know it's just a wall of vines with fluttering green leaves, my namesake, but it gave me moments of comfort just the same, especially after I agreed with Martin that maybe he ought to go ahead to the city and find us an apartment, get things set up so that I could follow as soon as I was ready. He promised to phone every day and visit every weekend.

And he did so throughout the winter, bringing me brochures from various florist shops and other little presents from time to time. He even got a gig downtown playing backup in some club. My lung and the half dozen ribs that had punctured it were healing more quickly than the doctors predicted, as were my broken leg and wrist. What wasn't going as well as they'd hoped was, to use their lingo, the series of surgical reconstructive procedures on my face. I'd flown into the windshield hard, hadn't fastened the seatbelt which was an insane oversight but there it was, and I paid for it with a long gash on my forehead and another on my cheek, as well as a shattered chin. A surgeon in Cooperstown did most of the work and while I usually loved it when Martin was around, during the months they kept regrafting and revising, and my face went from scarred to swollen-and-scarred to misshapen-and-scarred, I was just as happy when he called saying this weekend or that wasn't good for him to get upstate, he had a crucial stint here or was obligated to finish a five-nighter there, that he loved me and missed me and would come next week for sure. God knows I wasn't used to what I saw in the mirror, and even when girlfriends I'd known since the days of those daffodil plantings came over to keep the invalid company I felt ashamed not merely because my face was a devastated distortion, at least in my eyes, but because this didn't need to have happened. Margaret need not have been drunk, sure, but her responsibility was hers to govern and I had no say in the matter and she already paid big-time for her lack of judgment. For me, my head was a kaleidoscope of moving plans and thoughts of marriage and jostling flowers and wondering if I could get off early to see Martin about some damn thing I've forgotten what possibly it could have been that mattered so much I got distracted, blew through a stop sign and hit that sheet of heartless ice. She was plastered; I was in a rush. Now

I live with my mother, and Margaret's husband lives by himself. As for Martin and me, I knew where we were headed by the time April showers brought inevitable May flowers.

I proposed on Christmas, the same day Margot discovered she was pregnant. To celebrate both blessings we had corned beef sandwiches and Dom Pérignon. When she called her mother to tell her our news, the woman asked her daughter how went it with the freelancing—though her graphic design commissions had been slowed by the move, she had a few faithful clients and lived modestly on savings between jobs—when would she finally get to meet the famous James and how was the not-drinking going? My fiancée said work was fine, promised we'd drive to Vermont sometime soon for a long weekend, but failed to answer the last question. Still, Margot knew she would have to cut back because of the baby. I poured her from a second, cheaper bottle of champagne and phoned my sister in Philadelphia. Both my parents were dead, one of stomach cancer, the other of heart disease, so there wasn't really anybody else for me to share the news with. Margot seldom mentioned her dad except to say she didn't like him, and if she didn't neither did I. I'd always remember thinking that day how my future bride and I had grown inseparable, like the espaliered pears that grew together, latticelike, over at the inn where we first met. We set the wedding for Valentine's Day so the baby, due late April, wouldn't be born out of wedlock.

Sobriety wasn't Margot's calling but with my moral support, I who reminded her it was only a matter of a few lousy dry months, she disciplined herself to stay off the hard stuff, drinking wine and the occasional port. I guess I took up the slack by drinking for both of us, but seldom in her presence. Some good souls I'd known over the years, whenever I bothered to venture out into local bars before I met my wife, became happy-hour companions—companions insofar as we drank in the same room. From my stool at the far end of the bar I assumed they no more wanted to chat, emote, sermonize, argue, or in any real way engage than I did. Truth was, I missed drinking with Margot, but now that she and I had moved in together—my place because of the catboat—I felt it important not to bedevil my poor darling by hammering right under her nose. When she worried she was becoming fat because of the pregnancy, and that I would meet some beauty at the bar, I could only scoff. She knew as well as I did that bars were for one thing only, especially now that I was living with the mother of my child-to-be.

Her miscarriage in January brought these concerns to an end, and together we went on our first extended bender. When I phoned in to work with the tragic news they generously gave me the week off, which I spent behind locked doors with Margot in a fluctuating state of alcoholic philosophizing and comatose despair. Her mother pled to come help see us through our grieving but her daughter told her truthfully we were in no condition to see anyone. My sister sent a magnificent blooming amaryllis, which Margot dropped on the floor, breaking the clay pot and scattering soil and bulbs. We never got around to opening the envelope with her sympathy card. Instead of waiting for Valentine's Day, we pulled ourselves together toward the end of that black week and flew to Reno. We'd later have a good laugh when my sister said Reno was where you went for the quick divorce, not a wedding, but the knot was tied and we were again, after our own fashion, happy.

The first time he came over to see me I was three weeks out of my fifth reconstructive and was for a change not feeling all that bad about myself. I'd taken to gardening in the back yard, wearing a huge floppy straw hat because the sun was apparently detrimental to the healing scars, and was tilling soil for a bed of peonies when my mother came out back and told me James Chatham was on the line asking if he could visit. Always protective, especially now that Martin and I were no more, she shook her head no while covering the receiver of the cordless with her palm, as if he could hear her gesture somehow. I told her he was more than welcome. Time had come for us to meet face-to-face and talk. After all, who had suffered more from the accident (his wife aside, whose suffering was over forever) than he and I? It was right that we finally meet, or meet again really since during my months of nights I'd had an abundance of time to think about things, everything imaginable, and during the hours spent wandering the often frustratingly vague halls of memory I remembered him, recalled having known him better than I initially thought in those first confusing days after the collision when I was nothing more than an anesthetized dreamer who kept herself alive by picturing different roses and assigning them their names, Coral Creeper and Applejack and Marie Bugnet with its pure white tousled petals and a fragrance that would make the cloven-hoofed devil himself swoon.

Whiskey sours and daiquiris, mint juleps and sloe gin fizzes, the flagrant highball days and even the dull ones of dry Bordeaux having receded into the mist, we settled that spring and summer into the spirits that worked best for us. Margot drank gin on the rocks, her preference being Tanqueray; I became a Scotch man, and while I liked fancy single malts—Oban, Glenfiddich, so forth—my poison of choice was Johnnie Walker. *Johnnie walked me where I needed to go,* I said, a fatuous joke that never failed to make Margot smile. *Johnnie be good.* We had things under control. Back at her computer Margot was someone to watch in the graphic design world—uneven, yes, but when she was on her game just brilliant. As for myself, I was reliable, got the job done, worked slow and steady as Aesop's dusty tortoise. Binges were masqueraded as the flu, a leveling allergy attack, a sudden family emergency that called us away for a few days.

After we sank our catboat in shallow water, a heavy October wind having pushed the wide-beamed oak-and-cedar craft into a rock mere wading distance from the shore, I quit drinking Scotch. The debacle was without question my fault and I'd been through a fifth of Johnnie when I lost control of the *Margot,* as I'd rechristened her the year we were married. To Margaret's respectful bewilderment, I seemed to get away not just from the whiskey but all booze for a few weird months after the accident—that I only drank beer she found both inspiring and frightening. We even managed during this period of remission to take the train down to visit the Met and indulge in hot dogs and root beer in Central Park. Margot pointed out a little flock of birds chirping crazily and flailing about in the top of a cherry tree, telling me they were drunk, which made me laugh. No, really, she said, she'd read about this in one of her bird behavior books—they loved consuming berries fermented by the sun in the highest branches. Soused sparrows, go figure. Soon after that I came over to Tanqueray, if only because it made shopping for the liquor much easier and saved money since we bought by the case.

Evenings eventually witnessed a new routine in which rather than always drinking together we spent some quality time alone, me retiring with a bottle downstairs, where the catboat was dry-docked, to work on repairing its ruined hull; Margot curled up on the sofa with a magazine, smoking in front of the television. We spoke about having another try at parenthood, and although our lovemaking was sporadic, Margot did get pregnant again, and once more miscarried. As depressing as she'd found her prior failure to carry our child—I already had names in mind, Margaret if it was a girl, Dylan if a boy—she now descended into an inconsolable depression of weeping day and night, bingeing until her speech was too garbled to understand, though I knew the gist of what she might be trying to say. Third time was not going to be the charm in the years that winged by, day by blurry day, since our love evolved into a sibling companionship rather than what in the beginning was something else. I remained beautiful in my wife's eyes despite my puffiness and bloating, while Margot grew gaunt and angular, her skin transparent and long hair now shimmeringly more white than brown, which I frankly adored. We leaned on each other more and more, reflecting one another like the facing mirrors in a García Lorca poem Margaret memorized when she first moved up here, and sometimes recited. *Woodcutter, cut down my shadow.*

Rarely did we argue, but when we did the fireworks blinded all measure of reason. The precipitating problem was always some little thing that, fueled by the gin, turned incendiary. Why couldn't she vacuum once in a blue moon? Instead of pretending to work on my ridiculous boat, which was never going to sail again, why didn't I fix the lock on the front door so someone wouldn't murder us in our sleep? Why was this chicken burnt? Did I keep coming home so late because I was having an affair? How was it she always accused me of having the affair when she was the one home alone all day, drinking herself blind? How dare I raise my voice about her drinking when I was going through two quarts a night? Violence would follow these words, never visited by one of us on the other, but as inevitable as our morning-after apologies. Margaret smashed crockery and threw books. I punched the wall and stumbled over furniture, breaking my toe and cutting my hands on sharp edges as well as dull. Ordinarily soft-spoken, we thundered and wailed and wept. Usually tender, we spat and raged. Chairs were overturned, bottles flew. I slammed the door, screaming I never wanted to see her again. She barricaded herself in the bathroom, threatening to slit her wrists. It wasn't until I tripped and fell into the old French doors that separated the living room from our bedroom, and opened up my forehead and cheek with the splintering glass, sending me in an ambulance to the hospital for surgery to remove fragments and getting stitches that would leave me scarred, that we finally sat down to talk.

Scars, I thought. His face was nothing like mine but his flesh had known the same kind of pain. And yes, I was right. I suspected we'd met before, back when we were young optimistic kids going to school thinking that the world was a place in which reversals of fortune happen to the oldsters but never to us, which in a way wasn't wrong since now we were people we'd have thought of as very old back then. Still, isn't it crazy how stupid young people are and how inevitable is the downfall, the comeuppance, how when we're young we know we're smart and when we're older we know we're not, and how there must be an instant when the transition takes place and how seldom any of us knows just when that moment was or why it happened. My curse and my blessing is that I do know, of course. But when my mother let James Chatham in and he and I shook hands and even tentatively gave each other a victims' hug, I remembered that hand and that same hesitant hug because years ago when we weren't such damaged goods we'd made this same gesture, kissed each other just like a girl and boy who don't know what they're doing do. It was the first time I was ever drunk, the ground whirling and sky spinning and my feet freezing cold, fireworks if I remember right so possibly the Fourth of July, I couldn't have been more than thirteen or fourteen but understood it was a rite of passage, which meant you had to suffer for a higher cause or something idiotic in that vein, but he did kiss me, my first kiss, and I never told a soul pretty much including myself since I erased the moment (it was under a tree, an ash, I think) from my mind until now. Crazy. We sat and talked about my injuries for a while and I asked him how he was getting along and though he said he was doing fine, as good as could be expected, I saw that his eyes were swimming, their rims red as wild poppy petals. I was sorry to see him go and when he asked if he could come back to visit from time to time I told him I wished he would, and he gave me his phone number. My mother and my friends didn't like him and thought it was unhealthy for me to spend any time with him given, as they saw it, his alkie spouse had maimed me for life, nearly killed me. What they didn't know and even James would never really know was the ineffable nature of the gaze his wife and I exchanged as we lay there not ten feet from each other in the snow that winter day, a contact so pure and even sublime I will never achieve it again, something so unspeakably marvelous it makes me feel only gratitude that I had it, held it, held her in my eyes, just as she held me in hers, dying. That James must have gazed into her eyes with a similar depth of compassion obsessed me for days after he came by to see me, and when my mother was out one afternoon I took the chance of calling him at work and asked if he'd like to get together again maybe away from my house somewhere. He took to the idea as if it had been his own and when I mentioned I was still shy about being seen in public he asked me if I'd ever been out on the river, and said my scars meant nothing to him if his meant nothing to me. To this day I find it hard to believe he can't remember that time we were kids drinking God knows what and kissed under a tree with not a flaw on either of our bodies nor many strikes against us yet. I suppose it's all just booze under the bridge.

The drinking had taken Margot and me to a precipice, and we had no choice but to back away into sobriety or jump. A warm May breeze flowed through the room with its promise of summer. In the sane morning light, undecorated by alcohol, we glimpsed for a brief moment just how ravaged, how unexpectedly destroyed, how diminished, how cheated by booze we were. This had to stop. Margot proposed a contract, binding as our marriage vows, in which we would solemnly agree not to partake anymore, until such time as we both felt we could do so with restraint like normal human beings. In complete accord, I typed the agreement and both of us signed and dated it, then had one last eulogizing drink before we walked through the house pouring every last bottle down the drain. Afterward we made love and in our exuberance planned a Vermont trip to see her mother and the family homestead, which I still had not visited. Other itineraries came to mind, too. Philadelphia, Atlanta, the Met again. Why not Europe? When I was there I was always too smashed to see anything. From Montmartre to the Bridge of Sighs, from Valladolid's *Ferias Mayores* to the windy Acropolis, all was a perfect tabula rasa cycled into oblivion by Armagnac, grappa, and Macedonian *Náoussa*. Maybe the moment had come for me to revisit all those places with my bride—after five years of marriage we were still newly wedded so far as we were concerned—and have the honeymoon we talked about but never got around to sharing. See what had lurked beyond the hazy veil.

That first week of sobriety was far harder for Margot than me, not because I wasn't supposed to mix alcohol with the antibiotics— that had never been an impediment—but because of the prescriptions for pain management and the sedatives I'd been given, which nicely blunted the edge of my withdrawal. Seeing the tortured, enervated glaze that complicated her already nervous eyes, I naturally shared both pills with my wife, figuring what was fair for the gander, and so forth, imagining these would help her decompress a little, ease her back from that cliff we'd articulated and decided to defeat. The turnabout was as immediate as it was shocking. What for Margot was a reminder of that month when she tried this before, was to me pure revelation. The universe of fragrances, for godsake. I never knew my catboat had such a brackish fish-tangy smell. I'd forgotten that the sheets on our bed, after being washed, would have a scent. The wallpaper in Margot's small study stank: mildew. Our clothes reeked of smoke and of something else, despondency perhaps. Food had taste beyond hot or cold. The bloated travesty I'd grown used to seeing in the mirror whenever I made the mistake of looking had mutated into a familiar face, one my parents, were they alive, might have recognized, even acknowledged. I jokingly told Margot one evening, I remember you, to which she replied, Oh, no you don't, you were too drunk. We both regarded it as some kind of miracle that, sober, we loved each other the same as when we were plastered.

As I healed and ran out of the masking drugs, my old craving resurfaced, and with it the terror that it had never receded or withdrawn its deadlock on me for a moment. I was naked again. I was suddenly dying out here. It was a matter not of hour by hour, but instant by instant that I quashed the impulse to return to the bottle. I crammed chocolate, spooned sugar from the canister in the kitchen, chased it with Coke. Knowing in my heart I was going to flunk this experiment—maybe tomorrow, maybe the day after tomorrow—I could only look to Margot as a beacon of hope and strength. She might survive where it was my fate to fail. She was doing so well. Clients loved her again. She spoke often on the phone with her mother. She'd taken to reading at night rather than staring at the television or into space.

The afternoon I came home an hour early to discover her lying on the sofa, delirious, clutching an empty quart bottle of Stoli to her chest, was as exhilarating for me as it was devastating. I had every right to yell the way I did and justly accused her of breaking our contract. I wouldn't have felt a more passionate rage, such an excited fury, if she'd been caught embracing my best friend—though, of course, I realized she was doing just that. We slept apart that night, Margot in bed, humiliated, and me on the couch, mortified by the inevitable. For weeks we drank in secret until our need to be together flushed us out of hiding. Life returned to normal as we began to appreciate once more that gift we'd cherished in times past. The gift that two recluses might somehow find a path from their individual hermitages to one they could share, like monks brought together to worship a wrathful, turned-on god.

How strange of Martin to phone the night before James was going to take me out on the river, Martin telling me how much he missed me and how things weren't going so great without his good-luck charm, as he always called me, despite the fact I never brought him or anybody else much luck and didn't appreciate the sentiment nor that he asked at the dead end of the conversation how my face was doing, as if my face was ever going to do anything other than be a living topographic map of this surgeon's success and that one's failure. Stranger yet was James picking me up in a cab since he didn't drive anymore and taking me to the jetty where his sailboat was moored and helping me step aboard, then getting us out into the surging Hudson, into the pristine winds that wafted and breathed as if right through me, reminding me what it was to be in the world again, forgetting I had a face. I never meant to like him as much as I did that day, to feel such an intimacy toward him, and resisted what I saw in myself, knowing that people sometimes tend to identify irrationally with others who have been through a kindred crisis. Not that James saw or felt or thought the same things I did. In fact I had to wonder how he thought or felt at all given how much he was drinking while we sailed downwind past the Kingston–Rhinecliff Bridge and the lighthouse and pretty mansions set back on their grassy rises beyond where the train ran along the rock-strewn shore. He offered me something to drink, too, and I accepted a plastic glassful of white wine so as not to look the prude but emptied it overboard when he was tending to the sail, tacking with the unearthly agility of a specter on the deck, thin as the proverbial rail he was though my friends said that before the accident he'd been different, fleshy and flaccid, which I found impossible to believe looking at the man who now sailed me through the pelting wake of an oil barge with such easy skill you'd never know he'd ever had a single drink in his life. He cast anchor and we had lunch, some sandwiches I'd brought along, and as the boat rose and fell gently in the dull brown water we talked about this and that and the other until it came around to her, to Margot, as he called her, Margaret whom I associated with Marguerite, the oxeye *daisy, the "day's eye" so-called because the flower opens its petals in the morning to reveal its center then closes them against the night. He asked if I could tell him whether she said anything to me when we were alone that day lying there, and I said he could ask anything but I wasn't sure I could answer in any way that would make much sense but that I'd try. And I did try. I told him we said nothing and everything, that odd as it might sound we made a covenant, became sisters who sensed we were in the midst of knowing something few would have or get to know in their lives, and that I'd hold the memory in myself as long as I could remember my name or hers. He sat quietly for a time and I said nothing either, wondering whether I hadn't already said too much, had misspoken, opened a wound without meaning to do more than help to close it, and he began to cry and I wept with him. It was then he did the strangest rightest thing, he chucked his bottle over the side of the catboat and held me in his arms never kissing me but holding me like a strong wind holds a sail.*

Honoring her with a halfhearted final double shot of who knows what, I swore off the stuff, swore on my mother and father's souls, vowed I was done forever with the nightmare, pledged that Margot wouldn't remain a martyr for nothing, that her spirit's better half, so to speak, would learn from her tragedy, move on toward the life she might have wanted for herself and her husband. I spent two months in rehab, flinching and trembling like a newborn during the first weeks before slowly, incrementally getting an upper hand on what they told me was a disease. Some days I seemed so full of strength I doubted that I ever had a problem in the first place; then an ogre would rise in place of the sun the next morning and I would find myself in a cauldron of craving, of aching, simply lusting for liquor. Worse yet were the long days of plateauing— speechless hours spent staring out the window across the lawn or listlessly attending my housemates' testimonial "qualifications" at the noon group meetings. My sister and mother-in-law and Ivy supported me, visiting me at the facility, writing letters of encouragement, and when the time came for me to return home all three were there to help me move into the new place, a studio apartment not far from where I grew up in that great blue Victorian house. It would not be wrong to say I was a new man. Yet it'd be terribly wrong to presume that despite everything I didn't still want to drink, because I did and will always want to retreat into that dreamier, more fluid life.

Ivy was back at the florist shop, managing it, in fact, and while too much bad blood had passed between me and the old law firm, I was hired into another outfit and found myself taking on whatever anyone else didn't want to handle. I threw myself into work and, as well, the inevitably blossoming romance with Ivy. Who would have thought horticultural shows, botanical gardens, or even the modest pleasure of having fresh-cut flowers given to you every other day with a note from your affectionate girlfriend could be so sustaining? Who'd have guessed that, sober, I had no stomach for sailing, got seasick as a landlubber and had to sell the catboat? Who might have believed it was possible for me to reemerge from that infernal maw into which I'd descended after Margot died, leaving me to bury her, I who wanted nothing more than to climb into the fresh-dug pit in the cemetery and lie there until snow and gravediggers' soil blanketed us both?

Some months after my small triumph, my return to life, Ivy and I went to Paris and we had a fine time of it as unabashed tourists impatient to visit every monument and museum. We took the train to Berlin, then down to Florence and Rome, and, on our last day, walking the ancient dirt paths of the Forum beside the invaluable clutter of tumbled columns and broken statuary, I asked her to marry me and she agreed. The bittersweetness of these itineraries, once meant to be toured together with Margot, was somewhat allayed by Ivy's own deep connection with her. But rather than casting a pall on our marriage, which Margot would, we both believed, not have wanted, we took her memory to be affirmative. We bought an eyebrow colonial farmhouse outside town, which had a view of the Catskills beyond the river, and fixed it up with our own hands. A year after we were married, Ivy gave birth to our twin daughters. A barn cat adopted us, so we called him Paw both because of his fatherly mien and outsized furry feet. I was made a partner in the firm. Three years elapsed without a drop.

Down in New York on a late November evening I attended a dinner with one of our more important clients, a wealthy weekender whose upstate properties we managed. I'd spent a long day in his midtown offices going over books and records with his accountant and another attorney, reconciling the numbers and discussing an acquisition he was considering—an annual consultation followed by the requisite dinner at a nice French restaurant just off Madison Avenue. We'd had a particularly strong year with him, and all of us were in a festive mood. Although I had a hotel reservation in case things ran late, I still had every hope of catching the last train out of Penn and sleeping in my own bed that night. For all my hard-won sobriety, it was always tough to sit with others who were there to enjoy themselves, have wine with dinner like people do, but I never anticipated how uneasy I would feel—stunned is the word—when our host ordered a bottle of Château Margaux for the table. The disease was near me, as palpable and alive as the waiter himself, who poured the vintage into crystal stemware set before each of us. Even the crisp, starched white of his sommelier's linen was dangerous.

I forced myself to concentrate on the vast bouquet of flowers that centerpieced our table, and thought of excusing myself and rushing to a telephone so I could hear Ivy's reassuring voice, but didn't. While normally I would have turned my glass upside down on the tablecloth long before the wine pourer reached me, tonight

I failed to do so, allowing him to fill mine in my turn, knowing it was not for me to drink. Yes, I would lift it during the toast and clink my glass against the others'. Yes, I knew it was insulting not to partake after the salutation. But yes, all the same I would have no choice other than to set the untasted wine back on the table and leave it there to decant for the rest of the long evening ahead, unless I believed that just for once in my life, given all I'd been through and learned, I could join my friends in this most simple, convivial act.

ACKNOWLEDGMENTS

My deepest gratitude to friends who encouraged me over the years while I was writing these dark stories, friends who themselves are full of light: Peter Straub, Martine Bellen, Pat Sims, Mike Kelly, Thomas Johnson, Micaela Morrissette, J. W. McCormack, Nicole Nyhan, and Can Xue. Thanks also to my inspiring colleagues at Bard College, among them Mary Caponegro, Robert Kelly, Edie Meidav, and Michèle Dominy. As well, I'd like gratefully to acknowledge the stellar work Lorie Pagnozzi, Maria Fernandez, Jerry Kelly, and Phil Gaskill did during the production of *The Uninnocent*.

I want to thank the editors who published early versions of these stories in magazines and anthologies: Betsy Sussler, M. Mark, Joyce Carol Oates, Raymond Smith (fondly remembered), Patrick McGrath, Howard Norman, Steve Erickson, Peter Straub, James Ellroy, Bill Henderson, Laura Furman, and the redoubtable Otto Penzler, who in many ways godfathered this collection.

To my perspicacious agent and friend, Henry Dunow; to my intrepid editors, Claiborne Hancock and Jessica Case, who nurtured this book into being; and, as ever, to Cara Schlesinger—blessings to all of you for believing in these stories and for your kindnesses along the way.

ABOUT THE AUTHOR

BRADFORD MORROW is the author of the novels *Come Sunday*, *The Almanac Branch*, *Trinity Fields*, *Giovanni's Gift*, *Ariel's Crossing*, and *The Diviner's Tale*. He has been the recipient of numerous awards, including the Academy Award in Literature from the American Academy of Arts and Letters, a Guggenheim Fellowship, and O. Henry and Pushcart prizes. Morrow is the founding editor of the widely acclaimed literary journal *Conjunctions*, for which he received the 2007 PEN/Nora Magid Award, and is a professor of literature and Bard Center Fellow at Bard College. He divides his time between New York City and a farmhouse in upstate New York.